GRAFFITI KNIGHT

GRAFFITI KNIGHT

KAREN BASS

pajamapress

First published in the United States in 2014
Text copyright © 2013 Karen Bass
This edition copyright © 2013 Pajama Press Inc.
This is a first edition.
10 9 8 7 6 5 4 3 2 1

www.pajamapress.ca   info@pajamapress.ca

The publisher gratefully acknowledges the support of the Canada Council for the Arts and the Ontario Arts Council for its publishing program. We acknowledge the financial support of the Government of Canada through the Book Publishing Industry Development Program (BPIDP) for our publishing activities.

 Canada Council for the Arts **Conseil des Arts du Canada** 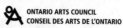 **ONTARIO ARTS COUNCIL CONSEIL DES ARTS DE L'ONTARIO**

Library and Archives Canada Cataloguing in Publication

Bass, Karen, 1962-, author
   Graffiti knight / Karen Bass.

ISBN 978-1-927485-53-8 (pbk.)

   1. Teenage boys--Germany--Leipzig--Juvenile fiction.
2. Graffiti--Germany--Leipzig--Juvenile fiction. 3. Freedom of
expression--Germany--Leipzig--Juvenile fiction. 4. World
War, 1939-1945--Germany--Leipzig--Juvenile fiction. 5. Leipzig
(Germany)--History--20th century--Juvenile fiction. 6. Germany
(Territory under Allied occupation, 1945-1955 : Russian Zone)--
Juvenile fiction. I. Title.

PS8603.A795G73 2013   jC813'.6   C2013-902728-9

Publisher Cataloging-in-Publication Data (U.S.)

Bass, Karen, 1962-
   Graffiti knight / Karen Bass.
[   ] p. : cm.
Summary: After a childhood cut short by World War II and the harsh strictures of Nazi Germany, fifteen-year-old Wilm seeks freedom of expression in a city governed by brutal police and oppressive Soviet forces. His graffiti successfully embarrasses the police, but it also endangers the people Wilm holds dear.
ISBN-13: 978-1-927485-53-8 (pbk.)
   1. World War, 1939-1945 – Children – Juvenile fiction. 2. Family life -- Germany -- Juvenile fiction. I. Title.
[Fic] dc23   PZ7.B388gra   2013

Cover design–Rebecca Buchanan
Cover photo–Aged Street Wall–Shutterstock/©donatas1205
Interior design and typesetting–Martin Gould
Map–John Lightfoot, Lightfoot Art & Design Inc.
Printed in Canada by Webcom
http://www.webcomlink.com/

Pajama Press Inc.
469 Richmond St. E, Toronto, Ontario, Canada
www.pajamapress.ca

To my friend Gisela.
Thank you for giving me the seed that became this story,
by sharing a bit of your father's tale
and encouraging him to share more.

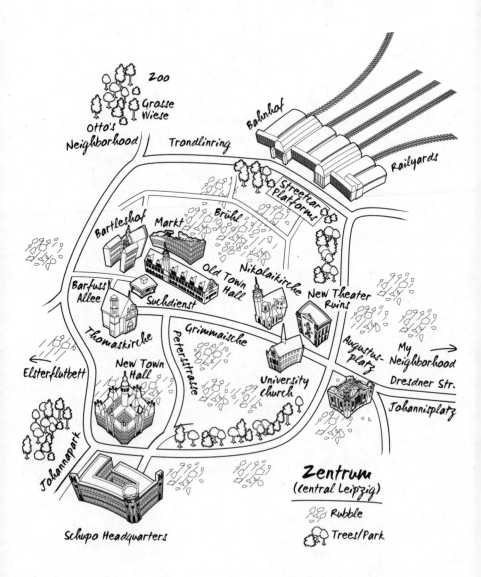

CHAPTER ONE

The broken windows of the building to the right watched our progress with the hollow stare of someone defeated and beyond caring. Georg and Karl eased around the corner in a crouch. I peered past the brick wall and spotted two *Schutzpolizisten* in the intersection half a block ahead. I dropped low and followed my friends along the path winding through heaps of destruction—crumbled walls that spilled chunks of stone and brick and dust into the alley.

Most days it was fun to play along. Karl had started the game two years ago, after the Soviet Army occupied Leipzig. We tried not to be noticed by Schupos, because they worked for the Soviets, but we'd also spy on them, pretending we were behind enemy lines, collecting intelligence for the American army in the hope they'd return. Failure meant a small punishment, usually a dare. But I wasn't in the mood for games today.

I straightened. The police were still there, backs to us, watching the street. I frowned at the blue uniforms and their tense, guard-dog postures. Something was up. My chest constricted, making it hard to breathe.

Karl grabbed my wrist and yanked me to my knees. "Keep your head down, Wilm," he whispered, pointing beyond the rubble. "Patrol in the intersection."

"I spotted them a block ago, *Dummkopf.*"

Behind a broken wall five meters away, Georg sheltered under a claw-footed bathtub suspended midair by a skeletal hand of green pipes that protruded from crumbling plaster. He signaled that another patrol was approaching, then scuttled to us like a two-legged crab. "What's going on? There aren't usually this many Schupos out. We've seen six since we left school. Is all of Leipzig is like this, or just our district?"

Beside the exposed bathtub was half a bedroom clogged with rubble. A picture hung crooked above a crushed bed. "Maybe they're looking for us."

Georg swatted my head. "You think that's funny, Tauber?"

"Sure. We're no threat to these guys." I sneered. "You don't even know what end of a pistol to hold."

I knew. Uncle Bruno had taught me to strip down and reassemble the Luger he kept hidden in his barn. One night, right after the Soviets arrived, my older sister, Anneliese, and I were at his farm when a terrific thunderstorm rolled in. He took us to the forest beyond his west field and, under the cover of the thunder, we fired the Luger until we ran out of ammunition. Uncle Bruno said I had a good eye, but Anneliese was a natural.

Georg glared at me, a look that said he wanted to hit me again. I tilted my chin and gave him a target. A slap was one thing, but he wouldn't punch me. He'd never been a fighter.

"Sssst." Karl got our attention. "Look." A murmuring Schupo swept his arm and pointed in one direction, then another. The others nodded and one pointed in the opposite direction.

"A search?" Georg peered between two slabs of broken wall, my taunting forgotten.

"Maybe," Karl replied. "At the Stag's Horn there've been rumors about a weapons stash."

I snorted. "Those drunks your mom serves in her pub eat

rumors for breakfast and drink them for supper. I suppose they're planning a revolt. Kill the police, kick out the Soviets with a few Mausers and hand grenades."

"I didn't say that." Karl raked his fingers through his sandy hair, a sure sign he was frustrated. It didn't matter what he did to his hair; it was always neat. He and Georg were opposites: fair and dark, tidy and messy. I was in the middle. Karl continued, "I only said there's a rumor. The Schupos listen to rumors too. And they hate the idea of anyone except them being armed. Half the time I think someone puts these ideas out there to see the police running around in a panic."

"You're crazy if you think kicking in doors and scaring families is a sign of panic." Had they already searched our block? No one was—wait. Anneliese might be back from work. I needed to get home.

I peered over the top of a rubble pile that smelled faintly of charcoal. The Schupos' clean navy-blue uniforms contrasted with the drab, mostly ruined street. Even the sky was dreary, though the morning's rain clouds had been replaced by a gray sheet. Backs still to us, the four Schupos watched a figure hobble toward them on crutches.

My body clenched at the sight: the familiar arc of crutches, the way the man swung forward, head down, looking for cobblestones that might trip him because he hadn't adjusted to having half a leg. My father paused at the corner, cap pulled so low that most of his face was in shadow. He didn't look at the police as he started across the street. As he did with the Soviets, Father tried to pretend the Schupos didn't exist.

They didn't let him. One stepped in his way, forced him to stop, and asked him something in a low voice. Father kept his head down, but I could see his chest rising and falling rapidly.

No doubt the Schupo could hear him huffing the way he did when he was getting angry.

"Leave me alone." His voice was gruff. Too loud. "I know nothing."

He moved to skirt the two patrols. The officer who'd spoken to him grabbed his arm and spun him back. A crutch clattered across the cobblestones. Father started to fall but a shove from another officer kept him on his foot. His other crutch dropped to the ground.

The four men surrounded Father and pushed him back and forth between them, never letting him fall. "Dirty Nazi!" one yelled. My hands curled into fists. Anyone the authorities didn't like got called a Nazi or a reactionary, but no one in our family had been a Nazi. Ever. I'd gotten into two fights last fall when older students had called me that. The first Schupo shouted, "You're hiding something. Tell us!" He backhanded Father.

I shot up and started over the broken wall, but Karl and Georg dragged me back. We rolled and struggled as I fought to escape, our grunts and scrapes echoing the other attack. We landed with me on the bottom, face down in a murky puddle, my ear and neck in water that lapped at my mouth when I tried to jerk free.

Karl's breath was hot on my other ear. "Don't move."

The sounds in the street had changed to thumps and the expelled breaths of someone being hit. I pictured two Schupos holding my father's arms, keeping him upright while the other two pounded him. I tried to heave Karl and Georg off. Rough stone scraped my cheekbone as they pushed me back down. One of them I could've beaten, but not both.

A thud came from the other side of the rubble. I stared at the crumbled stone, still charred in places. They had dropped him. He was lying in the street, maybe staring at the same pile of debris, smelling the same musk. Leave him now, I thought. Leave him.

I held my breath, strained to hear what was happening. No footsteps. No talking. The hush was suffocating, and I lifted my head to speak. Then—the sound of something hard hitting something soft. Boots against flesh. I flinched with every thump, felt every strike in my legs, my back, my gut. I tasted mud and knew Father tasted blood. He groaned at each blow, swore. Finally he cried, "Shoot me, you cowards! What kind of animals beat a one-legged man? Shoot me and be done with it!"

Silence. My breathing came in short bursts. After a minute the police muttered among themselves. They marched away, footfalls heading in two directions. Georg rolled off my legs. I pushed Karl away and stood. My cheek stung when I wiped it. Both friends scowled at me. Georg's hair stood up in clumps. "He didn't mean that, did he?" he whispered. "He couldn't have wanted them to shoot him."

They had no idea, and I wasn't in a mood to tell them.

I scrambled over the rubble pile and retrieved the crutches. It took a few minutes to get Father up, and even with the crutches he swayed precariously. When I set his cap on his head, he looked up, surprise blanketing his features as he realized who was helping him.

"Where did you come from, Wilhelm?" Father dabbed at a cut on his lip, then at another on his brow. His hands were bleeding too, as if he'd tried to ward off blows. "Could've used your help sooner."

"I tried," I muttered, and sent Georg and Karl an angry look. They kept their distance, uncertainty etched on their foreheads. My book satchel dangled from Georg's grasp.

Father shifted and his knee buckled; I caught him and helped him to the remnants of a low wall. "Stay here. I'll find a way to get you home."

His frown dared me to offer a solution. We had no car, not even a bicycle. They'd been buried under debris years ago when our first apartment was bombed.

I snapped my fingers. "Frau Nikel's wheelbarrow."

Father's lip curled. "Perfect. It will make my humiliation complete. You can wheel me to the pharmacy. That's where I was headed, to see if Herr Busch has any pain medication. Damned lost leg is on fire. Couldn't get anything done so they sent me home early."

His voice faded as he spoke and I realized his new injuries were paining him more than a nonexistent leg. I raced off, cursing under my breath, and returned in ten minutes.

Karl carried Father's crutches on his shoulder like a pair of rifles, Georg packed our satchels, and I pushed the wheelbarrow. As we headed to the pharmacy, curtains on either side of the oddly deserted street fluttered to mark our passing. The neighborhood was taking note. Word would travel fast. Heinz Tauber had been beaten by police. What had he done to deserve it? What could they do to avoid the same fate?

As the wheelbarrow bounced along, Father spoke through gritted teeth about the beating. He seemed proud of how he'd held up. "I'll be sore for days," he informed us. Anger darkened his gray eyes. "Next time those swine try to beat me I'll grab one of their pistols and turn it on them."

I tried to imagine that, but could only see him falling as he grabbed a weapon. And the other policemen shooting him before he hit the ground.

CHAPTER TWO

There was no medicine at the pharmacy, but our neighbor sold Father a bottle of black-market *Schnaps*. He settled in his chair in the living room, had a few drinks while he waited for supper, and another while we ate.

The potato soup looked suspiciously thin. I swirled the spoon through the broth and fished out a lone piece of sausage. My stomach picked that moment to growl. Mother sighed. I ate the sausage without looking up, tore my dark bread into chunks and dropped them into the soup, ate each soggy bit and tried to pretend it was juicy sausage. My stomach wasn't fooled. And it wasn't full when I finished, but I knew better than to ask for more.

As usual, Anneliese disappeared into her bedroom as soon as the meal ended, so I helped Mother clear off the table while Father left the table to drink. Not that I had a choice. He expected one of us to help clean up and Mother never called Anneliese back.

After I dumped the wash water, Mother said, "Get my sewing basket and your trousers so I can mend them. They should be dry. What were you doing to get them so dirty and tear the knee? Fighting at school?"

"Wilhelm tore them. Let him mend them," Father called from the living room.

"I don't know how to sew." I crossed my arms. "That's women's work. Get Anneliese to do it. She sews all day and would have it done in a minute."

Father's voice boomed, "Do as you're told. Soldiers in the field repair their own uniforms."

"I'll show you how in a minute," Mother said. Her lips pressed together in silent reprimand against my protest. She turned away to fold the tea towel and straighten everything. I stared at her back. There had been a time when she used to smile.

Had I been eleven? Father in uniform, home on leave. We'd gone for a picnic in the park by the zoo, Grosse Wiese. I tried to score on Father, who guarded his makeshift soccer posts. When I finally got the ball past him, he swept me onto his shoulders and laughed. And Mother laughed at our celebrating. Had that really been us? It was hard to believe now.

Mother's lips pressed together always signaled the end of the argument, so I sat at the table with my almost dry trousers and the sewing basket. Threading the needle was easy; I'd done it all the time for Mother when I was younger. I stared at the tear in the knee and saw in my mind Father's encounter with the police. Saw the blows I'd only heard. It had been so casual. Like they had every right to beat him. Like he was their prisoner.

Prison. Why had I never realized that before? Leipzig was our prison and had been since the war ended. The Soviets were our wardens, but the Schupos were our prison guards. I was a prisoner. In my own home. Guarded by my own people.

A touch on my shoulder made me flinch. "Don't hold the needle so tightly," Mother said. "Relax." She explained how to tie a knot in the thread, how to turn the trouser leg inside out, and what kind of stitch to use. She watched my first few pokes at the tear and said I was doing fine.

I didn't feel fine. Concentrating on each stitch kept my mind off my thoughts until Father decided to retell the story, even though no one wanted to hear it again.

Mother inspected my work. "Good job, Wilm." She showed me how to tie off the thread.

A lie. Next time I saw these trousers my sloppy repair job would be replaced by Mother's neat stitches. Father had to know that. I couldn't figure out why he had bothered to make me do it.

I moved to the sofa and picked up my page of mathematics notes to prepare for tomorrow's test. The smell of cheap alcohol seemed to ooze out of Father's pores. I studied him from the corner of my eye.

"What are you looking at?" When I hesitated, he snapped, "Answer me. Why are you staring?"

The anger lacing his words always made me bristle. "Haven't you had enough?"

At the table, Mother looked up from the newspaper. "Wilm ... don't make trouble. Show some respect."

"That's right," Father said. "I'll decide when I've had enough. I'm one big bruise and feel like ground-up pork. If a few drinks ease the pain you should be happy. Lately you've been getting too big—" He broke off and stared. Not at my face. Lower.

What was he looking at? Since when was asking a question making trouble? Mother told me the same thing every day when I left the house. Don't make trouble. Father hadn't been making trouble today either, for all the good it had done him.

He raised his glass, took a long swallow, then said, "You are wearing my trousers."

Mother spoke in a rush. "I should have told you, Heinz. I didn't think you would mind. Wilm has outgrown everything he owns so I altered two pairs you never wear. Even your trousers are getting too short for him. I think he will be as tall as Bruno."

At the mention of her brother, Father's face lengthened. He emptied his glass. "The doctors saved his leg. He hardly even limps anymore."

Mother lowered her head. I tried to concentrate on my home-work. We had heard the same story time and again, but when he was drinking it was impossible to change the subject.

"That's because he had German doctors," Father muttered. "Good doctors. Not like those American slaughter-masters that got hold of me."

I was tempted to leave the apartment, but that would probably just make things worse. And I couldn't even hide in my room—the living room was my bedroom. I tried to shut out his droning voice.

"Why didn't they let me die on the battlefield?" Father rapped his empty glass on the shelf beside his chair. "I was their enemy. They should have let me die. My unit left me for dead. Why couldn't the Americans have done the same? There's honor in dying on the battlefield."

His voice cracked on that word: *honor*. I didn't mean to, but I looked up. His pale gaze captured mine. With tears clinging to his lashes, he whispered, "What honor is in this, Wilhelm?" He slapped the thigh of his amputated leg. "What hope for any honor at all?"

I fled. His mournful voice followed me. "They should have let me die."

When I slipped into her room, Anneliese shrank back against the wall, then released a long sigh and relaxed back against her pillow. "Wilm, you startled me."

"Sorry. I couldn't stay out there."

Anneliese didn't ask why. The silence sat heavily between us. Shadows rimmed and emphasized her pale eyes and the pallor in her cheeks. Her hair was lighter than mine, dark blond like Mother's but dirty. Every morning she wore an old pair of my trousers and scurried to work in the back room of a seamstress's shop, and every night she hid in her room.

"Could I sleep in here tonight?" I asked, breaking the silence. Her eyes widened and again she pressed her back to the wall. What was that look for? I pointed to her worn area rug. "On the floor. Please? Father's talking about the battlefield again. He might go on for hours and I have a test tomorrow."

After a moment she nodded. I retrieved my bedding from the linen closet before she changed her mind, laid it out on the rug, and stripped to my underwear. When I glimpsed myself in the mirror on the dresser I flexed my muscles, sucked in my stomach, and braced my fists on my hips while I studied my torso, looking for signs it was filling out. I released my breath and turned to see Anneliese watching. Heat burned my cheeks.

In a quiet voice, the only one she'd owned for the last year, she said, "You look like Uncle Bruno. You even have his brown eyes and straight nose."

"Mother said I'll be as tall as him." I raised my fist and clenched my arm to form a muscle. "I hope I'm as strong as he is." Not weak like Father. I immediately regretted the thought. He'd been different before the battle that took his leg.

When I burrowed into my blankets, Anneliese told me to cover my eyes. I rested my forearm across them. Like all of the other sixteen-year-old boys I knew, I really wanted to see a girl, any girl, naked, but it didn't feel right to look at my sister that way. I needed to think about something else.

"He told them to shoot him," I blurted.

The bedsprings squeaked as Anneliese shifted. Her voice was almost directly above. "Who?"

"Father. He dared those police to shoot him."

She sighed. "Death in battle."

Of course. Why hadn't I seen it? "An honorable death. He'll never get it now but it's what he wants."

"Some days death would be ..." Another sigh.

"Forget that. I want to be around to see the Soviets leave. I want to know ... what freedom is like." I frowned into the darkness. "Don't you want that, Liese?"

She didn't answer so I kept talking. "Do you ever wonder if we'll be happy again? It seemed like we were happy before the war, even at the beginning. Weren't we?" I paused. "I remember you being happy. Ernst would write and say he had leave and you'd get all fluttery. You'd spend hours getting ready! What happened? Why did you break up with him?" I had liked Ernst. He'd dated Anneliese since early in high school. He had taught me soccer moves, teased me, and wrestled with me. He had called me little brother, and I remember hoping he'd marry Anneliese so he could be my real brother.

The bedsprings squeaked again. "Good night, Wilm."

I hoped she'd speak again and soften the darkness. It was the most we'd talked in ages. But the silence rained down on me. I whispered, "Did I say something wrong?"

Her breath hitched quietly, as if she were trying to muffle tears, and I inwardly cursed myself for being an idiot.

CHAPTER THREE

The mathematics instructor, Herr Bader, called me aside as the class filed out of the room. "Herr Tauber, how do you think you did on the test?"

I glanced behind his desk to the neatly made cot in the corner, the shelves fashioned out of three stacked crates, the sparse collection of belongings. I frowned at the pile of test papers. When he repeated his question I said, "Not good, sir."

"You are capable, but your marks continue to languish. Why would that be?"

If only he'd stop pestering me. None of the other teachers bothered, but they were scantily trained New Teachers, recruited from farms and factories to replace the ones who hadn't returned from the war. Herr Bader had always been a teacher. I shrugged. "Not studying, I guess."

He inhaled slowly, as if drawing judgment into his lungs. "Stop guessing, figure out the problem, and solve it. As it stands, you are wasting my time and yours. Decide what your future holds, Herr Tauber, and act accordingly."

He dismissed me and I left, biting my tongue to keep from saying what I really wanted to say. What good was mathematics in this broken city? Did it help fill the stores with food? Or my stomach? Did it help us afford a bigger apartment so I could have my own room again? Did it provide heating? Did it get me trousers and boots that fit?

He was right about one thing: mathematics was a waste of time. School too, but Mother and Father insisted I keep going; they dreamed of me going to university. I would rather help Uncle Bruno. At least farmers didn't go hungry. I could hardly wait for the weekend when I could work beside him on his farm.

I grabbed my coat and satchel, and met Georg and Karl outside. As we jogged down the steps Karl said, "Some guys are meeting at the park to kick a ball around. And since Georg has the best ball, they want us to come."

Father had stayed home from work to nurse his wounds, so home was a good place to avoid. "Sure." I flung my satchel over my shoulder. Georg ducked, but the bag still brushed his dark hair. His foul look made me laugh.

"What did the accountant want with you?" Karl asked, using his nickname for Herr Bader, who could do amazing sums in his head faster than we could on paper.

"Wants me to get serious or stop wasting his time."

"He never says that to me."

Georg gave Karl a gleeful look. "Why would he bother? You're the worst mathematics student he's ever had the misfortune to teach."

"Then why am I passing and Wilm is failing?"

I gave Karl a shove and he stumbled sideways. "Because you cheat."

He swung his book bag at me. As Georg and I bolted down the street, Karl yelled, "Cowards! Say that again, I dare you!" We were all laughing when we got to Georg's apartment. We collapsed in a heap on the outside staircase. Georg took our satchels inside so we wouldn't have to carry them to the park. He didn't live in an apartment but rather in one of the hovels in the inner courtyard. Even though we'd been friends since kindergarten, he always seemed embarrassed when we were in his home, so we usually waited outside or met elsewhere. His family had had a nice apartment before the war, but their landlord had evicted them after Georg's father and brother died in the same battle. Finishing high school and going to university was his best chance to get his mother out of that place. Compared to him, I lived in luxury. His soccer ball, originally his brother's, was his prized possession.

"It's true, you know," Karl said as he smoothed his sandy hair. Not that it was messy.

"What?" I sniffed, catching a whiff of musk. Was he wearing cologne?

"That I cheat."

"I know. I've seen you. I swear Herr Bader is blind. Either that or he wants you to pass so he doesn't have to teach you again."

Karl reclined with a grin, his elbows on the step behind him. "At least I'm good-looking."

"Which helps you pass mathematics?"

"No. Only cheating does that. But it attracts girls. Much more important than mathematics."

I couldn't argue with that. We fell silent as a group of girls strolled by. They always traveled in groups. Two of them giggled and peeked at us from the corners of their eyes. The third was bolder. She flipped a braid over her shoulder and smiled at Karl. She was pretty and her baggy coat seemed to hide nice curves. She didn't look at me.

That's the problem when your best friend is good-looking. If a girl bothered to talk to me or Georg, it was usually so we could introduce her to Karl. He thought this was hilarious and offered to let us have his leftovers. I didn't like the thought of kissing a girl who wanted to be with someone else, much less my friend. I could imagine it, but I didn't like it.

The route to the park took us past the street I used to live on, still clogged with debris. Our apartment building had only partly collapsed, so we hadn't been crushed as we hid in the basement's bomb shelter during the raid. Many people weren't as lucky. That night I'd seen my first freshly dead person up close. The blank eyes and mangled body came to mind every time I walked by.

On the far side of the park a squad of police was drilling. The other guys from school cheered when they saw us. Georg held up his ball and they cheered louder.

We chose up sides for a game, though the teams were small. Georg and I ended up on the team that lost the coin toss. We stripped off jackets and shirts, and ran onto the field in our undershirts. It didn't take long to warm up in the mild spring weather.

Twenty minutes later a wild kick sent the ball over the head of our goalie. I raced to get it, then stopped as if I'd run into a wall. A policeman stood in front of me, holding the ball. Behind him sat the squad that had been drilling. The Schupo spun the ball between his index fingers, then cupped his hands onto the ball to stop it. "We decided to have a break. Feel like taking on real men?"

I hesitated as my gut churned, then glanced over my shoulder to see the guys hovering by our makeshift goal. I shrugged and got a few nods in return. "You have a game," I said. "We'll even let you keep your shirts on." The policemen laughed.

A few guys backed out, claiming they had chores. I watched the police strip off their jackets, belts and holsters. Had any of them had a hand in my father's beating? I didn't realize my jaw was clenched until Karl flicked it.

"Relax," he whispered. "You look ready to hurt someone."

I rubbed my jaw. "I'm not an idiot."

"Good. This is just a game."

I nodded. "A game that can get rough. Especially with no referee."

Karl narrowed his blue eyes. "I thought you said you weren't an idiot."

I started to smile but stopped as I noticed one policeman stretching. His build, the way his arm jab, jab, jabbed at the sky. It was so familiar, but it couldn't be. Then he turned. And it was. Ernst Weber. He stepped over his neatly folded jacket, nodded at something another Schupo said. I'd mentioned him last night to Anneliese and now here he was, as if speaking his name had conjured him. I shivered. I'd never imagined him joining the police, even though a lot of ex-soldiers had been recruited because of their training and discipline. It made sense, but Ernst a Schupo? I didn't like it.

"What are you looking at?" Karl asked.

"Anneliese's old boyfriend, Ernst Weber."

"I remember him. We were always catching them kissing in your living room." Karl opened his mouth as if to shout at Ernst.

I clamped onto his arm. "Don't! If he doesn't recognize me I don't want to say anything."

"Why?"

I thought of my father's bruised body. "I'm not sure we're on the same side anymore."

Karl snorted his scorn. "This is a game, Wilm. Frau Nikel's wheelbarrow is too far away to carry you home."

It was annoying sometimes how he knew my thoughts. We'd been friends for too long.

The sun broke through the clouds as we lined up. I stood facing Ernst. He nodded but didn't recognize me. Not surprising. We'd last seen each other three years ago, when he was recovering on leave from an injury he received in France. My change from scrawny boy to someone the same height as him, who had to shave once a week, was as good as a disguise.

Their striker tossed the ball up. Karl headed it to me and I started down the field. Ernst came at me. He didn't even try for the ball, just tripped me then dribbled the ball down the field. I inhaled a whiff of grass, picked myself up, and brushed off.

The game got rougher. I stopped counting the number of times I hit the ground. But Schupos got tackled too. Sometimes fairly, sometimes not. My elbow bruised more than one set of ribs. I savored each collision.

Thirty minutes later, the Schupos looked ragged. In a burst of speed, Georg and I zigzagged down the field, passing the ball as we went. He faked out a halfback; I circled a fullback and passed to Karl, who slipped the ball past the goalie. We were still down two goals but we all piled on Karl in celebration.

We rolled off him to find a Schupo, the one who had suggested the game, waiting to get our attention. "We're done. Thanks."

Karl replied, "But we're just getting warmed up."

"Some of us have evening patrol. Maybe another day."

I retreated to my pile of clothes before I could ask who they were going to beat up tonight. I kept my back to them, stripped off my filthy undershirt, and wiped my stinking armpits with it. While I was buttoning my shirt I noticed a woman walking toward us. She wore a fitted jacket that showed off her figure and heels that gave a sexy curve to her legs. Her skirt swayed nicely.

She was passing by when she spun to face me. "Wilm Tauber?"

My eyes rose from her neckline to her face. I stared for a moment before it hit me. "Johanna Fahr." My gaze bounced down to the generous cleavage mostly hidden by the V-necked shirt and jacket, then back up. "You've grown." We were the same age but she looked older. And classier.

She laughed. "Quite a lot since you and I played doctor in my grandmother's sewing room."

Heat pooled in my cheeks at the thought. That was seven years ago, when we were nine. Her grandmother had looked after us while our mothers went to some sort of bandage-rolling meetings each week. I could remember Johanna's slight form, the first, the only girl I'd seen naked. No sign then she'd have an hourglass figure. We had lived in the same building and played board games on rainy days. Until we were twelve she was my best friend after Karl and Georg. I cleared my throat. "I didn't know you were still in Leipzig. My mother never knew where you moved after our apartment was destroyed."

"We moved in with Mother's cousin on the north side of town. For the longest time I couldn't bear coming back to this district. Oma was killed that night."

"In the same raid?" She nodded and I said, "I'm sorry. Your grandmother was nice. Made the best gingerbread in Leipzig."

"She did, didn't she?" Johanna's smile showed off surprisingly white teeth. Was she getting real toothpaste from somewhere?

I tucked my shirt into my trousers. "What brings you here?"

"I'm meeting my boyfriend. His friend escorted me. I thought they were drilling but I find them playing soccer. Here he comes." Her smile reappeared and she waved. "Ernst! Come meet an old friend. I lived one floor above him when we were young."

I didn't turn, just worked on breathing evenly. Johanna was five years younger than Ernst. What did she see in someone that old? When had he started dating her? Recently? Right after he broke up with Anneliese? Or had she broken up with him? I'd never known, and Anneliese certainly never talked about it. No one did. It was like he'd ceased to exist, except here he was.

Ernst came up to us as I shrugged into my jacket. I balled up my undershirt and stuck it in my pocket. Ernst extended his hand. "A friend of Johanna's? Glad to—"

He blinked several times, then gripped my shoulders. A wide smile almost made him look my age, like he'd looked when he'd been dating Anneliese. "Wilm Tauber! I didn't recognize you out there. You play a dirty game. That's not what I taught you." His smile hadn't dimmed, and his tone held amusement, not judgment.

Something inside of me responded to his happiness, and my grin matched his. "Your first play of the game wasn't exactly a clean tackle."

"Times change, little brother." The old nickname made my momentary joy evaporate. Big brothers don't walk away like he had. He seemed to sense the change. He stepped back and slipped his arm around Johanna's waist, pulled her close. "You've grown," he said.

"That's what Wilm said to me." Johanna laughed.

Ernst hesitated. "I'm sure." His eyes narrowed in a clear warning: keep your distance from my girl. He might as well have shouted it. Then his expression softened again and he nodded. "It's good to see you again, Wilm." He started to turn away.

This was my best, maybe only, chance to find out what had happened between him and my sister. "Ernst." He looked over his shoulder, then joined me when I motioned for him to step aside. Out of Johanna's hearing I asked, "Why did you and Anneliese break up?"

At her name, his face turned to sunbaked clay. It took a few seconds before he said, "I like my women … untouched." His voice cracked on that last word, like he couldn't contain his anger.

Whatever I'd expected him to say, it hadn't been that. Was he saying my sister had cheated on him? Anneliese would never do that. A bolt of hatred shot through me.

I returned what I hoped was an equally hard look. "I'm sure you don't keep them that way."

"I don't like your tone, little brother."

Hand in pocket, I turned my folding knife over and over. His uniform filled my vision. How could I forget, even for a minute, what Ernst had become? "Don't call me that. No brother of mine would hurt Anneliese ... or sell out to the Sov—"

His fist plowed into my gut and I folded. My forehead pressed against the ground as I tried to catch my breath. Over my wheezing I heard him say, "Change the attitude. And learn to keep your mouth shut."

"Go to hell," I whispered.

But he was already walking away.

CHAPTER FOUR

On Saturday I rose with the sun, eager to get to Uncle Bruno's farm. I would take a streetcar east to the end of the line, but it was another hour's walk beyond that before I'd get to Engelsdorf. I'd stowed my bedding and was scrounging in the kitchen for breakfast when Mother entered the room. Her hair was tied up in a kerchief and she wore the dark skirt she liked for cleaning. She put on an old jacket.

Then she spotted me. "Why are you up so early? School doesn't ..." She buttoned the jacket with jerky motions. "Wilm, you can't keep skipping your Saturday classes."

"I'm not missing anything important. And Uncle Bruno needs my help." An exaggeration, but one that usually worked with Mother. I changed the subject. "Why are you up so early? I thought you were going to stop working on the rubble piles."

"We ... need the extra rations my work brings."

Every night worry wrinkled her brow as she studied the ration-card changes listed in the newspaper. I knew things were sometimes tight, but I hadn't realized that Mother needed to work for us to make it through. I hesitated, then offered the piece of drying cheese and the bread crust I held. "You'll need this more than me." When she didn't take the food I set it on the counter and spun away so she wouldn't hear my stomach growl.

She touched my arm. "I know you don't like me doing this, but it's the only way for me to make money."

Trümmerfrauen. Rubble women. I hated seeing groups of them clearing up the mess made by Allied planes. Hated more that Mother was one of them. What if she set off an unexploded bomb? The work had been forced labor for all women in 1945 and part of 1946. No exceptions. If they didn't help, their families didn't get any ration cards. Now it was voluntary, but was it really voluntary when a family needed food? I headed to the door.

"Wilm, take this food. You need it."

"Uncle Bruno will have something when I get to the farm."

As I opened the door, she sighed. "I'll write you a note for school when you get back tomorrow. And ... don't make trouble."

I closed the door quietly, resisting the urge to slam it.

When I got to Uncle Bruno's farm, I found him inspecting his potato field. I crouched beside him, plucked a tiny weed, and smoothed the soil I'd disrupted. He gave me a nod, then squinted down the row. "Weed the field, and watch for those beetles I told you about."

My stomach chose that moment to growl. He turned his squint on me. "No breakfast?"

"Mother needed it. *Trümmerfrauen* duty."

"There's half a loaf on the table. Eat before you start." He stood. "I'll be in the barn until noon." He strode toward the farmyard, his limp hardly noticeable. His tall, lanky form didn't look strong, until you noticed his powerful hands. He didn't look back. He'd given his orders and knew I'd follow them. I liked that about Uncle Bruno. He treated me like a man.

My stomach growled again and I sprinted to the house. Rye bread waited uncovered, as if Uncle Bruno had expected I'd need to eat. I tore off a chunk before I noticed the pat of butter on a plate by the bread. I wolfed down the chunk, cut a ragged slice, spread the butter, inhaled the delicious aroma, then gobbled it down. I cut another slice, covered the remaining bread with a cloth, got a long drink of water, and headed outside, nibbling as I went.

Butter was one reason I loved coming to the farm. It was hard to get in Leipzig, even with ration cards. Uncle Bruno had to give most of his milk to the authorities—even more with the Communist SED government than with the Nazis, and they'd been pretty demanding—but he always skimmed some for himself. He had caches of supplies and food all around the farm. I never asked where. I only knew where he hid the Luger in the barn.

I also loved escaping the destruction. We lived twelve blocks from the *Bahnhof*, which wasn't the best place to be during a war. Train stations were always targets, and Leipzig's was no exception. Our district was hit hard, large chunks of it wiped out in a gigantic bombing raid by the British. Other areas of the city had barely been touched, but housing was so tight we'd been lucky to find a place near our first apartment. I lived among ruins. At the farm, where things were green and growing, I breathed something other than dust.

A morning spent weeding left me hot and sticky. And hungry. Always hungry. The aroma of frying onions greeted me when I walked into the house. Uncle Bruno usually worked through the day, carrying bread, cheese, and water with him. He was cooking for my benefit. I absorbed the mouth-watering smells.

Georg was always hungrier than me, but Uncle Bruno wouldn't let him come to the farm. He was leery about anyone except family and a few trusted neighbors visiting; he claimed SED informants were everywhere. At least he let me take food back. Georg didn't mind gifts.

"Get in here while it's hot," Uncle Bruno called from the kitchen.

I kicked off my filthy boots and washed in the basin of tepid water by the coat rack. In the tiny kitchen, Uncle Bruno sat, sleeves rolled up to his elbows. A cast-iron pan in the center of the table brimmed with fried potatoes, onions, and sausage. Saliva flooded my mouth. I sat as Uncle Bruno poured me half a glass of milk, emptying the jar. "Drink up. Don't want it going sour."

I downed the milk. It was room temperature, and had already been skimmed of cream to make butter, but it still tasted wonderful. I piled food onto my plate. "I should live here."

Uncle Bruno snorted. "That's your stomach talking. You have to finish school."

"Why? What will it get me?"

"A future."

"There's a future here. I could help you farm."

Uncle Bruno took a smaller helping than me. "Maybe not. The bigger farms are all collectives now. Farms this size could be next. And ..." He began eating.

After a few forkfuls, I asked, "What were you going to say?"

He laid down his fork. "Might get married. No future for you here then."

I almost choked on a potato. "Married? But ... You've never. When ...? Who ...?"

A faint smile appeared briefly. "Neighbor's cousin near Taucha. Lives on a farm. Knows the life."

"Have you met her?" His gaze let me know it was a stupid question. "B-but—"

"Do I need your permission?"

My face heated and I returned to eating. I tried to imagine Uncle Bruno with a wife and family. He'd been alone as long as I could remember. With men scarce since the war, any able-bodied man was popular. Would girls consider Uncle Bruno a catch? He caught me looking.

"What?" He set down his fork again.

I shrugged. "It's hard to imagine you with a wife." He kept staring and I searched for a different topic. "I ... saw Anneliese's old boyfriend, Ernst Weber, the other day."

His eyes narrowed. "You tell Anneliese?"

"No. His name came up the night before and she cried so I decided not to say I saw him." That got a small nod. I added, "He's a Schupo."

When Uncle Bruno kept his silence, I spilled the whole story. The impromptu soccer game, how rough it got, my conversation with Ernst after he recognized me. Uncle Bruno's serious expression never changed. "What did he mean?" I finally asked. "Anneliese would never have stepped out with anyone else. She loved him like a crazy person."

Uncle Bruno poured us some artificial coffee and set mine down with a nearly empty bowl of sugar. He got his cup and sat. His expression reminded me of his barn when it was shuttered against a storm. Uncle Bruno closed down like this sometimes. I could ask until I was breathless and no answers would come. I stirred in some sugar and took a sip, winced against the scalding liquid. Then I told him about Father getting beaten and his drunken complaints.

"Don't be too hard on him."

"He doesn't hesitate to be hard on me."

"Does he beat you?"

"No. But he frustrates me so much sometimes I could hit him."

"Don't. You'll be done school and gone soon enough."

"Anneliese didn't go. She's twenty and still at home. Last night I asked her to come with me today, but she ignored me."

"Country roads aren't safe for girls. Leave her be."

The shuttered look returned. We finished our coffee in silence and went back to work. All afternoon, as I plucked weeds,

I thought about Anneliese and our summers spent on the farm. Uncle Bruno had made us do chores in the morning, but he let us play after lunch. We stalked cows, pretending they were Saracens and we were crusading knights. We swam in the nearby stream, made rafts, and invaded Istanbul. At nights we filled the darkness with our hopes and dreams until Uncle Bruno silenced us with the threat of extra chores.

At the end of one row, I rested by the fence and watched a crow preen. Its head popped up and it squawked, "*Ha, ha, ha,*" as if mocking me for working in this heat. I recalled Anneliese's hearty laughter. It had rung like the bell in Johannisplatz church. Now only the bell tower remained, but the bell itself had been silent for a long time—like Anneliese's laughter. I missed how it had made Father smile; even Uncle Bruno's stone face had usually cracked under its peals.

The evening was sultry, so after supper we sat by the garden on the bench my grandfather had carved for my grandmother. In the west, clouds piled up.

Uncle Bruno nodded at them. "Storm's coming quick."

I repeated a comment he often made about storms. "Maybe the heat will break."

"Probably." He glanced at me. "Got some more ammunition."

I gaped, wanting to ask how he had acquired ammunition, barely daring to breathe. He nodded. "If there's thunder, you could learn to brace against the Luger's kick." His mouth twitched. "If you aren't too tired."

I leaped up. "Never!"

The clouds darkened, boiled higher, blocked out the sun. Their shadow blanketed the garden. In the distance a fork of lightning cut through black clouds. The air thickened with the smell of approaching rain.

Uncle Bruno said, "I'll close the windows. You clean the pistol."

I bolted, containing my whoop of joy until I was inside the barn. The workhorse snorted. In the stall farthest from the door, I edged past Uncle Bruno's remaining milk cow, pried up the loose board on the bottom of the stall's manger, and removed the double-wrapped weapon. Up in the loft I unwrapped the oil-scented rag. I stroked the Luger's wood-grain handle and ran my finger along the barrel. My finger came away smelling like oil.

Somewhere that weapons cache Karl had told us about was rusting away. If anyone ever found it, the guns would be nearly useless. But tonight I had both a pistol and ammunition, which was better than a hidden stockpile any day.

A small box had been stored with the Luger. I opened it, removed the cleaning kit, and set to work. I finished with thunder rumbling overhead. Uncle Bruno called me. I tucked the Luger under my belt. As I climbed down the ladder I glanced toward the back of the barn and the silence registered on me. Uncle Bruno's sow was gone. He threw a raincoat over my shoulders and hustled me outside. As we crossed the field I almost matched his long strides.

In the forest, Uncle Bruno pushed aside some brambles and pulled out a target of painted wood, propped it against the thicket then braced it with rocks. He explained how to improve my stance, and passed me the bullets. I loaded the clip, pumped a round into the chamber, and planted my feet shoulder-width apart with knees bent, like he'd said. From beside my left shoulder, he whispered, "Take off the safety. Good. Wait for the thunder."

I remembered the empty pen in the barn. "What happened to your sow?"

"Authorities took her for butcher." Bitterness filled his words.

"But she almost ready to give birth!"

"Told them that. Told them more piglets would feed more mouths. They didn't listen." The pistol lowered a fraction. Uncle Bruno tapped my left shoulder. "Steady."

I raised the pistol again and sighted down its barrel in the growing murk. "When are they going to leave, Uncle? When will we have our freedom back?"

"Freedom's for the rich and powerful. When was the last time any of us had freedom?"

I couldn't answer. I'd felt free when I was younger, but maybe that was just the freedom most children feel knowing they have parents taking care of them. That wasn't what Uncle Bruno was talking about.

Lightning flashed. Seconds later thunder rumbled and I fired. And again.

The pistol's kick reverberated up my arms.

A miniature bolt of electricity surged through me. With a start, I realized what it was: power. Holding this pistol made me feel powerful. Was this what freedom felt like?

I smiled grimly and waited for the next roll of thunder.

CHAPTER FIVE

Dusk dimmed the sky as I arrived home on Sunday evening. I could smell the *Schnaps* when I closed the door. Father had been drinking heavily all week. To soothe his aching body, he claimed.

"Wilm," Mother called from the kitchen, "I'm glad you're home. I was wondering if you had decided to stay another night at the farm."

It had been tempting. I went to the table where she was sewing a button back on one of Father's shirts and pulled the package I'd carried so carefully from inside my coat.

"What've you got there?" Father demanded.

"Cheese. A bit of butter. Some sausage." Father rose from his chair, maneuvered his crutches, and stumped over to stand behind me. The smell of *Schnaps* grew stronger. I untied the cloth bundle and opened it. Mother smiled. Anneliese appeared at the other end of the galley kitchen. Her gaze darted from the table to me to Father and back to me.

Behind me Father huffed. "We aren't taking charity from that man."

My hand slid into my pocket and my fingers began turning my pocketknife over and over. I managed to keep my voice calm. "It isn't charity. It's my pay for two day's work."

"We aren't taking it."

"It isn't yours. You can't make that decision."

"Wilm ..." Mother tried to calm me with gentle tones. "Don't make trouble."

"I'm not. I brought home food. It's mine to give away or keep." My hidden fingers turned the pocketknife relentlessly. Father's light eyes seemed to swirl with shadows.

He spoke through gritted teeth. "While you live in my house, you obey my decisions."

"And what's your decision, Father? To let us starve while you drink our food money?"

He struck so fast my cheek was stinging before I realized he'd slapped me. One crutch clattered to the floor. Mother gasped and Anneliese fled. The front door slammed. I cupped my hand over my cheek and trembled with the desire to strike back. "Why do you hate Uncle Bruno? Because he never lost his leg? Or because he can feed us better than you can?"

Father roared, "I hate him because he stole my son!"

We glared at each other for a full minute. "He didn't steal me," I finally whispered. "But the war stole my father. He left to fight and never returned. I don't even know who you are."

His face reddened and he raised a fist. When Mother cried out he unclenched his fist and pointed at the door. "Get out. Don't come back until you can show respect."

I bolted to the door, paused with my hand on the knob. "Don't you dare throw out that food. It's for Mother and Anneliese. Not you."

I slammed the door behind me and thundered down the stairs. At the bottom, I hesitated. No curfew any more but patrols harassed young men out after dark. I jogged back up, then paused on our first-floor landing and eyed the closed bathroom door, which was where Anneliese was likely hiding. I continued up two more flights, climbed onto the roof from the dormer window on the top landing. A ladder was bolted to the incline beside the window. I scrambled the short distance to the flat roof and sprawled near a chimney radiating warmth.

It sickened me to think Father might throw out food to spite Uncle Bruno. Father's words—"because he stole my son"—flew around my head. I liked Uncle Bruno. But that didn't mean—

My own words slammed into me and my stomach clenched. I'd accused him of being a stranger, not the father I'd known. I'd thought it before, but I'd never said it, not even to Karl or Georg.

Father already hated what the war had done to him. Now he'd think I hated his loss of a leg as much as he did when that wasn't it at all. He'd never been an angry or critical man, never drank so much. And he'd sure never hit me. I remembered his patience when he'd taught me things—like when he'd run down the street behind my bike, balancing it as I learned to ride.

That was part of the problem. No more running. Walking was a challenge. I knew he hated those crutches, and that he couldn't seem to adapt. I'd seen other men who had adjusted, even one who worked on a building site, balancing on his only leg while he shoveled sand.

What was the difference? Confidence? Father had lost his along with that half leg. Maybe he didn't know who he was either. Which made what I'd said even worse.

Did I hate him? I didn't think so, but I'd hated how he didn't—couldn't—stand up to those Schupos. Couldn't physically stand up to them because of his leg; couldn't mentally stand up to them either. I covered my face. Oh God, that was it. His body was his prison like Leipzig was everyone's. He was even more powerless than I was. And I wanted him to be ... the man he used to be. The one who had the power to protect his family. I hated how powerless he'd become.

If only time could be rewound like a movie reel. I'd take back those words. I don't even know who you are. An apology wouldn't erase them; they were carved inside both our skulls.

Anneliese joined me on the roof an hour later. She sat close and hugged her knees to her chest. "I hoped I'd find you here."

Faint light rose from the streetlamps that were working. Anneliese was a dark form, features hidden. I couldn't remember the last time she'd sought me out for anything. I didn't move for fear of scaring her away.

Her sigh was soft. "I heard you go down then back up."

"You were hiding in the bathroom?"

"You know me well enough to know that."

I propped myself on my elbow. "I don't know you, Liese. I used to, but you've changed since you and Ernst broke up." I hesitated. "Sorry. I know you don't like talking about him. It's just ..."

"Just what?" The question seemed like an invitation. I hoped it was.

"I wonder sometimes about you and Ernst. This weekend I asked Uncle Bruno a question about you and he closed up the way he does, turning into a bolted oak door. It made me think he knew something."

A long pause. Then, "Why were you talking about me with Uncle Bruno?"

I struggled with whether to say anything.

"Wilm? Please?"

I'd say the most awful things to my father, but I found it hard to say anything hurtful to my sister. "I was in the park the other day with some guys. A squad of Schupos had been drilling and challenged us to a soccer game ..." I hesitated. "Ernst was one of the officers." She inhaled sharply. I continued, "He didn't recognize me until after. Before he left I asked him why you and he had broken up. He was awful, hinted about you being unfaithful ..."

Though Anneliese was a short distance away I could almost feel her tense. Her silhouette shrank. "I know you didn't cheat on him," I blurted. "He's a jackass to say that. You loved him more than he deserved."

The night wrapped us in a silent cloak of cool air that seemed sharp with Anneliese's hurt. We heard footsteps in the street. Two pairs of boots slapping the cobblestones in cadence. A patrol. When the sound faded Anneliese said, "We should've told you."

I didn't like the sound of that. Did I really want to hear more? Anneliese's fingers brushed my arm. "I'm cold. Can we sit back to back? Like when we'd go up to the roof on our old apartment to watch the moon?"

"Sure." We shifted around. It amazed me how much smaller she was than me. A reversal of how it had been years ago, when I'd tilt my head and rest the top of it against the back of Anneliese's neck. Now she was doing that to me. Clouds hid the moon.

Anneliese said, "Do you remember the day I went to the train station to meet Ernst?"

"You mean when the British released him from the prisoner-of-war camp?" I felt Anneliese nod. "I remember Mother at breakfast, saying you could see him after work."

"She told me it wasn't safe."

"You laughed."

"I don't remember that." She drew in a shuddering breath. "Wilm, she was right."

I tensed. "Why?"

"Please. This is hard." Reluctantly I waited.

"I went to the train station. Ernst's train was late, but I was so excited. The only thing in my mind was that he was coming home." A long pause and Anneliese continued in a quiet voice. "Suddenly I realized there were uniforms in my way. I stood on tiptoe to see over them. I said excuse me, excuse me, because I saw a train approaching on the track Ernst's train was to arrive on. I didn't pay them any mind until one grabbed my shoulder. There were ..."

Another breath vibrated from her ribs into mine. She whispered, "Four of them. I think there were four. Soviet soldiers. I tried to back away. They pushed me to the side. To some crates, I think. Maybe a table. They ..."

Her breathing was shallow. I'd turned to stone. I wanted her to stop but couldn't open my mouth. She said, "After the first one had ... finished, I struggled to get away. I saw Ernst, standing in the flow of people." Her voice gained strength. "I cried out to him. Lost sight of him. And the Soviets took turns r-ra ..."

I remembered coming home from school that day. Anneliese was in her room and not to be disturbed, Mother had said. She was distraught over breaking up with Ernst. I gulped in some air. "Why didn't he help you? Why didn't anyone help?"

"Because they were Soviets. They attack whomever they choose. They kill whomever they choose. To interfere is to die. Where have you been these last two years?"

"Playing games, I guess." I squeezed my eyes shut. My limbs trembled. This horrible thing had happened a year ago. A whole year. But this was the first time I'd heard it.

"Wilm? Are you okay? I didn't mean to upset you. I wanted you to understand, to know what I've been through. I don't want you to hate me like you hate Father."

Father hadn't done anything to help Anneliese either. But what could he have done? I couldn't stop shaking. "I could never hate you, Liese. And I don't hate ... I just want our old father back, the one who could protect us."

"Only listening to Mother would have protected me, and I was too foolish to listen." She moved so suddenly I almost fell over. "I'm going inside. Please come down."

"Not yet. I can't ..." Couldn't face our parents. They hadn't told me. No one had told me.

"I'm sorry I didn't tell you sooner. Before tonight, when you stood up to Father, you always seemed like such a child. But you grew up without me noticing. I'm sorry for that too."

I listened to her leave and struggled to draw air into my lungs. The slight breeze carried the smell of burning coal. It stung my eyes. The attack had happened a year ago, but for me it felt like it had happened today. I couldn't think, couldn't breathe ... couldn't block the images forming in my mind.

Those soldiers had battered Anneliese's soul so much that she flinched when her brother walked into her room. Little reactions were suddenly explained. The looks of fear, the cringing. Why she dressed in boy's clothes to get to work. Why she scuttled from one safe haven to another, never went out, never saw anyone. Never laughed or smiled.

As surely as the war had stolen my father, those Soviet soldiers had stolen my sister.

I wasn't cold anymore. My feelings whirled so fast I felt dizzy. I hugged my stomach, hoping to stop its churning. But raw fury kindled deep inside, getting hotter and hotter until it pumped through me with the heat of a foundry's furnace. I thought I might burst into flames. I howled and shook my fists at the ghostly outline of the cloud-shrouded moon.

A block away, a dog answered in mournful tones.

CHAPTER SIX

I didn't return to the apartment until after Father left for work the next morning. Karl called our mathematics instructor "the accountant," but it was my father who counted numbers in a job he hated. Herr Bader had begged to keep his job, a job where he taught slobs like me who didn't want to learn, a job he loved with a passion that puzzled everyone. The SED almost hadn't let him keep his position because he had been a Nazi, yet from what I'd heard he'd only been a Nazi so he could keep his job. And so many others were in the same position. The world was turned inside out and backward.

Anneliese was leaving for work when I walked in. She whispered, "I'm okay. Don't worry," and slipped into the hall. How could I not worry?

As she started down the stairs, the lights flickered then went dark. Another power outage. I'd heard that much of the city had few power problems, but here so many lines were damaged that we weren't so lucky. Anneliese's footsteps continued down. At least the back room where she worked had a window so she'd have some natural light.

Mother greeted me cheerfully, like the previous night hadn't happened. I saw by the lunch waiting on the table that Father hadn't thrown out my food. "Could I take extra? For Georg?"

Without comment she sliced more cheese and sausage, wrapped and placed it in my lunch tin, along with the promised note for Saturday. Before I could escape to school she said, "You need to take out the ashes, Wilm."

I had slept so little I didn't have the energy to ask her why they hadn't told me about Anneliese. I still felt confused about it, but mostly I was so numb I couldn't think.

All my satchel had in it was my lunch tin. I slung it over my shoulder and trudged downstairs with the pail of ashes and out the back door. Frau Nikel was hanging her wash on one of the communal clotheslines strung the width of the courtyard's north side. She snapped a pillowcase and called a greeting as she pinned it in place.

The acrid odor of the ash pit hit me and I almost sneezed. None of the six manhole lids on the metal plate covering the recessed pit were closed snugly. The bricked-in pit was full. I dumped the ashes under the lid with the smallest gap and left.

Mostly I dozed through my classes. Lunch-break conversation was Georg moaning gratefully over the sausage and cheese. After school I spent the evening on the roof.

Every time I tried to think it hurt. Worse, thinking brought back the images Anneliese's words had drawn. I saw it over and over again. The movie playing in my mind made me so sick I threw up the *Abendbrot* of cheese, sausage, and bread that Anneliese delivered to the roof. Better to be numb and not think. I came down from the roof only after I knew everyone would be in bed.

I stumbled through the days, hardly sleeping at night and struggling to stay awake in class.

Thursday afternoon in mathematics my eyes refused to stay open. A tapping on my shoulder made me jerk my head up. I blinked and tried to remember where I was. Light filtered through dirty windows and backlit Herr Bader's thinning hair. He smelled like cabbage. I mumbled an apology and glanced around. The other students were gone.

"I am at my wit's end with you, Herr Tauber." Herr Bader slammed a mathematics book on my desk. I flinched. "Study Chapter Twenty-three," he said. "You have a test tomorrow. Pass it or you fail the class. And return the book. It is the only student textbook I have."

I retrieved my satchel and stuffed the book in. "Thank you, sir." The weight of the bag felt strange. Other than my lunch tin, it usually contained only scraps of paper on which to do homework.

As I was leaving, Herr Bader spoke again. "Is there something you'd like to tell me about, Herr Tauber? You are not usually so blatantly inattentive. Trouble at home, perhaps?"

My knuckles whitened as my grip on the doorknob turned vise-like. "No, sir."

"No, there is nothing going on? Or no, you don't want to tell me?" He sighed. "Never mind. Go home and study."

I pried my fingers off the doorknob and left. Head down, I walked home, kicking at pebbles. I skirted around some workers replacing paving stones.

At the corner of my block I paused. Two apartments on the east side of the street had been bombed in the war and the blast had blown out every window in our apartment building. Finding replacement glass had been difficult, so ill-fitted panes rattled in the wind. All that remained of the bombed apartments was a meter-high pile of rubble, packed down, mostly level. Some boys tossed a ball around the platform, insulting each other and laughing.

Anneliese and I had played ball games at the farm. Our favorite had been a version of Völkerball she'd created. We'd stand on opposite sides of the house and throw the ball over. If you caught the ball, you raced around the house to throw the ball and hit the other player. I usually missed. Not Anneliese. She'd race around a corner and smack me before I could dodge the ball. Bruises the size of potatoes would pepper my back by the time we were finished.

One of the boys missed and their ball rolled toward me. I
lobbed it back. They thought playing in the rubble was normal,
but I could remember Leipzig when it was whole. No parts missing. No one fearing attack ...

Something hit my back and I crashed to the pavement. My
palms slapped stone, then my chin. Someone stole my satchel,
rolled me over, and pinned my wrists. "Karl, you idiot!" My chest
heaved from the shock. I tasted blood. Spat it out. The gob landed
on his coat and he scowled down at it. I spat again. "Let me up."

"You're a traitor, Wilm. You'll be treated accordingly."

"Make sense, *Dummkopf*."

"We followed you. And you walked past two Schupos in plain
sight."

I didn't remember any police. "I wasn't playing your dumb
game. I was walking home."

"Dumb? Operating behind enemy lines isn't dumb." He
glanced over his shoulder at Georg, who was holding my book
bag and grinning. "What should we do with him?"

"Drown him? Tie a bag of bricks to his feet and throw him in
the Pleisse?"

Karl's smile turned wolfish. "Good idea. Unless he proves his
loyalty."

I spoke through clenched teeth. "I can't play your game today,
Karl. I have homework."

"That's funny. You slept through every class. How could you
have homework?"

Karl's grip loosened slightly and I used the chance to send
him sprawling. I stood, brushed off my trousers and coat. "Bader
caught me after class."

Georg laughed and wild tufts of hair bobbed. "How hard was
that? You were snoring."

I snatched my bag. "Right. See you around."

Karl grabbed my arm. "Tomorrow you prove your loyalty."

He was still playing the game, though I could see the worry in his scrunched eyebrows. He wanted me to tell him what was happening but wouldn't push. I nodded. Karl released me and walked away.

In the apartment I scrounged for food and found a note from Mother saying she was gone to an appointment. I was eating the last of Uncle Bruno's cheese when she walked in, still chatting to Frau Nikel, who lived one floor up. She said her good-byes as she closed the door. I had never realized before, but it seemed she always went with a neighbor to the store or, well, anywhere. I didn't remember her being so sociable during the war, or even when the Americans controlled the city.

When she greeted me, I asked, "Why do you always go places with someone else?"

Mother set her cloth bag on the counter and joined me at the table. She studied me so long that I brushed at my face in search of crumbs. Finally, she spoke. "There is safety in numbers, Wilm."

Safety. I swallowed. "Why didn't you tell me what happened to Anneliese?"

She drew a slow breath. "So she finally told you. I didn't say anything because ..." She touched the top knot on the kerchief holding her hair in place. "It changes nothing."

"It changes everything!"

"No. This is the world we live in now. Understand it. What happened was awful. But do you think Anneliese is the only woman to be attacked since the Soviets arrived? Far from it. The best we can hope is that they don't kill us or our men when they're finished with us."

"The best? How can you accept that?" My fists were clenched so hard they ached. I forced them open and pressed my palms against the table. "Have you ...?" I couldn't say it, couldn't bear to think of my mother being attacked.

"I had a close call once. A drunk Soviet soldier forced me down an alley. His commanding officer must have seen because he followed and stopped the man."

"Does Father know?"

"I never told him. But he knows about Anneliese."

"If it happens so much why don't any men or boys mention it?"

She drew another long breath. "I think they hope that if they ignore what is happening it will stop. They are helpless too. It's a form of punishment. We must bear up under it."

"Bear up! Where's the justice in that?" I stood so fast that my chair fell over. "Anneliese shouldn't have to bear up. What if she's attacked again? It could destroy her."

Mother began to cry. "There is nothing we can do, Wilm. Don't you understand? If your father tries to say anything they might shoot him. All we can do is survive each day and hope it gets better."

"This is insane. You didn't start the war. Anneliese didn't start the war. But you can both be punished on a drunk soldier's whim? And you have to clean up the rubble to have the privilege of eating? And no one can protest without getting shot? I can't stand this."

I snatched my book bag and headed for the door.

"Where are you going?"

"To the roof to study. I hate mathematics, but at least it makes sense."

CHAPTER SEVEN

I dropped the test on Herr Bader's desk. "Don't move, Herr Tauber," he said.

I clasped my hands loosely behind my back while he pulled out a marking key and studied my test sheet. I fixed my eyes on the blackboard.

"Tauber," Karl called from the back of the room. "You aren't a Hitler Youth anymore."

I'd hated being in the HJs with all their practice soldiering and military discipline, and had joined only because it was the law. Yet I'd fallen into military parade-rest position. I crossed my arms. Head still bent, Herr Bader said, "Herr Heinig, you would be advised to pay more attention to your test and less to your fellow students. Keeping your eyes on your own paper would be a nice change."

The students snickered.

I longed to see Karl's expression, but didn't turn, only stuffed my hands into my trouser pockets. My fingers twirled my pocketknife as I waited. Herr Bader laid down his pen. "Herr Tauber, you have some explaining to do."

Clamminess seeped from my hairline, down my face and neck. "I swear I didn't cheat."

"I know who cheats." I thought I caught a flicker of amusement in his expression. "No, you need to explain why, when studying merits you a mark of ninety-two percent, you rarely study?"

Warmth had just returned to my cheeks. They went cold again. Ninety-two percent? Karl would harass me mercilessly about such a high mark. "I found this chapter interesting, sir. It used mathematics in …"

"In practical ways?"

I nodded, relieved he understood.

"Then it's fortunate for you, Herr Tauber, that the next chapter is also about practical mathematics. Do try to stay awake for the lectures."

Now my cheeks went hot. "Yes, sir." I returned to my desk and slid low in the seat, not responding to Karl's spitball that hit my arm. I hadn't meant to do so well. Now Herr Bader would expect it all the time, but he was going to be disappointed. I wasn't going to wind up an accountant in a brickworks factory.

After school, as we walked to Karl's apartment, he chanted like a child, "Teacher's pet. Teacher's pet." He shut up when my fist connected with his shoulder. We stashed our satchels in his apartment and sat on the building's front steps eating day-old bread and cooked turnip slices.

"I wish we had honey," Georg said.

"I had real honey at Christmas. Enough for a whole slice of bread," Karl replied. "It was so much better than that artificial stuff we usually choke down."

"At least we get jam once in awhile," I said.

"When do you get jam?" Georg replied. "I haven't had that for months either."

I didn't reply, or mention that I'd had real honey at the farm a few weeks ago. Uncle Bruno had traded three eggs for it. But my favorite was still raspberry jam. The clerk would scoop it from the store's bucket and drip ruby-red sweetness into our jar, and I'd carry it home to enjoy on warm bakery bread. It had been the highlight of shopping when I was young. I closed my eyes and licked my lips.

The bitter smell of turnip cut through my memories. I wrinkled my nose and let Georg gobble down my last slice. Needing to get my mind off food, I said, "I'm ready to prove my loyalty. If I have to."

"You have to." Karl grinned, cleared his throat, and deepened his voice. "You must go to where the vipers watch the searchers."

A riddle. I thought for a moment. Nodded. "You mean the missing person's registry office beside the old town hall. So I go to Markt and do what?"

Karl sprang up. "Reconnaissance. You must spy out the vipers and report numbers. We'll watch from a distance to make sure you don't betray us. If you do, you'll wish the vipers had struck you down with poison."

I fought the urge to roll my eyes, but Georg's wink injected some fun into this mission. Anyway, it was better than going home. "Sure. Then I'll beat you at a game of Mensch Ärgere Dich Nicht."

"As if you could," Karl replied. "I'm king of the board, undefeated for sixteen games."

"Then the odds are against you." I stood. "Let's go."

"As you wish. Your life hangs on the results."

This time I did roll my eyes. I told myself it was a bit of fun, but it had been hard to think about having fun since Anneliese shared her secret. She'd want me to enjoy myself, pretend I was still a boy.

We headed along some narrow *Trümmerbahn* tracks. In Johannisplatz we stepped aside to let a train of coal mining cars piled with rubble go past. I spun my knife in my pocket like I was making a cocoon. I couldn't hold it still. Why was I so nervous over a game?

In Augustusplatz—the Soviets wanted us to call it Karl-Marx-Platz—a massive banner covering half the New Theater's ruins warned us about the beetle Uncle Bruno had taught me to watch for. "The fiend of the potato fields," the sign said. I didn't think potato bugs were the real fiends in Leipzig.

By the university church, the only undamaged building in the square, I slowed down.

"Dragging your feet, Tauber? A sign of guilt," Georg goaded me.

"Sure." I nodded at the church. "Do you think we'll get accepted into the university?"

"You, maybe," Karl replied. "Georg for sure. Me? The shock might kill my mother."

I grinned. "Why?"

"Tavern owner is the highest we've ever climbed." Karl nudged Georg. "It sounds like our traitor is trying to distract us, comrade."

The Soviets and their German communist lackeys used that term. My jaw clenched, so hard it hurt. I pretended to yawn and forced my thoughts to the mission. I imagined central Leipzig, nicknamed Zentrum. "Grimmaische Strasse here runs straight to the market. Let's jog two blocks north, circle the rubble field on Brühl and come at Markt from a side street."

Karl and Georg grinned. The hunt was on. Fifteen minutes later we crouched in the archway of the Barthels Hof building. Its courtyard opened behind us and on the far side of that was another access to the yard—our escape route.

Our doorway was in the northwest corner of the market square and offered a clear view of the one-story registry building in the middle of the south half. I could remember when market stalls filled the square. I had loved the noise and excitement, had loved the way the old town hall had presided over it. I was glad to see repairs happening on the roof and tower that had burned in a raid. Now there were a few cars around the outer edges of the square, some people cutting across Markt, and only a few vendors hawking their food to the passersby.

I studied two military trucks parked where a big statue had once stood on the north side of Markt. No police in sight. They'd be on the other side of those trucks, if they were around at all.

Hand in pocket—to look casual—I left Karl and Georg in the doorway and sauntered past the bombed-out buildings lining the north side of the square. Still no police.

I reached the first truck, parked parallel to its partner, and paused by the waist-high back wheel. Loud voices came from the far side of the second truck. I eased past the wheel well so I was between the two vehicles, the smell of diesel thick. I clutched my knife tighter as if that would slow my heart's hammering. A game. It was a game.

Through the windscreen and side window I spotted a cluster of seven Schupos, all clean and well fed. I checked over my shoulder to make sure no one was around. Most civilians gave military vehicles wide berth. Today was no exception.

Beyond the seven police, four Soviets strolled into view. They halted, chatting as they watched the police watch the people.

Four. Anneliese had been attacked by four Soviet soldiers. Maybe these four. My breathing sped up. I inhaled deeply to ease my jitters. For a second I wished for a more dangerous weapon, something from that secret cache Karl was always going on about. I gripped my knife.

And suddenly I was calm. I watched them as options spun out, a spiderweb of possibilities interconnected like the vaulted ceilings in Nikolaikirche. A part of my mind floated above the square like an eagle. And through that imaginary eagle's eye, I looked down, saw tiny soldiers positioned by tiny trucks. Their line of sight didn't include the entrance of Barthels Hof. I had a clear retreat.

Karl wanted a game; he'd get a game. But this time I was going to make the rules.

I checked around again, ducked down, and scuttled to the truck farthest from the police. I could see their feet. One was kicking at a loose cobblestone. None of the feet broke the circle.

There would never be a better time.

I drew my knife, flicked it open. I jammed the blade deep in the rubber of the front wheel, sawed it back and forth as I worked to lengthen the cut. Then I yanked it out and stabbed the back tire too. The other side of the truck was too exposed so I pocketed my knife.

Forcing myself not to run, I quick-marched toward the Barthels Hof archway. I had almost reached it went something popped. Loudly. The weight of the truck must have blown one of those gashes wide open.

I darted through the doorway, past Karl and Georg, and into the courtyard. "Come on! We have to leave!"

In the square, people began to shout.

CHAPTER EIGHT

We shot across the courtyard, through the other exit to Barfuss Allee, and headed west. After a few blocks I slowed to a brisk walk. Karl and Georg caught up but were too winded to talk. We reached Johannapark, zigzagged around greenery, and collapsed on the bank of the canal, Elsterflutbett. I leaned against a tree facing toward central Leipzig so I could spot any pursuit. The park was quiet.

"What was that bang?" Georg said. "It sounded almost like a gunshot."

I shrugged. "A tire blew."

"You seem pretty sure of that," Karl replied. He studied me then pushed his fingers through his light hair. "You didn't."

"Didn't what?" Georg asked. "What didn't Tauber do?"

"Yes, Karl," I said. "Didn't what?"

"Let me see your knife."

We glared at each other for thirty seconds before I tossed my knife to him. He opened it, flicked his thumb at the blade, then stabbed it into the earth. "*Scheisse*. Rubber crumbs on the blade. What did you do? Forget the police, the Soviets will be furious. Those were Soviet trucks."

"Why should I care about angry Soviets?"

"Because angry Soviets toss hooligans in jail, call them Wolverines, make them disappear, like what happened to Rolf, that boy a year ahead of us."

"I wasn't caught. And I'm no Wolverine. I was glad to get out of the Hitler Youth. I'm not going to conspire with other ex-HJs against anyone."

Georg was looking from Karl to me and back. "Why are we talking about Wolverines? If someone hears us they might turn us in."

"You're right, Georg." I stood and stretched. "So don't use the word, Karl. You were the one who wanted to play a game. Now you're complaining that I changed some rules?"

Karl jumped up and gave me a shove. "Because you're acting crazy!"

"I saw seven Schupos, four Soviets. You want crazy? Crazy is playing at being behind enemy lines but never sabotaging the enemy if you have the chance."

"It's a bloody game!" He shoved me again. Harder.

I'd had enough. I tackled him and we rolled around, each struggling to get on top. We pushed apart, got up. Started swinging. My reach was longer. I landed two shots before Karl clipped my jaw. We traded stomach punches, clutched and grabbed and jabbed each other's ribs. Georg yelled at us to stop. I poured my frustration into every hit. Karl pounded me right back.

All at once pain gripped my ear. I staggered back to see that the man with my ear locked in his fingers held Karl the same way. He was strong for an old man. Karl and I both yelled, "Let go!"

"Not until you explain yourselves."

I grabbed his wrist and tried to pull his hand away but he tightened his grip. I yelped. The old man said, "I will relax my hold if you both stop squirming and answer my questions."

"Why should we?" I asked through gritted teeth.

"Because you are scaring the ducks."

Karl and I went still. Stared. And Karl thought I was crazy. The man smiled. "Isn't that better?"

I started to nod but a needle of pain shot through my ear. The duck-loving crazy man wore a tweed jacket, dusty, old but not frayed. His hair was white and thick as a thatched roof. His hands were strong like Uncle Bruno's.

"So. Two hooligans making trouble?" he asked.

"Not hooligans," Karl answered. "Friends."

"Ah. I could tell. Do the friends have names?"

I prayed Karl would keep silent. "I'm Karl. This is Wilm."

Idiot.

"Wilm. Short for Wilhelm?" Karl nodded and the man said, "Karl and Wilhelm, and ..." Georg offered his name. The man smiled. "A pleasure, Georg. I am Otto Steinhauer. Since we have become so suddenly and intimately acquainted you may call me Otto." He nodded at each of us in turn. "Now, Karl and Wilhelm, I shall release you so you can properly thank the man who saved you both from a severe beating." He dropped his hands.

I cupped my hand over my ear and bit my lip to keep from swearing. Karl muttered his favorite, "*Scheisse.*" Who did this old man think he was? He continued smiling mildly and tapped tobacco into a pipe.

"Tobacco?" Georg said. "Are you rich?"

The old man laughed. "No, but my services are in demand so it is easier for me to get certain restricted items than for most people."

"What services?" I asked, still coddling my ear. "Spying for the SED?"

"I am not a spy, though I do work for the SED."

I backed up a step. How much of our talk had he heard?

"Don't get skittish, young friend. I am only an engineer, contracted to inspect bridges." He pointed to the bridge spanning the canal at the north edge of the park. "I was inspecting the pilings when a flock of startled ducks almost swept me from my feet."

Then I noticed his rubber boots. He saw my downward glance and raised salt-and-pepper eyebrows. "Am I passing inspection?"

I slipped my hand in my pocket, hesitated when I realized my knife wasn't there. "A man can never be too careful."

"True. A man should always be careful, especially in these times." He dropped the unlit pipe into his breast pocket. "What made friends mindlessly attack each other?"

I retrieved my knife from where Karl had stuck it in the ground. I almost sighed in relief when my fingers tightened around it. "Only a game. A little fun." I felt Karl's glare.

"I remember roughhousing with my friends. This looked more serious than that," Otto Steinhauer commented. "But I can see you don't want further inquiry. I should get back to work at any rate. Drop by some time. I always enjoy intelligent company."

He strolled along the bank toward the bridge.

"Crazy old man," I muttered.

He called back, "I'm neither crazy nor terribly old. And I have excellent hearing."

Karl punched my shoulder and gave me a look that clearly warned me to be quiet. A little late.

Silent and sullen, we walked south beside the canal. My chin started to ache, along with a few spots on my ribs. I inhaled the smell of earth and grass and river. Most of the city was blanketed by harsher smells, bitter coal and diesel. I hardly noticed except when they were absent. When I inhaled too deeply my left side pulsed; I'd have bruises tonight.

When we reached the next bridge, Karl led us to the middle of the span. We leaned against the railing and watched the distant figure of Otto Steinhauer splashing beside the bridge he was inspecting. It was quite new, with clean, straight lines and ends that looked like white wings sweeping up the green banks. I liked its modern look and hoped it wasn't damaged.

"Why'd you do it?" Karl asked.

"Not your business."

"You made it our business. We were with you. The police could arrest us all."

"They won't."

"You'd better be right."

I was. No Schupo had seen me. No passerby would get involved. We were safe. And if the Soviets were upset too, even better.

"You still haven't told us why." Karl's voice was tense.

"A little payback."

"What have they done to you?"

Anneliese's secret still felt too raw to share. I shifted to rest my hip against the chipped stone wall. "What haven't they done? To all of us?"

"Shut up, Wilm. You sound like a real Wolverine."

"I don't want the Nazis back. They destroyed the whole country. All I want is some justice."

"I know about Soviet justice. My father is experiencing it in one of their prison camps," Karl whispered and turned his attention to the water. "You'd better hope you don't get it."

CHAPTER NINE

I sat cross-legged on the roof and traced the initials scratched into one side of my pocketknife's handle: E-W. Ernst Weber. I flipped the knife over and remembered the ceremony we'd made of etching my initials into the wood on this side when Ernst gave it to me for my twelfth birthday. It was a good knife. Krupps steel. It made the triumph all the sweeter, using this knife to strike back. My lucky knife.

Satisfaction surged as I recalled stabbing the knife into rubber, and the sound of the tire blowing out. If only I could have seen the expressions on those Schupos' faces. Half of them had probably thought they were under fire and had drawn their pistols. Or hit the ground.

Someone clattered up the ladder toward the roof. I stood, stashed the knife in my pocket, then grinned when Anneliese appeared. I rushed over, clasped her forearms, and whirled around.

She held tight, looking uneasy. "What are you doing?"

"Celebrating!"

We spun and spun, and I laughed at her wide-eyed expression. Then Anneliese smiled. Small, wavering, but definitely a smile. The first I'd seen in a year.

I halted, released her. The world kept spinning. I grabbed my knees to stop from falling, and Anneliese dropped to the roof. I sat beside her and propped my elbow on an upraised knee. I couldn't stop grinning. "Do that again."

"Do what?"

"Smile."

"That's silly." She brushed flyaway hair from her face. She eyed me curiously, forced a smile, but it died immediately. "Maybe next time."

I bit back a sigh. At least she had tried.

She picked at her skirt hem. "Why are you so ... giddy?"

"It's hard to explain, but I feel happier than I have in years. More free." More powerful.

Anneliese stood and adjusted her waistband. "Then I hope I don't ruin your mood."

"You couldn't."

She wrinkled her nose. "Don't be too sure. Father dislikes that you've been eating *Abendbrot* on the roof since you two argued. He said Mother's kitchen isn't a delivery service and you should join us for the evening meal."

I grimaced, then reconsidered. My father had asked for my presence. Was it an offer of truce?

"Wilm? Will you come?" Anneliese looked half hopeful, half fearful.

I couldn't refuse. Didn't want to. "Anything for you, Liese."

She almost managed a smile.

Anything, I repeated silently.

Monday after school I was bored, restless. Karl and Georg had chores, and I knew if I went home there'd be a note telling me to mix some coal dust to form into briquettes. Who wanted to be stuck inside kneading brown stinking dough on a sunny day?

I walked to central Leipzig along the busiest streets, where bomb damage was already cleaned up. So many streets, like the one

I used to live on, looked like the war had just ended. Clogged by rubble, deserted. I preferred roads where life made the stones hum.

I stopped near Thomaskirche, with its charred tower, to scan the market square. The missing person's registry was quiet. I stared at the spot where the Soviet trucks had been parked and relived the sabotage in my mind. I touched my knife. That small act of defiance had felt so good. I'd tried to hold onto that feeling over the weekend but it had faded. I hadn't gone to the farm on Saturday and the boredom of everyday life had once again taken over.

Beside me, on the grassy lawn by Thomaskirche, a Soviet officer showed a little boy how to scatter breadcrumbs for the birds. They laughed with delight at their success and threw more crumbs as the boy's nervous mother watched. How could Soviets be so nice to children but so cruel to everyone else?

A Schupo and his woman strolled across Markt, arms linked, enjoying ice cream. When was the last time I'd had ice cream? I tried to re-create the taste in my imagination, but it couldn't overcome the memory of cold potato and sauerkraut from lunch.

The Schupo changed direction and headed toward me. I raised my gaze from the rivulet of melted ice cream trickling over his fingers. Ernst Weber. He stopped in front of me. "Why the angry look, little brother?" He stressed the nickname, as if daring me to contradict him, though he'd said it with a smile.

Hand in pocket, I squeezed the knife as I arched my eyebrows and wondered if his smile was mocking or real. "I'm trying to remember what ice cream tastes like."

"Oh, poor Wilm," Johanna declared. She held out her cone. I blinked at it. She nodded. "Take it. Really."

I thought Ernst tensed, but it was so slight I wasn't sure. I gave Johanna a rueful smile. "No, thanks. Ernst wanted to treat you. Enjoy it." I walked away, my stomach clenching in protest.

Ernst called that I was smart. I waved, acknowledging his words, but didn't look back. After working so hard to hide my disgust I didn't want him to see it now. I never knew I was a good actor.

When I reached the Elsterflutbett, I realized my feet had been taking me in the direction of the odd, duck-loving engineer. Am I crazy? He almost ripped my ear off. But still, he was interesting somehow.

Otto Steinhauer sat under a linden tree on the far side of the bridge, studying a sketchpad. I crossed the bridge and sat astride the end of the white concrete railing. Five minutes later he noticed me. Surprise flickered across his face. He left the sketchpad and strolled to the bridge. "Well, well. Young Wilhelm. I'm frankly surprised to see you."

A bit surprised myself, I shrugged. "My ear recovered quickly."

A nod. "To what do I owe this pleasure?"

I said the first thing that came to mind. "How old is 'not all that old'?"

"Fifty-three."

Eleven years older than Father. To needle him, I whistled. Smiling, he asked, "Old?"

"Very."

"Through your eyes, perhaps."

"They're the only ones I can look through."

Otto Steinhauer laughed. "True. Come with me. Let's put that quick wit to work."

He pointed at the sketchpad on the ground under the tree. "Tell me why I drew a picture of the bridge before inspecting it."

The pen-and-ink sketch was detailed, the lines bold, full of confidence. Like its owner? I considered the bridge, wanting to ask where it got its strength when it was flat instead of arched, how it survived the traffic, how much damage would weaken it.

So what good was drawing the bridge? I studied the meticulous sketch, details visible even in crosshatched shadows. That was it. "You have to pay close attention to the bridge to get that much detail in your drawing."

Otto nodded. "Not all engineers do this, of course, but I find it helps me to better see the structure so I know the areas that might need inspection."

I sat on the grass near the tree. "How will you fix it?"

"It might not need it. How would you fix it?"

My eagle's eye swooped over and under the bridge. "It seems pretty new, made of big blocks of concrete. I think you'd need to remove broken sections and completely replace them."

Otto nodded. "With extensive damage, yes. The trick is for the repairs to not look out of place so the aesthetics aren't compromised."

"The what?"

"Aesthetics. The pleasing way it looks. Having the bridge remain visually appealing doesn't concern most governments, which makes it difficult to satisfy them and me."

Otto sat under the tree and stretched out his legs. He retrieved a jar of water from behind the trunk and offered it to me. I took a mouthful, swished it around, and let the cool liquid trickle down my throat.

I set the jar between us. "How do you figure out things like how much weight it can carry?"

"That's called load-bearing. I apply physics. Also called practical mathematics."

I grinned.

"You look pleased."

"I've been failing mathematics all year. Then we had a chapter test on practical mathematics and I got the highest mark."

Otto took a drink, passed the jar to me again, and pulled out his pipe. "I am not surprised."

"Why?"

"When you considered my questions, you didn't seem to be looking at the bridge in front of you so much as somewhere in your mind. I would guess you excel with spatial tasks and can see things in three dimensions. Many engineers have that skill and are good at practical mathematics, but often don't understand abstract aspects of numbers."

"You sound like a teacher."

"I did teach. I taught Wehrmacht lieutenants how to build portable bridges from prefabricated engineer corps pieces, or from available materials. I taught explosives experts the stress points on a bridge, and where to place charges to collapse different types of bridges." He tapped tobacco into his pipe but slid it back into his pocket instead of lighting it. "Destroying things is easier, but building things is much more satisfying."

I paused with the water jar partway to my lips. Was he still talking about bridges? I set the jar down. His green gaze, so direct, trapped mine.

After a moment he said, "An odd coincidence occurred the day we met. That night, a fellow in the SED told me a Soviet truck had been attacked in the market, only meters from a group of policemen. This brazen attack happened shortly before I saw three young men enter the park and get into a violent argument."

My gaze lowered.

"Never!"

I jerked my head back up.

"Never look down or away when an official accuses you of something. To do so underscores your guilt. Do you understand, Wilhelm?"

"I prefer Wilm."

"Good. You kept your voice steady. Though I suspect you are shaking inside."

He was right. I swallowed.

"Do not swallow when I am looking for an answer. Do it when I am talking and slightly less attentive to your actions. You must know what your body is saying, not only your mouth."

"Why are you telling me this?"

"I heard you and your friends talking. I know you did the deed. You chose to play a dangerous game. Do you know what makes it so dangerous?"

I plucked at the grass and shook my head.

"Because they don't consider it a game. What seems insignificant to you, like slashing a tire, could land you in a prison camp. Like when playing poker, you should always know what the stakes are before you begin to play."

"You're not going to turn me in?"

"No."

"Doesn't that make you guilty too?"

"In a way."

"Then why help me?"

"I saw how you studied that bridge. You like bridges."

"Since I was little. There are three on the way to my uncle's farm. I can never resist balancing on the railings."

"If you saw the bridge spanning the Rhine River at Cologne you would want to climb the girders like a monkey." He was right again. I'd love to scale girders.

"I was no different at your age." He peered into the distance. "I was several years older than you are now when my world was first upended by war, the Great War. Aptitude tests sent me into the engineering corps. That was a filthy, awful war. I never imagined I'd be in another. We who survived thought it had been the war that would end war. After all that destruction I only wanted to build. Now there is so much to rebuild that I sometimes feel overwhelmed."

Attention still far off, Otto fell silent. I plucked a new blade of grass and chewed it. He was strange but he seemed trustworthy. After all, he hadn't reported me to the police.

Otto started and looked around, as if trying to figure out where he was. "My apologies. My mind drifted. What was I talking about?"

"Rebuilding."

"Ah. That made me think how objects are often easier to rebuild than lives."

"Did someone you know get hurt in the war?"

"My wife died in a bombing raid in Berlin in 1943. My son decided the biggest threat facing German citizens was the Allied bombing campaign. He left university and took to the air to protect the people."

"He was a pilot?"

"A fighter pilot, and a good one I was told. He had the spatial sense that you and I share. But he was shot down during the Battle of Dresden. The sheer size of the British attack cost many fighter pilots their lives. For nothing. The city wasn't saved." He paused before speaking again. "Did you lose family in the war?"

"Half a leg." His eyebrows curved into bushy S's. I explained, "My father lost half a leg. He'd admire your son. He wishes he'd died on the battlefield. Now he's a bookkeeper at a brickworks factory and hates it."

"He might not hate it."

"He says he does."

Otto tapped the pocket cradling his pipe, forehead furled in thought. "If you don't mind me asking, does your family have enough to eat?"

I shrugged. "Not always."

"Then perhaps your father hates working indoors instead of having a physical job, and is frustrated by being unfit for one."

"Why would he want to spend his days firing a brick kiln or slogging at a construction site?"

"Because the SED gives more generous ration cards to men who do physical work, and higher pay to buy that extra food, which lets the family eat better."

"Really?"

Otto nodded. "It bothers a man when he cannot put food on the table or keep a roof over his family. Or if his wife must work to make up the shortfall. This starvation economy is enough to make a man do something drastic." His salt-and-pepper brows arched again. "Even keep hidden the identity of a would-be saboteur."

"A successful saboteur."

"Hmm. You had your moment of foolish glory. Please do not take more risks."

I remembered what he'd said earlier and held his gaze. I didn't say anything.

He blew out a breath, then pulled a foil packet from his jacket pocket. "Before I return to work, a treat." He unwrapped the foil to reveal chocolate, broke off two squares, and gave me one. While he enjoyed his, I stared at mine.

"Aren't you going to eat it?"

I rubbed my brow. "Georg had stale bread and moldy cheese for lunch today. Maybe I'll save this for him." My stomach twitched, another protest at refusing good food.

"When did you last eat chocolate?"

"Christmas."

"Almost five months ago."

"Georg hasn't had it for two years. The Americans were here.

We'd offer to run errands. The soldiers who spoke German would say, 'Get lost, boys. We aren't supposed to fraternize.' Half the time they'd toss us some chocolate as they turned away." My chocolate started to melt. "Georg tells that story whenever we see a chocolate display and wish we had money."

"Eat your chocolate. I'll give you a piece for Georg."

I licked my palm clean of delicious, velvety goo. Otto tore off a piece of tinfoil and wrapped a chocolate square in it. "Keep this away from your body heat. Georg might not like having to lick his chocolate from the creases of your pocket." I thanked him and put it in my lunch tin.

Otto stood. "I enjoyed our visit, young Wilhelm. I mean, Wilm. You are good company when you become talkative."

"I'm not usually."

"Not what?"

"Talkative. Not with adults, at least."

"Then I feel honored."

"Right. But ..." I closed my eyes, told myself not to swallow. "Can I trust you?"

"Yes."

"Of course you'd say that."

"Why did you come today, Wilm?"

"I don't know. You interested me. I liked that you were fixing the bridge. Maybe because of that I wanted to see ..."

"If I could be trusted. Yes." Otto pulled a ring off his pinkie finger and gave it to me. "A token of my trust."

"What is it?" I squinted at the coat of arms on its flat face.

"It is my graduation ring from the Berlin School of Engineering." He closed my fingers around it. "It is gold so has value. I would prefer you keep it as a reminder of a possible future, although I cannot stop you from trading it for food."

I turned it over and read the inscription inside: Otto Wilhelm Steinhauer—1922—Honor Roll. We shared a name. I slipped it on my finger, then changed my mind and put it in my pocket. "I'm not as hungry as Georg. Thank you."

He offered his hand. I shook it. His hands were powerful, like I'd expected. I flexed my hand and jogged toward the bridge. My palm slapped the flat-topped balustrade. I hoisted myself up, balancing easily on the twenty-centimeter-wide surface. Halfway across the span, I pivoted and pretended to almost lose my balance. Otto stiffened and stepped toward the water, as if preparing to dive in and save me if I fell.

Maybe I could trust him.

I grinned and waved. He shook a fist at me but I could tell he was smiling. I ran the rest of the way along the railing, leaped off, and wove my way through the trees beside the road.

CHAPTER TEN

The days were quiet, but every night my mind spawned visions of Anneliese's ordeal. Mother didn't even ask me to not skip school on Saturday morning when I headed to the farm. I slept better there so didn't ask Uncle Bruno about Anneliese's secret in case it revived the nightmares. And I sure didn't tell him about sticking those tires. We barely talked.

I arrived home on Sunday afternoon after a damp, miserable walk back to the city.

The heavy oak door of the apartment building was streaked by drizzle and the brick walls had wet tiger stripes. I pushed into the gloomy entrance and shook out my jacket. Water droplets sprayed everywhere. I rubbed my hair; water ran down my neck. A warm bath would be great, but Mother would only have her usual small pot of water heating.

As I trudged up the flight of stairs, I wondered if Karl was home. I might be tired from the walk, but the idea of spending a whole afternoon with my grim family tasted like sour milk.

I stepped inside the apartment, called a hello, and hung up my coat. Mother returned a greeting from the table. I cut through the living room, halting when I saw visitors.

Two Schupos.

My mouth went dry. Otto had changed his mind and reported me. So much for trust.

At least his lesson in facing authorities was going to get tested. I looked each officer in the face. Strangers—that was a relief. If one had been Ernst I couldn't have hoped to stay calm.

The older, bald one ordered me to join them. We only had four mismatched chairs so I dragged over the crate that was Father's footstool and settled between Mother and the younger officer. My outward control gave me a shot of courage. I sat as tall as possible, but was still below everyone's eye level.

"We were just talking about you," the balding officer said.

I made myself keep eye contact. I would admit nothing, but my mouth was parched and I wasn't sure I could talk. I waited for him to continue. Mother seemed to realize my problem and got me a mug of water, commenting about my long walk. Would drinking it tell them my mouth was dry from being nervous? I kept my hands on my thighs.

I couldn't believe I'd been wrong about Otto. Worse, they would search me, find the ring, and charge me with theft. I'd found a strip of leather from a broken bridle at the farm and hung the ring around my neck. My skin went cold. The ring was a hot circle against my chest, branding me with guilt even though I hadn't stolen it.

"Do you know why we're here?" Baldy asked. The younger officer was probably watching for reactions. Know what your body says, Otto had warned.

"No." More relief. My voice worked. I rubbed my cheek nearest the young officer and used the movement to hide my quick swallow.

"We received an anonymous tip." Baldy claimed my mug and drank half the water.

Anonymous. That didn't sound like Otto's way of doing things. I wasn't sure what Baldy wanted me to say so I just raised my eyebrows in what I hoped was a questioning way.

Baldy leaned forward. "Do you know anything about that?"

"No."

"Not very talkative, are you?"

I shrugged. I knew I should be scared, but it was like my brain was a series of rooms. The fear was there, but it was locked behind a door.

Father wore a frown. Whenever I shrugged he accused me of having a bad attitude. Baldy also frowned. I knew I'd better speak. "What was it about?" Fear started to scratch at the door, like a cat wanting to get out. I mentally stuffed a towel along the threshold.

"Someone"—he squinted at me—"reported that some *Schutz-polizei* patrols beat your father in the street for no reason a few weeks ago."

Relief rolled off me so strongly I worried Baldy would smell it. They weren't looking for a weapons cache or investigating the tire incident; they wanted to find that informant, probably arrest him. It could be ugly if I said the wrong thing. "Schupos never beat someone up without a reason." I glanced toward Father; his eyes seemed full of icy shards. I almost smiled. The fear retreated to the corner of its room at the base of my skull.

Baldy drained my mug and slammed it down. "Are you telling me this anonymous tip was right?" His cheeks flushed.

"I have no idea, officer."

"The tip also said you wheeled him down the street"—he checked a small notepad and continued—"in a wheelbarrow."

"Yes, sir."

"Why don't you tell me what happened?"

I looked him in the eyes. They were brown like mine—we were both full of it. "My friends and I were fooling around after school, climbing around ruins. We climbed over one pile and my father was lying on the street. I helped him to his feet—foot—but he must have hurt his ankle when he fell. I borrowed Frau Nikel's wheelbarrow to get him home."

"You didn't see anything?"

"No, sir." *Heard it, though, you red-faced swine.*

"How did your father fall?"

"I didn't see."

"How do you think he fell?"

I glanced at Father again. His frown screamed, *Shut your mouth.* I leaned forward, as if telling a secret. "He doesn't like people feeling sorry for him, but sometimes the rough cobblestones trip him. That must be what happened."

Baldy nodded slowly, like he sympathized but knew better than to embarrass the one-legged man. This was starting to be fun. Baldy pointed at the empty mug. Mother refilled it while he continued, "Did you notice any *Schutzpolizei* patrols in the area?"

"A few on the walk home from school."

"What were they doing?"

I shrugged. "Patrolling."

Father's breaths were starting to come in short bursts. He slapped the table. "Officer, you are wasting your time. My son doesn't know anything. As I told you, there's nothing to know."

"So it seems." Baldy lifted the mug and guzzled down the water. He closed his notepad, tucked it away, rose. Except for Father, we all stood. "We need to question a few more people. If you hear anything that helps discover who leveled this false accusation, we'd appreciate you telling us." He gave me a long look, his forehead wrinkled like the bridge of a pig's snout. He beckoned his partner and they left.

Father pointed to the window. "Make sure they go."

I cut to the living room window, kept to the side, and peered into the street. The Schupos paused on the front step, put their hats on, and walked away. When they disappeared around the corner, I turned toward the table.

Father poured himself a glass of *Schnaps*.

"They're gone," I said.

He jabbed his finger at me. "If I find out you gave that tip I'll beat you like they beat me."

I braced my knuckles against the table. "I don't think you could. But you won't need to try because I didn't do it."

"You better not have. You and that cocky attitude. Sitting there almost smirking."

I'd have to watch that. Authorities wanted obedience and bootlicking. Just like Father. We glared at each other. I tried to remember what Otto had said, that here was a man frustrated by being unable to properly support his family. But Father's belligerent look seemed to say he was mad at the world, and madder at me.

He downed the *Schnaps*. "So you think your father can't give you a beating?"

I started to shrug but caught myself. "Probably not. I work on the farm on weekends. You work in an office."

"A real man." He grabbed the mug, splashed some *Schnaps* into it, then refilled his own glass. "If you're such a man, drink with me."

This was different. Head down, Mother fiddled with her apron hem. I stood behind the chair Baldy had occupied and eyed the top of Mother's head. I'd never noticed gray before, but there were some streaks spiraling out from her crown. I picked up the mug.

Father raised his glass; I raised the mug. He downed his drink in one smooth swallow; I did the same. And folded over coughing.

The mug slipped from my fingers; its handle broke against the chair leg. I coughed and coughed as if that could douse the fire in my throat. The heat burned downward and flowered into pain in my chest, not a pale strawberry blossom but a bright sunflower of pain. Fist pressed against my breastbone, I gasped. Gradually the pain withered and I straightened up.

A sneer twisted my father's lips and his eyes narrowed. I gripped the back of the chair, failed to hold his mocking gaze, and studied the brown *Schnaps* bottle instead. Father poured himself a third drink, downed it, and slammed the glass on the table. I flinched. He said, "You aren't a man until you can drink like a man."

The words formed silently on Mother's lips: don't make trouble. I clamped my mouth closed and stalked to the door. As I was sliding my first arm into my damp jacket's sleeve, Mother spoke from the kitchen. "Wilm? Where are you going? You just got home."

"Somewhere I'm welcome." I jammed the other arm into its sleeve. She appeared at the end of the galley kitchen. Worry contorted her face and she kept darting looks at Father. One hand cupped her neck, as if hiding a wound. Father and I fought and she was wounded. I opened the door, then gave her an apologetic shrug. "I'll be at Karl's."

"Be home before dark. And—"

I held up my hand. "Don't say it."

The rain had cloaked the city's usual bitter smell of brown coal with the earthy scent of wet stone. I turned up my collar and stuffed my hands in the jacket pockets.

Why couldn't I get along with Father? No matter what I did or said, he took it in the worst way. He hadn't even thanked me for saying he didn't get beat by Schupos, and he'd assumed I'd given them that tip. It didn't help that I always reacted to his needling. We were like two tomcats fighting over territory.

I rounded the corner. When I looked up I spotted the two Schupos at the end of the block, smoking under the grocer's awning. Turning around would draw their attention.

My chest oozed warmth that spread to my head. I could understand why Father drank if he'd somehow learned to skip the throat-burning, gut-wrenching pain. And now I knew why some people called alcohol liquid courage. I didn't feel one flutter of fear.

The Schupos watched me come. When I was almost to the awning, Baldy said, "Young Tauber, out again after just getting home?"

"I'm going to visit a friend."

"The friend you were with the day in question?"

It took me a few seconds to realize it was an important question—and that hesitation put both Schupos on alert, like tracking dogs on a scent. The warmth blanketing my mind made things fuzzy and I doubted I could lie convincingly. I nodded and walked past.

They fell into step behind me.

I halted and half turned. "You have another question?"

"We have a few questions, for your friend. We'll follow you so we don't get lost." Baldy offered an unfriendly smile.

I kept walking and tried to think how to warn Karl to deny everything. I couldn't focus my thoughts. At Karl's apartment, the Schupos muscled past me and had Karl alone in his kitchen before I could say anything.

I waited on the worn sofa. Dread scattered any trace of warmth. Karl's kitchen had a door, so their voices were muffled. I played with my pocketknife, returned it to my pocket, and studied the water stain on the ceiling near the window. My thoughts were colder than the Pleisse River in December. How much trouble did a person get into for lying to the police? The door finally opened. The Schupos left without looking at me.

Karl plopped on the other end of the sofa. Neither of us spoke for two minutes. When I did, it was in a whisper. "What did you tell them?"

"I didn't know anything, didn't see anything, didn't know how your father fell."

Breath whooshed out. "How did you know that was our story?"

"It'd be anyone's story. No one willingly gets on the wrong side of the police. You should hear some of the stories told in the beer hall. Always in quiet voices." Karl sometimes helped his mother and her business partner by cleaning tables. "Once in awhile a Schupo walks in when a story is half told and"—he snapped his fingers—"the subject changes."

"Do they come in often?"

"There are some regulars. They always sit at the same table, the one with padded benches and a good view of the room."

Someone knocked. I went cold again. "They're back?"

"That'll be Georg. He's going to help repair two of my match-stick models. You're the surprise visitor." He crossed the room. "Why are you back from the farm early?"

"No work for me in this weather." I pulled out my knife again. "When the Schupos left our apartment I had an argument—"

"With your father. Again." Karl reached for the doorknob. "At least he's around, Wilm. Mine's in a Soviet POW camp. Georg's is dead. You're lucky."

He opened the door. I muttered, "I wish I felt lucky."

Georg entered, stomping his feet. He spotted me. "Tauber? Food man!"

Karl shushed him. As usual, his mother was using her Sunday afternoon to catch up on sleep.

I'd forgotten about the food. "The breast pocket of my jacket. All I could scrounge from Uncle Bruno were a few slices of early tomatoes."

Georg lunged to my jacket and claimed the waxed-paper packet.

"I have bread for a sandwich," Karl offered.

We retreated to Karl's bedroom where Georg ate his sandwich and I looked out the window so I wouldn't have to watch his eye-rolling gratitude.

"Don't lean on the wall," Karl said, as if he hadn't told me a hundred times that the brick had been poorly caulked after partially collapsing. Karl expected it to fall apart some day. The plaster was a maze of cracks.

I leaned against the scratched dresser and surveyed the street while I told Georg about the Schupos' visit, and explained what to say if they questioned him.

"I claimed I was the only one with you," Karl said.

"I think I said friends, plural. I don't know what Father told them."

We both stressed to Georg how important it was to stick to the story. He looked anxious, which worried me. He wasn't like Karl and me. He couldn't lie to anyone he felt deserved respect—mother, teachers ... police.

Karl and Georg settled on the floor to work on Karl's models. I'd had some in our old apartment, before the bomb. With my bedroom now being the living room, I didn't have anywhere to keep stuff so hadn't replaced them.

While they worked I said, "I've been thinking ..." I joined them on the floor and rested my elbow on my upraised knee. "The day Father got beat, there were extra Schupo patrols around."

"Right," Karl replied. "We thought they were searching for that cache of weapons Mom heard rumors about."

"I think the rumors are true." That got their attention. They both laid down their models and stared at me. "And I think we should find those weapons."

The silence stretched for a long moment. Finally Karl said, "You're crazy."

"Remember what you said, Tauber?" Georg's clumps of hair quivered. "I do. You mocked people who'd hide weapons, said Mausers and grenades wouldn't defeat the Schupos or Soviets."

"Wilm, you're scaring me," Karl added. "First you slice Soviet tires. Now you turn reactionary, a regular Wolverine. Don't kid yourself. You can't win."

I kicked him in the chest. He would've somersaulted backward except he hit the bed with a grunt. He moved onto the bed, out of my foot's range, and rubbed his chest. "What was that for?"

"You haven't let me explain, *Dummkopf*." I stood, paced the length of the room and back. "I want the Soviets gone. Now more than ever. But they have all the power and a few weapons won't change that."

I did another lap of the room as my idea took shape. "We find the weapons, lead Schupos to them, and they tell their Soviet masters."

I searched Karl's face for understanding. His shoulders lifted in defeat. I knew Georg wouldn't see it; he was too trusting. But I'd expected devious Karl to get it. I folded my arms. "If we lead them to something so important, they'll think we're their friends."

Karl grumbled a choice phrase. Georg's eyes widened as his regard bounced back and forth like a ball between two buildings in a narrow alley. Karl's fist struck the wall so hard the window rattled. "You'd only want them to think we're their friends if you want to hit them again."

I shrugged. "Nothing big, nothing serious. I want to ... embarrass them. Powerful people hate being embarrassed." The way Father hated me talking back.

"Why?"

I stuffed my hands into my pockets and retreated to the window. I focused on an elderly woman walking with a tattered umbrella, pushed away the images trying to fill my vision.

Karl snapped his fingers. "You said, 'Now more than ever.' Explain, Tauber."

Georg often called me by my surname, but Karl only did when he was angry. I needed my friends to pull this off. I had to be honest with them. I had to tell them about Anneliese.

I can do this, I told myself. I turned away from the window.

CHAPTER ELEVEN

It's strange, being watched by your friends because they don't trust you. I only needed them to be my lookouts, to warn me if someone happened along. Especially someone in uniform. They hadn't agreed or refused. But once I decided to act they'd watch my back. That worried them. They were so jumpy, any feint made them flinch. What was the word Otto had used? Skittish.

When I visited Otto on Tuesday after class, he asked, "Keeping your knife in your pocket?"

I kept my expression neutral. "For now." I liked that he didn't lecture me about risks.

I helped him examine footings above the waterline for three hours. He gave me two Deutschmarks. More than I'd earned. Georg was right: Otto was rich. I already had plans for the money.

The next day as we left school, I told Georg and Karl I'd treat them to a movie. We all loved movies; unfortunately, Soviet movies were grim things. Didn't those people know how to have fun? Still, a serious movie was better than nothing.

"Where'd you get the money, Tauber?" Georg asked. "Don't say you stole it."

"From a Soviet general." The color drained from Georg's face. I punched his shoulder. "Can't you tell when I'm joking? I did some work for Otto, the engineer from the bridge."

"The crazy one who tried to rip off our ears?" Karl asked.

"He's not so bad." I nudged Georg. "Where do you think I got that chocolate last week?"

"Wait," Karl said. "You had chocolate? You didn't give me any."

"Sorry, Karl. He only gave me one extra piece."

He kicked a car tire as we walked by. "You always give your extra food to Rohrbach. What are you, his mother?"

He was fishing for a reaction. I smiled. "So go home and pout. You'll miss a hot sausage."

Karl grabbed my arm, his eyebrows high. "How much money did he give you?"

"Enough for sausages and a movie. Don't worry, though. Georg and I will split your sausage. It won't go to waste." I winked at Georg. His tufted hair bobbed as he nodded.

"That's because I'll be eating it. What's for dessert, *Mutti*?" Karl grinned.

"No dessert for you, little boy. If only the girls knew, they wouldn't bat their eyelashes at you." Karl swung but I was already running. I heard his boots pound after me. I laughed as I dodged a cluster of women outside a cigarette shop, jumped the outstretched legs of two men slumped in a doorway, and charged around the corner.

Right into a group of girls. They screamed as two fell against the wall and the others stumbled out of my way. I halted in their midst as heat crept up to my hairline, flushing my face darker by the second. Karl veered around the corner and crashed into me. I lurched but stayed on my feet. A few girls gasped.

I gave an apologetic shrug to the pair I'd knocked into the wall. "Sorry. You okay?" I never knew what to say to girls. I sounded like a lame idiot.

Karl pulled me into a chokehold. "Thank you, ladies, for helping me apprehend this dangerous criminal."

That drew giggles. I elbowed Karl in the gut and he released me. The prettiest girl gave Karl a sweet smile. I didn't know any of them—I knew hardly any girls except Anneliese—but they looked familiar. Three from our grade, the others younger. The skinny one beside the smiling girl eyed me. She was cute, even if her nose was pointed. "Doesn't look dangerous," she said.

Georg joined us as Karl slapped my back. "Wilm's looks are deceiving, Ruth." It figured he knew their names; he probably knew the name of every girl in Leipzig. He slicked back his already neat hair and eyed the prettiest one. "We'd love to chat, Klara, ladies, but Georg and I need to relieve this criminal of ill-gotten gains."

"Where?" Klara asked, as if they might mug me right in the street. I swear her eyelashes really were batting. I almost burst out laughing.

Karl sent me a warning look. "In a cinema, where no one will see us emptying his pockets."

The one named Ruth said, "If you're going to a cinema in Zentrum, don't take the tram to the train station. A delivery boy told me there's a crowd gathering."

Crowds didn't gather in Leipzig unless trouble was brewing. There had been a few hunger protests over the winter, but that had been starving women and children. A crowd would mean police. Tension coiled inside. I asked, "The *Bahnhof*? Did he say why?"

"No, but they're getting noisy."

Police would be there for sure. Maybe a riot would start. "Let's go see," I said to Georg and Karl, and strode away, eager to spy out the situation.

"I told you," Karl said. "A dangerous criminal. Next time I relieve him of his booty I'll take you to the cinema, lovely Klara."

I heard the girls giggle and I broke into a jog. Let him flirt. I was on the hunt. My friends caught up two blocks later. Karl grabbed my arm, forced me to walk. "What's your hurry?"

"I don't want to miss it." We turned onto Dresdner Strasse. Tram rails ran down the middle of the street. An eastbound tram dinged its bell as it pulled to a stop past the intersection. A block west, a tram was parked on the westbound tracks. I sprinted to it. The driver said he'd been radioed orders to stay where he was. These tracks went to the *Bahnhof*. The rumor was right.

Eight blocks. By the time I arrived it might be over. Georg and Karl caught up again and I shoved my satchel at Georg. "Meet me at the cinema on Petersstrasse. I want to check this out."

"We want to see too," Karl replied.

"Stay out of it." I jogged down the tram's tracks. Karl called me back. I kept going.

A delivery truck honked its horn and rattled past. I swerved aside. Its back had only a chain where a tailgate should be. I raced forward and dived onto the truck bed, smacking my shoulder against a wooden crate. When it continued straight at Augustus-platz, I jumped off and ran north.

Gathering onlookers craned their necks. The closer I got to the *Bahnhof*, the more crowded it became. Lots of muttering, but people on the fringes wouldn't know the story. I wedged between clusters of people, wove my way toward the doors of the train station's East Hall.

A cordon of police blocked the entrance. People pushed forward, demanding entry. I asked a man in a gray suit what was happening. He ignored me and joined the shouts to be let inside.

I was only two meters away when a burly man barged out of the station and bellowed, "They aren't letting anyone off the train!"

A woman at the front screamed. Shouts and jostling started. An elderly woman beside me was pushed and started to fall. I held her upright and asked what was happening. Tears flowed down her cheeks. "My grandson is on that train. He was a British prisoner of war. The train is full of prisoners of war coming home. He wrote and asked me to meet him."

They aren't letting anyone off the train. The realization rolled through me the same way it was rippling through the crowd. The Soviets were keeping those POWs captive. Sending them east to join Karl's father and thousands of others in camps. They must have stopped for supplies.

The rage was savage. My thoughts splintered in a thousand directions. I wanted to hit back, like everyone around me. I pressed forward. One row of the seething crowd separated me from the cordon of Schupos. Several had wrestled down the big man who'd gotten out of the *Bahnhof* and were beating him. A pistol butt cut his forehead and blood gushed out.

I could almost hear Otto's voice. They don't consider it a game. I whispered. "It's not a game, Otto. Not any more."

But I didn't want to end up like that man. I had to keep it game-like, not get caught by emotion. The rage cooled, replaced by the calm I'd felt in Markt. My eagle's eye soared above the crowd—I could do anything so long as the target wasn't looking.

The man on the ground roared like a wounded bull, drawing the attention of the Schupo nearest me. My hand whipped out. I tore a metal service bar off his pocket and stepped back, letting shoving people take my place. I slipped the rectangular pin into my pocket. These service bars were awarded for good work, which meant I'd hit a Schupo who was good at licking boots.

Someone must have noticed my action and decided to join in. I glimpsed the Schupo fighting off someone tearing at his coat. A button flew into the air. I smiled.

That was fun, but the crowd felt like a trap. I had no room to maneuver and uncertainty wedged into my thoughts; I needed to get free. I pushed away from the domed train station.

In the middle of the mob, at the streetcar platform, I squeezed passed a one-armed veteran standing at attention, quietly singing "Deutschland Über Alles."

Now that would embarrass the Soviets. I pitched my voice lower than normal and joined in the third stanza of the anthem:

"Unity and right and freedom / For the German Fatherland."

The veteran stood straighter and his voice gained strength.

"Let us all strive to this goal / Brotherly, with heart and hand."

A few people looked alarmed but some joined in. Then more. Like a windstorm out of nowhere, the song swept to the edges of the crowd.

"Unity and rights and freedom / Are the pledge of fortune grand / Prosper in this fortune's glory / Prosper German father-land."

The singing grew louder than the shouting. I escaped the crush, walked faster as I neared the edge, no longer singing. The crowd started the anthem from the beginning.

Some Schupos at the back of the crowd appeared dismayed. Would they beat their own people for singing a song? It was banned, after all. I bet some wanted to join in.

I slipped between islands of people and kept to a fast clip as I passed the last onlookers. But not so fast as to draw attention. I was a student who had taken a wrong turn and wanted to leave so I could go to a movie with friends.

My heart was thundering a drumroll of victory. Halfway to the cinema, near Nikolaikirche, I heard popping from the direction of the *Bahnhof*. Minutes after I got to Petersstrasse the guys arrived. They spotted me and started to race. Karl won, Georg three steps behind.

"*Scheisse.*" Karl panted. "Did you see that mob? I thought they were going to rip Schupos' arms off. What was that about?"

I leaned against the nearest building and crossed my arms. "A train of POWs. The British released them but the Soviets won't let them off the train."

Understanding lit Karl's eyes. "They're sending them to camps. How'd you find out?"

"I made it almost to the doors." I showed the service bar. "Close enough to get a souvenir."

Karl reached out but I stuffed my prize back in my pocket. He snarled, "Get rid of it."

"Don't worry. No one will find it." There were more people around now. I peered down the street. "Is it breaking up?"

"Gunfire will do that," Karl said.

Georg nodded. "Why do you think we got out? Schupos at the doors fired over the heads of the people. Everyone scattered."

That was the popping I'd heard. Had they shot the man I'd seen being beaten? Arrested him? Others at the front were likely arrested too. It was good I'd left. The trick would be to act as if I'd never been there. "We have an hour. Let's get sausages."

"Food man!" Georg whooped. He dragged me away from the wall.

We got food to go from a café and settled on the knee-high wall trimming part of the lawn beside Thomaskirche. I sniffed my hot sausage. This had to be what they served in heaven. I took a bite, chewed slowly, savored each dribble of grease, licked my lips.

Georg groaned and took a bite that made his cheeks bulge. Karl, mouth full, nodded his thanks. We ate in silence, listened to snippets of conversation flowing past: "... heard prisoners on the train begging ..."; "... beaten then they turned on a Schupo ..."; "Everyone should have been arrested ..."; "... the poor families ...";

"... woman fainted and her arm was broken ..."; "... never thought I'd hear those words again. Do you think the soldiers on the train heard?"; "I hope so."

I hid a smile by gulping down some Fanta. The orange sweetness coated my mouth and bubbles tickled my nose. I wiped my mouth with the back of my hand. Karl peered at me.

"The anthem," he said.

I shrugged. "I heard it. So?"

"I saw you smile. You heard it? Or started it?"

His voice vibrated with tension. I glanced around. No one was nearby. "I swear I didn't start it." Karl relaxed, until I added, "Though I might have helped it along."

He jumped up, knocked over his Fanta. I rescued it so he only lost a swallow and held it out to him as he shouted, "You're a bloody fool, Tauber!"

"Stop yelling, Karl. Do you want to attract Schupos?" He clamped his jaw shut and glared. I smiled. "No one will remember anything in that crowd. For sure not a guy with dirty hair, dirty eyes. Adults don't remember my face any better than girls. If I looked like you I'd be worried."

Karl grabbed his Fanta and leaned down so we were nose to nose. "There were POWs on that train. Families in the square just wanting—" He made a strangled sound, then whispered, "This wasn't a game."

"It started as your game. We're behind enemy lines, remember?"

"That isn't funny, idiot. Come on, Georg. We're leaving."

"Fine." I stood. "But I'm going to a movie. I'd rather have company."

Georg was caught between us again, his gaze a tennis ball. "Please, Karl? I haven't seen a movie since ..." He released a slow breath. "If you really don't want to go ..."

I could see it in Karl's face. He wanted to go. But his rawness over the POW train had fed his anger at me. He was almost spitting. I needed to offer a truce. "You're right, Karl. I was stupid. Next time I'll be more careful." I hadn't felt stupid, but it was what Karl needed to hear. I'd felt the same surge of power as when I'd slashed those tires. I liked that feeling.

He didn't look happy about "next time," but he let it pass. "I'm always right. You need to learn that, Wilm, and start listening to me."

I inclined my head. I'd listen if he had anything good to say.

Karl returned a nod. "Let's go to the cinema early and get good seats."

Georg guzzled down his soda and threw the bottle into the air with a victory shout. It tumbled end over end in a high arch, crashed into an alley, and glass sprayed like shrapnel. With any luck a Soviet truck would run over the pieces.

We got good seats. At least, they were in a fine spot. On those wooden benches I was afraid to shift for fear of getting splinters somewhere tender.

The movie was a bad idea. Soviets liked documentaries. This one was about the Great Patriotic War and the mighty victories won fighting the evil Nazis. Lots of dead bodies—Germans, Soviets, civilians. When the film showed straggling lines of starving German prisoners, Karl bolted from the theater.

We found him slumped in the alley against the wall of the cinema, tears tracking down his face. He didn't even try to hide them as we crouched on either side of him.

"One of them looked like Dad," he whispered. "I couldn't tell for sure." He banged his head against the brick wall. "Soviet *Scheisskerle*. They won't even let us write to him. We don't know if he's ... He could be hurt, or starving, or ... We don't know. Now more men—more families ... won't ... know. I just want to know."

Over Karl's head, Georg's look begged me to stop the pain
we were witnessing. At least Georg and I knew our fathers' fates.
Even death had to be easier than not knowing.

I clasped Karl's shoulder and he raised his face. His features
contorted. "I'll help you, Wilm. Anything you want. You're in
charge."

Now I was listening to him. Listening hard.

CHAPTER TWELVE

Planning was easier than execution. Huddling in Karl's bedroom, tossing out ideas, was great fun, but even we realized that most had problems with the actual doing. Or rather, with the not getting caught part.

I thought Otto would be good at planning and doing. Why did he know how to face interrogations? I wasn't sure he'd help me after warning me not to take more risks, but if I spent more time with him maybe I'd get a chance to ask.

At school on Thursday everyone was talking about the near riot. Not mentioning what I'd done was harder than not talking back to my father. Karl, Georg, and I agreed that no one at school could know; no one in our families either. Safer that way.

After school, Karl and Georg went to sniff out rumors about the weapons cache and I showed up at Otto's work site. I asked if I could come every day and learn about bridges. That much was true. He seemed pleased.

I helped clear foliage from the base of the bridge so Otto could examine its condition. Soon I stripped to my waist, though I often took breaks while Otto explained things to me.

On Friday we had a mid-chapter quiz in mathematics. As soon as I finished I knew I had a high mark. If only all mathematics were this easy.

As I handed in my quiz, Herr Bader caught my eye. We held

opposite ends of the paper, neither releasing it. The shadows under his eyes were pits today. He whispered, "I saw you at the *Bahnhof* on Wednesday. What were you doing, Herr Tauber?"

"Curious. I'd heard there was a crowd." I hesitated. "Why were you there, Herr Bader?" I expected a verbal whipping. Students didn't ask questions; they answered them.

His brows lowered over his eyes like the brim of a cap. "My cousin was on that train."

"I'm sorry."

I released the paper. Today we were allowed to leave class once we handed in our tests, so I grabbed my coat and satchel and headed toward central Leipzig. Zentrum was the fastest way to get to Otto's bridge. I skirted the south side of the new town hall, in sight of the police station. I'd started taking that route to gauge how many police were around. Today, there were none.

I was almost to the new town hall's main doors when I noticed Johanna Fahr sitting on a bench, swiveling her head as if looking for someone. Ernst Weber, no doubt. He wasn't in sight so I sat and said hello.

"Hello, Wilm. Shouldn't you be in school?"

A mother's question, but spoken by a young, beautiful woman. The fitted skirt and jacket showed off her curves. New clothes. Hardly anyone in Leipzig could get new clothes, except, apparently, people with connections to the SED or Schupos. "I'm not skipping class." I rested my arm on the back of the bench. "Why aren't you still in school?"

"I finished grade eight. I'm not going to university so had no need of *Gymnasium*."

"Why not? You're smart enough."

Johanna bit her lip and frowned down at her silky blue gloves. It seemed warm for gloves. "Things are hard for women in this city,

Wilm. My family was slowly starving. And after I was almost ..."
She exhaled and closed her eyes. "I knew I needed protection. If
I had the protection of the right man, then my family wouldn't
starve."

I frowned across at the police station and considered her
words. Ernst Weber was her shield. The other Schupos and the
Soviets would leave Johanna alone because they knew she belonged to one of them. It was smart.

She whispered, "Don't hate me, Wilm."

I swung my attention back to Johanna. We had been friends a
long time ago. Now, staring at me, wide hazel eyes almost glowing
from a sheen of unshed tears, she looked like that little girl again.
If my gaze didn't dip below her neck. I shrugged. "We all do what
we can to survive."

She smiled and dabbed at her eyes with a handkerchief.

"Are you waiting for Ernst?"

"Yes. I work half days for a town administrator and—" Her
hand shot out and touched my wrist. "Oh, I must sound like I'm
using Ernst. He told me you were close once. Please don't misun-
derstand. I appreciate him. He might seem harsh in public, but he's
quite sweet when we're alone. And he's so protective. He won't
let me walk home alone. If he can't make it, he sends someone.
But he seems to have forgotten today."

Ernst knew it wasn't safe to let a pretty woman walk alone. At
least he took his responsibilities seriously. But he was just serving
his own interests. If Johanna did get attacked, he'd likely desert
her like he had Anneliese and find someone else untouched. "I'll
walk you home." Had I really said that? Walk Ernst Weber's girl
home? What was I thinking?

Johanna's face brightened. "Thank you, Wilm."

Her smile made me realize I wasn't thinking about Ernst.

She lived with Ernst in a neighborhood several blocks southwest of the new town hall. Fancy apartments. Not much bomb damage and even that had been cleaned up. We chatted as we walked, about nothing, everything, whatever came to mind. Favorite flavors of ice cream, movies we had enjoyed, dancing, the farm, Otto and his bridge repairs, memories. Not the war, or the hard parts of living, or Ernst.

When we reached her apartment, we talked outside for another fifteen minutes. Johanna leaned against the wrought-iron railing. "Would you like to come in? I could make coffee. Real, not *Ersatz*."

Alone with Johanna. I could imagine doing more than talking. She was so beautiful, her mouth so kissable. I stared at her lips for a few seconds and swallowed. A woman with a pram and an Alsatian dog walked up the street. A witness.

I blinked. Was I crazy? I didn't want to get fresh with Johanna, and not because she was Ernst's woman. She was the first girl I had talked to without choking. I didn't want to ruin that with clumsy flirting—and it would be clumsy. I didn't know how to approach a girl. Kiss a girl.

"No thanks," I finally replied. "Real coffee would be great, but I have to get to the bridge before Otto wonders where I am."

"Oh. Some other time then."

I agreed. We both knew there'd be no other time so long as Ernst was in her life. I turned to go but Johanna said, "Wilm? We were friends once, right?"

"Sure."

"Could I think of you as a friend again?" Her smile was wistful, as if implying she didn't have friends. How could someone so pretty, living a rich life, not have friends?

As I hesitated, her smile wilted. "Sure. We never stopped being friends, Johanna. We just didn't see each other for awhile." I left her by the door, her smile bright again.

Johanna's house was three blocks east of the canal so I cut over, then walked beside it toward Otto's work site. He was digging along the bridge's base above the waterline. He spotted me walking along the bank and met me on the bridge.

"You are coming from a different direction. You needed different scenery, did you?"

"I walked a friend home."

His bushy eyebrows curled into their questioning S's. "A girl?"

"Yes." I held up my hand. "Not a girlfriend. She's a childhood friend, and has a boyfriend."

"A trusting boyfriend."

"No, he was an absent boyfriend. He never lets her walk home alone but he didn't show up today. I happened along so ..."

"Didn't show up? I was thinking he was a schoolmate. He must be older."

Five years older. "He's a Schupo."

Otto's hand clamped on my shoulder. "You don't want to get on the bad side of any police officers, Wilm."

We started across the bridge. "I know. I only walked her to her door. But it's odd no one showed up if he arranges an escort whenever he can't come."

"All available police are busy today."

I spun toward him. "What happened?"

"You haven't heard?" I shook my head and he pointed northeast. "An explosion in a factory near the edge of the city."

"Accident?"

"My source in SED says no."

I scanned the skyline for signs of smoke. "A bomb?"

"Probably. No injuries, just some damaged equipment that was set to be dismantled and transported to the Soviet Union."

"Father said they weren't doing that anymore, that they preferred to take goods now."

"Usually. But these dismantlings still happen. Unfortunate because in this factory the workers had taken great pride in rebuilding and getting back to decent production capacity."

"Too bad they don't dismantle the SED and take it east. The Soviets already own every man in it."

"Think what you must, but never say such things aloud. Ever."

I could only shrug. "Do you think the workers blew it up rather than let the Soviets have it?"

He replied, "Given what happened on Wednesday, I do think that."

I closed my eyes. I could see that man in front of the *Bahnhof* doors bleeding while Schupos beat him. Those workers were right to hit back. I didn't realize I was nodding until Otto's grip on my shoulder tightened. "Wilm? Were you there?"

My eyes flew open. "The factory? No."

"You know I meant the train station. Don't lie. I see the truth in your face. You were there. Did you get into trouble?"

"Would I be here if I had gotten into trouble?"

His hand dropped. "I fear for you, my friend."

"I'm fine. I know what I'm doing."

"So say all young men everywhere. You think you are untouchable, yet experience is a cruel teacher. But enough of that. Come." Otto led me to the linden tree he liked to sit under. "I don't need your help today, but I have something for you." He opened a leather briefcase, pulled out a book, and handed it to me.

A History of Bridges. My fingers skimmed the title. "For me? Really?" I was grinning like a fool. You'd think he had handed me a whole carton of cigarettes for trading on the black market.

"Yes." His eyes seemed to reflect sparks of sunlight. "Would you like to see what I am doing today before you take your book home?"

I left my satchel and book on the grass and followed Otto to the shore, where he pointed and talked. I didn't hear any of it. My mind was on the book. First the ring, now this. Why? Because we shared some abilities? Was I a replacement for his son? Was he luring me into trusting him? No. Not that. He could be trusted; I would stake my life on it. In a way, I already was.

His hand came down on my shoulder again. "Did you hear anything I said?"

"No. Sorry."

"Go home. Read your book, dream of girls, or whatever was filling your mind."

"Not girls. I'm not good with girls." I scooped up a flat rock and skipped it. It left a dark brown smudge on my fingers. I picked up a similar one.

"Not being good with them doesn't mean you don't think about them."

I snorted in agreement, turned the rock over, then held it out. "This rock isn't muddy but it's getting my fingers dirty."

Otto barely glanced at it. "Bituminous shale. There isn't enough bitumen in it for efficient burning like its cousin, bituminous coal. Brown coal, you'd call it. The rock is common enough, but quite unimpressive. Not at all eye-catching. I expect many people go through their whole lives without noticing it."

I considered the smudges on my fingers as an idea began to sprout. "You're right. I don't think I've ever noticed it. Maybe I'll take this one home." Into my pocket it went.

"Boys and rocks." Otto pulled out his pipe, then returned it to his pocket untouched as a scowl dropped over his brow. "Make sure that little rock doesn't fly through any windows, Wilm. Understood?"

"It never occurred to me, Otto. Really."

"Good."

I'd told Otto the truth. My idea had nothing to do with windows. On Sunday night, Karl and I snuck out after dark, keeping a sharp lookout for patrols. They assumed young men were only out in the middle of the night if they were getting into trouble. Maybe they were right.

On Monday morning, the light-colored stones of the SED headquarters near Augustusplatz had a dark, streaky scrawl:

S – *Sowjetisches*
E – *Eigentum*
D – *Deutschland*

The Soviet Property of Germany. It wasn't original but it made the point, especially after the train of POWs and the factory blast. The Soviets owned the SED and their henchmen Schupos.

Bituminous shale was handy. I hoped it was hard to scrub off.

CHAPTER THIRTEEN

For the second night running, I stayed in Anneliese's room and pored over Otto's book. When Anneliese asked what I was doing, I told her about him. How we'd met when Karl and I had been roughhousing, and Otto had separated us. I didn't say why we had been fighting.

She was excited in her quiet way. She called Otto my benefactor and said he obviously wanted to be my mentor. Big words. Dare I hope it was true?

As I slid the book onto her shelf, the spot she had said could be its home, I paused. "Liese, since you don't work on Wednesday afternoons ..."

From her usual perch, wedged into the corner on her bed, she peered at me. "What?"

I pushed the book until it thunked against the wall, and then turned to face her. "Come with me after school and meet Otto."

"I don't think so, Wilm."

I sat on the opposite end of the bed. "You seem better since we talked that night on the roof. You smile sometimes. You even spoke once at the table." I laughed. "Father almost fell off his chair."

Her only response was wide eyes. Silence wasn't a refusal, so I plowed on. "You go to work, Liese. You're already getting out. This is only a bit farther. I'd be with you." She still didn't look convinced. "Nothing will happen. If it did, you know I'd protect you."

Anneliese nodded like a woodpecker drilling a hole, short quick nods. "Of course."

"Say you'll come." She bit her lip and I said, "You could see the park. Being by the canal almost smells like the farm. The grass and leaves tickle your nose. The ducks paddle around. It's cooler by the water. You could sit under a linden tree and watch me sweat."

"Is that why you're so stinky today? What made you sweat?"

"If you want to know, you'll have to come see."

Anneliese made a face at me. "Now you're teasing."

"Say you'll come."

She closed her eyes and splayed her fingers, then inhaled as deeply as she could.

I tilted my head. "What are you doing?"

"You're so brave, Wilm. Maybe if I breathe in the air around you, I'll inhale some courage."

My grin broke out. "You're coming."

"Shhh," she whispered. "Don't tell me. I might chicken out."

This unexpected ray of silliness made me want to laugh. I managed to reply solemnly, "I'm going to bed. I'll see you after school, Anneliese."

She repeated, "Shhh," and I left her to keep breathing in courage.

The next day after school, I ran all the way home, thundered up the stairs, and burst into the apartment. "I'm home!"

Mother was still doing her *Trümmerfrauen* shift, so Anneliese was the only one home. I hung up my satchel and followed my nose to a pot on the stove. Stew. Please not horsemeat, I thought.

Anneliese entered the kitchen and I turned with a smile, then hesitated. "Aren't you going to change?"

"I don't think so. Do you mind if I pretend to be a boy?"

"No. You can wear my jacket. It's baggier than yours. Get your cap and I'll help you tuck all your hair under it."

Anneliese disappeared into her bedroom. I wrote a note to Mother telling her we had gone to the Elsterflutbett. I was sure we'd be back well before either she or Father finished work, which was good since they might forbid the trip if they were here.

Anneliese reappeared, tucking her hair under the short-brimmed cap she had claimed from me last summer, though at the time I hadn't known why. I helped her hide a few escaped tendrils. "Your face is too clean. We'll fix that downstairs."

I opened the door. "I'm glad you're coming, Liese."

She laid her hand on my wrist. "You give me courage. And ... I want to see ducks again."

She and my duck-loving engineer would get along fine.

In the foyer downstairs, I rubbed my fingers in traces of coal dust on the floor near the apartment below ours. Herr Flickinger often left a pail of coal sitting there for days. I figured he counted the number of briquettes in the pail so he could make sure none of his neighbors were stealing them. I wondered if he kept track of his dust too.

"This is silly," Anneliese said as I smeared some dust on her nose, cheeks, and chin, then added a dab by her eyebrow.

"You look like my little brother now. Max. Could I keep my face clean when I was thirteen? Mother hounded me. Get some on your hands."

On the street. I whispered, "Try to walk like a boy, Liese ... I mean, Max. Longer steps. Kick rocks or something." After a block of coaching she started to get the idea. We both balanced on curbs, swung around poles, and kicked at anything loose.

"Race you to the corner, Max." I gave her a head start but still beat her. We both started laughing. I punched her softly on the shoulder. "Max, you laugh like a ringing church bell."

She clamped her hand over her mouth and I winked. The day shimmered with heat that bounced off the sandstone and brick buildings. I had my sister back. I was the protector now, but we were outside, tramping down the pavement past street-level shops, with teenagers hanging out of windows in the apartments above, women gossiping outside the shops and children playing tag around them, old men smoking on steps.

I wanted to hold every sensation in my mind forever.

We walked in silence for two blocks as Anneliese soaked in the sights, places she hadn't seen for over a year. "Look," she said, "Puttkam's Grocery. Frau Puttkam used to have the best pickles. Weren't they from the Spreewald?"

"I think so."

We stopped at the corner store and peered through the always-sparkling glass. Frau Puttkam appeared in the doorway with a broom. "Get away, you hooligans! You're marking my glass!"

I lurched backward. Beside me, Anneliese smothered a chuckle.

"What's that, boy?" Frau Puttkam's voice turned shrill. "You think it's funny?"

"No," I said. "We were only remembering your famous pickles. How great they were."

She scowled. "I can't get them anymore. So leave. Go." She waved her broom in our direction and we darted across the street.

It was hard not to laugh. We ran for a block until Anneliese called for a rest. She leaned against the wall of a cigarette shop, gasping. I joined her, propping one foot on the bricks so my knee stuck out. "What's wrong, Max?"

"Haven't run in so long. Too hard." She pressed her hand against her ribs and rested her head against the bricks with face upraised to the sun and eyes closed. "This is nice."

The bricks were almost hot with only my shirt protecting my skin. I closed my eyes and thought about how cats liked to lounge in pools of heat. And lizards. And snakes. But dogs preferred the shade.

The bell above the cigarette shop's door dinged as someone went in or out. I caught a whiff of tobacco. It made me think of Otto, always filling his pipe but never smoking it. Maybe today I'd ask him why.

Shadow darkened the inside of my eyelids. I opened my eyes. Stared into the blue eyes of Ernst Weber. They were dark wells under the brim of his police hat. Dark and dangerous.

He rested his palm flat against my collarbone with his thumb curving around my neck. No pressure, but its weight felt threatening. "So the person who told me you walk by every day was telling the truth. I thought I'd made it clear you were to stay away from Johanna."

"I don't know—"

Ernst pushed so my back pressed against the wall and the edges of the brick dug into me. "Don't try to lie, little brother. You aren't good enough at it."

I forced my jaw to unlock. "All I did was walk her home." He pressed harder and I squinted against the rough-edged discomfort. "I saw her outside the new town hall, waiting for you. Only you were late." He leaned, pinning me with his weight. "Heard ... Schupos were called to ... factory accident. Must've been where you were. I just ... walked her ... home."

The pressure eased. "Did you think about doing more than that?"

How was I supposed to answer that? Yes, Ernst, I wanted to go inside and strip her naked so we could play doctor like we used to do when we were young. That would get me a beating. "No." I forced myself to keep my eyes open as I waited for the first blow.

The pressure eased a little more. "You don't think she's pretty?"

I frowned. "Johanna's very pretty. But she's with you, Ernst. She likes you."

One eyebrow quirked a little. "Yes. She's beautiful, and she's mine. Don't forget it."

I almost smiled. Johanna had only said she appreciated him, which wasn't the same as liking. Instead I nodded, quickly, like I was afraid. "I won't forget. Ever." No, I wouldn't forget how he just watched while my sister—

Anneliese. I'd forgotten she was beside me. My gaze flicked right. She was there, staring.

Ernst noticed my glance and gave Anneliese a sneer. "Get lost, boy."

Go, Anneliese. Go. She didn't hear my thoughts, stayed rooted to the spot. Her breaths came in short puffs like Father's did when he was upset. Ernst's hand slid up to my neck as he focused on this new annoyance. "Boy, I said—" He blinked repeatedly, pushed me away. "Anneliese."

I landed on my knees. Scrambled up. Ernst braced his arms on either side of Anneliese and she cowered against the wall as he bent close. People skirted way around us, no one willing to get involved in Schupo business. I touched Ernst's wrist and he backhanded me, a blow that barely grazed my temple because his attention was on my sister.

I crowded as close to him as I dared. "Leave her alone, Ernst," I hissed.

He ignored me, stared at Anneliese just like she was staring at him, with wide, horror-filled eyes. "Why?" he finally whispered. "Why did you go to the train station?" It was a pleading question. Where was the sneer he'd had after that soccer game when he'd said untouched?

Anneliese's lower lip quivered. She looked like a rabbit trapped by a fox. For a moment I thought they were only going to stare. Then words poured out of him, an indistinguishable murmur. The more words, the paler Anneliese got, and the greener Ernst turned. All I heard was wanted, couldn't, hate. Anneliese sobbed.

I reached for Ernst's arm again. His face solidified, as if a mask had dropped into place. His fingers wrapped around my neck but he kept his gaze on Anneliese. He spoke louder, steel in his voice. "Tell your brother to stay away from Johanna. I've fended off one Russian lieutenant who wants her. Wilm will be easier than a bug to crush. If he even goes anywhere near her I can, and will, protect her."

Ernst pulled back and gave me an almost friendly smile as I rubbed my neck. "I like you, little brother. You'd make a good *Schutzpolizei* candidate if you got a better attitude. But going near Johanna isn't smart, and neither was bringing your sister anywhere near me."

"If I'd known you were around, we would've gone a different route." I marveled that I could sound so calm. I considered yanking his pistol from its holster and shooting him, like Father had wanted to do after he was beaten. But I'd probably wind up being the one shot. "Come on, Anneliese. Let's go home."

I reached for her hand. She gave a choked cry and ran down the street. I raced after her, caught her easily but she hit and scratched and wouldn't stop struggling. A nail raked near my eye. I grabbed her by the upper arms, plopped her down on some steps. I retrieved the cap that had fallen off during our tussle and moved to place it on her head.

Anneliese scooted backward up the stairs. "Don't touch me!" She huddled by the door, shivering under the baking sun. I stood dumbly, cap in hand. I don't think she saw me. She saw four Soviet soldiers. Ernst had managed to catapult her back into that train station. I glanced around but he was gone.

How could I have been so stupid? I told her I'd protect her. But I'd made things worse. I set my foot on the bottom step. She screamed and cringed.

Something brushed my arm. I jumped. Ruth, the skinny girl who thought I didn't look dangerous, laid fingers on my forearm. "What's wrong?"

"My sister ..." I squeezed my eyes shut. Ruth had no idea how dangerous I was. I had destroyed a year of healing in one short walk.

Her fingers flexed into a sure grip. "I've seen girls like this before, Wilm."

"You have?"

She actually rolled her eyes. "You boys are clueless. Stay back. Better yet, walk toward your home slowly so I can follow with her. Don't look back. Okay?" She started up the steps, then paused. "What's her name?"

"Anneliese."

"Go."

Six minutes later she coaxed Anneliese from her corner. Then I started out, following Ruth's quiet directions to slow down or speed up. I'd never felt so helpless. Those five blocks stretched like five trips to the farm. When we reached our apartment block, Anneliese was sobbing wretchedly and clinging to Ruth to stay upright. I opened the door, hid behind it, and held out my key. "First floor, left apartment," I whispered. Ruth nodded.

From the foyer I listened to them ascend. The stairwell was dark. I didn't know if the power was out again or if the one bulb had burned out. I leaned against the open door. Waited.

Ruth returned after ten minutes. "She's in her bedroom. What happened?"

I told her, keeping it brief. Her eyes widened. "I remember that attack. The whispers. How ... relieved I was it hadn't been me." She bit her lip. "Look, Wilm, this isn't your fault."

"Of course it is."

"No. I have a friend who ... She will be doing fine one minute, then the next she's so upset you can't touch her. Anything can set her off. Everyone tries to tell her to get on with her life, but she told me once that she feels ripped to pieces inside."

That's how Anneliese had looked. Like shredded cabbage. "I just wanted her to be happy. We were going to the canal, to see the ducks and smell the grass ..."

"Lucky her, having a brother who wants her to be happy."

With me as a brother, lucky was not the right word. "You don't have a brother?"

"He was eight years younger. Died in February in that typhus outbreak."

"Sorry."

"We're all sorry, aren't we? For a lot of things. I'd better go."

"Do you want me to walk you home?"

"I'll be fine."

"How far is it?"

Ruth smiled. "You aren't very observant, are you?" I gave her a scornful look and got another eye-roll. "You walk through my building every time you visit Georg. I'm on the second floor."

I gave her an apologetic shrug. So I wasn't observant. As she left, I grimaced. Otto had said I should always pay attention to my surroundings. If I'd done that, perhaps the day would have ended differently, with ducks and the smell of grass instead of with Anneliese trapped inside a terrifying memory.

CHAPTER FOURTEEN

Mother set a bowl of stew in front of me. I didn't lift my head, painfully aware of the empty chair across from mine. I licked dry lips. "I'm not hungry."

"Eat," Father said. He scooped a piece of meat onto his spoon and wolfed it down. I hadn't been able to keep the truth from Mother when she arrived home, and she'd told Father. He had known as soon as he walked in that something was wrong. The air was like half-frozen water, cold and impossible to breathe.

Why couldn't Ernst have not noticed me? Why hadn't I fought him off, grabbed Anneliese's hand, and run away before he said ... whatever awful things he'd said? All the unanswered whys ricocheted in my head, chipping away at my crumbling control. Father repeated his order. I replied dully, "I don't like horsemeat." Mother bought it because the butcher gave double rations if you did, but I could barely stomach it on a good day.

"You'll eat it. Every morsel."

His voice vibrated. I knew the warning that tone carried. I didn't care. I lifted my head. "I ... am ... not ... hungry."

His fist slammed the table. I didn't flinch. Father hobbled with one crutch to the cupboard, returned with a serving bowl three times the size of mine. He dumped my bowl's contents into the larger one, ladled in stew until the bowl was full. He pushed it toward me. Sat heavily. "You'll stay until that bowl is licked clean. Until it spews back out. Then you'll lick that up."

"Heinz," Mother whispered.

"Stay out of this, Gertrud. This selfish turd wants to shatter Anneliese's life again, make everyone's lives miserable, let him do it right. He can eat all our food, leave us with nothing." He toppled Anneliese's chair with his crutch. "Then he can get the hell out of my house!"

My chair scraped against the scuffed hardwood floor as I stood. I picked up the bowl and spoon. "I'll leave now."

The sound of Mother's crying followed me out the door. I sagged against the wall in the corridor and sucked in foul air. Where could I go?

The warmth of the bowl I hugged to my chest gave the answer. Georg's. At least the food wouldn't go to waste. I walked the block and a half as quickly as I could without spilling any stew. The streets were deserted. Everyone was eating.

My stomach clenched, for once protesting the thought of food rather than the refusal of it. The smell of the stew was making me gag. Worse than the horsemeat were Father's words. Their finality. At least he and I agreed on one thing: this mess was my fault. I'd talked Anneliese into going, but I hadn't protected her. I should've fought Ernst, even if he'd pistol-whipped me.

In the foyer of Georg's entryway, my gaze slid up the bannister. Ruth lived on the second floor. I wondered if those hollow cheeks and skinny legs were just the way she was, or if she was hungry too. This block was shabbier than ours, the entries more threadbare, more unemployed sheltering in doorways.

I owed Ruth a debt and there wasn't another way to pay her back. I started up the stairs. The second floor landing had five doors—that meant four small apartments sharing one bathroom.

I tried the door of one of the apartments overlooking the street. A barefoot boy, maybe ten, answered. When I asked about Ruth he pointed to the other street-side apartment and closed his door. The lock clicked.

Ruth flung open her door seconds after I knocked. "I saw you coming up the street."

"Oh. Well ... hello."

"Right. Mother always complains I'm rude." She clasped her hands in front of her gray skirt. "Hello, Wilm. How are you this fine evening? If you don't mind me asking, why are you holding a bowl of stew?"

Her mocking tone made a smile tug at my mouth. "I wanted to thank you. And ask if you'd like to split this stew with Georg and his mother."

"I know you've taken food to Georg before. He's easy to pry information from. You don't have to offer ..." She trailed off and bit her lip, her gaze on the bowl.

I'd seen that expression enough on Georg to know it meant hungry. "Take half. Please."

"I don't like charity."

"Weren't you listening? This is a thank you. Are you so rude you can't accept a thank you?" I extended the bowl. "Half. I do want to give some to Georg."

Ruth pursed her lips and took the bowl. "You called me rude. I only let my mother do that." She marched to the small counter that was her kitchen. She was too skinny, but still had a hint of curves. I tried to focus on her hair, a shade lighter than my mouse-brown mat and hanging in a braid fifteen centimeters below her collar.

While she spooned stew into a pot, I said, "Where is your mother?"

"Sick in bed."

"Anything ... contagious?"

Ruth returned with my bowl and pushed it at my chest. "A broken heart. Is that contagious?"

"It might be. Misery seems to be." It was the wrong thing to say. She just stared so I stumbled over my good-byes and retreated down the stairs.

I couldn't bring myself to ask Georg if I could stay so I returned to the apartment. I left the bowl outside the door and snuck onto the roof. With no coat, pillow, or blanket, my sleep was nearly nonexistent. At dawn, the rhythmic banging of a metalworks shop in the next block woke me. I was bleary-eyed and my mouth tasted of bile even though I hadn't puked. I felt as clean as Uncle Bruno's manure pile.

A hot day in the making. I could feel it in the sullen air, the way it smothered everything, not letting a breeze carry away the stink of coal and fumes.

I sat under the dormer window in the building's stairwell until I heard the familiar clumps of Father descending the stairs on his crutches. Only then did I go down to our floor and use the bathroom. Washed up as best I could with no towel.

I crept into the apartment, gathered my coat and satchel, and turned to see Mother watching me as she dried her hands on a tea towel. "Why couldn't you have eaten the first bowl, Wilm?"

I frowned at the ceramic tiles decorating the heater in the living room. "Could you get my book out of Anneliese's room? The one about bridges."

She did so in silence.

"Is ... she better today?"

Mother didn't answer. "Go to her shop and tell Frau Winter she's ill, but she could do some handwork if someone brings it here. And you can drop the sheets at the laundry to be ironed."

When she brought me the package of sheets, she said, "Give your father a few days, Wilm. I will try to convince him you couldn't have foreseen ..." She sighed. "Where will you sleep?"

"The roof, I guess. Neighbors will complain if I stay in the stairwell."

"I'll leave your bedding with Frau Nikel. I'd ask her to put you up but—"

"I'd rather sleep on the roof."

She got my lunch bucket. I took it and left.

CHAPTER FIFTEEN

I couldn't bring myself to talk, not to Karl, not to Georg, not to anyone. At lunch I gave Georg my tin without looking at it. They didn't ask questions. It made me think Ruth had told Georg what had happened, and that made me regret giving her the stew.

Karl and Georg told each other where they had searched for the weapons cache, but they were really telling me, wanting me to give them more ideas. When I didn't, Karl gave me a worried look and suggested Georg could help clean tables at the beer hall; he'd be an extra pair of ears listening for more rumors. I imagined aiming a pistol at Ernst Weber.

Early June and the afternoon was stifling. Windows open or closed didn't matter, though a bit more light filtered in with them open. No electricity today. Sweat dripped while Herr Bader lectured, his voice droning, sounding like the fan we'd had in our old apartment.

I woke to see students filing into the hallway. Herr Bader waved a sheaf of papers in front of his face and watched me leave, too listless to lecture me. I paused in the doorway, wanting to ask why he had to sleep in his classroom. The words wouldn't come. At least he had a cot, a ceiling.

Karl caught me on the front steps. "When are we going to hit them again, Wilm? Soon?"

I pulled away and started to leave.

"Wilm! Answer me!" I turned. This was my best friend. He deserved better. Still no words would come. Karl lifted his shoulders high and repeated, "Soon?"

I nodded and left.

Soon.

The word echoed over and over. Ernst was the one I wanted to hit. But I couldn't. He'd know right away who had done it. And I still cared enough that I didn't want to get caught.

My feet took me to central Leipzig on my way to the canal. On a side street I palmed my knife and scored a shiny black car. Only government officials drove cars like that. I pocketed the knife, tried to savor some victory from my small defiance. Nothing came. Good feelings were bricked off with the bad.

I found Otto under his favorite tree, sipping water and dabbing his sweaty brow. I sat on the grass in the sunshine. At least feeling the sun's heat meant I was feeling something. I took a drink of water when Otto offered but kept behind my high silent wall.

After awhile, Otto said, "You should join me in the shade so you don't get heat stroke. The sun is merciless today."

I stretched onto my back and let the sunlight continue to beat on me. I stared into the stark blue of the sky. My eyes felt rubbed by invisible sandpaper.

"You are a particularly stubborn boy," Otto said. "I would guess something has you upset."

I closed my eyes. I should have known Otto would see what Karl had seen, but unlike Karl he wouldn't leave it alone. Air stirred painfully in my lungs, making me inhale sharply before I resumed slow measured breaths.

Otto said, "Talking is a useful exercise. It can be an outlet for pent-up feelings."

My breathing turned shallow; I forced it back to normal. What was normal? Apparently, it was me and my father at each other's throats. It was me causing pain to my family.

"I like to think we have earned each other's trust, Wilm," he said. "Please tell me what is wrong. And you need to get out of the sun."

Why should he care if I shriveled into a husk? Why did he care at all? He was a crazy old man who couldn't see that everyone would be better off—

Water splashed on my face and neck. I sat up sputtering. Otto latched onto my upper arms, heaved me into the shade, then heaved again and sat me against the tree trunk. The thud vibrated through my muscles.

"Talk to me." Otto held me in place.

I tried to struggle. His shin settled across my knees. "Let me go!"

"Ah. You are not dumb after all."

I couldn't control my rapid breathing. "Let me go, you crazy old man."

"Perhaps crazy is another thing we have in common, yes? Tell me what is wrong."

"Why do you care? It's not your business."

"You came to me, Wilm, not the other way around. You lay at my feet like a hound needing succor." Otto's breath brushed my hot cheek. "You came to me. If you didn't want me to care then you should not have befriended me, because I do not like seeing my friends in pain."

He was right. I had come because I'd known he wouldn't leave it alone. Because he would demand that I talk. Waves of emotion crashed over me. He must have seen it. He released me and I rolled onto my side. His hand rested on my trembling shoulder as everything spilled out. Anneliese, the attack against her, Ernst, my father. Everything.

After I finished, too exhausted to care how Otto might react, his hand stayed where it was. It felt like an anchor keeping me from drifting out of this safe harbor.

Our family rarely touched, I realized. Why did we deny ourselves this ... What was it? Trust. A hand on a shoulder said, "You can trust me." Letting the hand remain replied, "I know." There was no trust in my family. We kept to ourselves, afraid to share our hurts, afraid the hand would be knocked away.

We were idiots.

"So you will sleep on your roof again tonight?" Otto's first question.

"Yes," I croaked, throat raw.

"Would you consider staying at my house?" The hand gently squeezed. "I ask only because it feels like a thunderstorm is coming. This heat. The heavy air. A rooftop won't offer much shelter when the heavens open."

Two thoughts hit at the same instant: I had left my coat at school, and my book would get wet. "Sure. Only tonight though."

"Will you go home again?"

"If I can. I have to try to make it up to Anneliese. I'd do anything for her. I wanted to make her happy, but instead I hurt her."

"You did not hurt her, Wilm. Understand that. It was not your fault that this police fellow ambushed you."

I rolled over, sorry to lose the comfort of Otto's touch but needing to see him. "Ambushed?"

His salt-and-pepper eyebrows quirked. "He did say he had asked about you. He wanted to catch you and threaten you because of this Johanna. I expect he waited for you in the cigarette shop. His turning on your sister was uncalled for, and might have been meant to hurt you. He sounds like one of those men who fail to see women as anything but objects to possess. If so, he would see your compassion for your sister as a weakness."

I sat up and wiped the sweat from the back of my neck. Couldn't a person be compassionate and strong? Otto seemed to be.

He gathered up his things and we walked through Johannapark back toward the city center. I picked up rocks as we went. "Where do you live?" I asked.

"Across from Grosse Wiese, not a dozen blocks from the zoo. I fear you will see it and declare me to be a Soviet-owned SED lackey."

"Are you?" I asked the question lightly, never considering it could be true.

"I am not a member of the SED and never plan to be. But they gave me these lodgings and they pay my wages."

At the church in the park we headed north, skirting the heavily bomb-damaged areas southeast of Thomaskirche. I'd never had reason to explore this northwest corner of Zentrum. The apartments and townhouses were slightly battered by the war but were finer than anything in my working-class neighborhood. Fancy trim along eaves, on lintels and window frames. Delicate wrought-iron fences. Painted fronts instead of bare brick or stone.

We came to an area of detached houses. They seemed big enough for three or four families. They had yards with ornate fences separating one tidy lawn from the next. They grew grass when they could be growing vegetables.

"Do you live ... in one of these?" I swallowed.

"I live in the yard of one, in a ground-floor addition that is a stand-alone apartment. It was probably for some family member who came to live with the original owners. The people in the main house aren't interested in the yard and told me to use it. I think you will find it adequate."

We entered the yard through a back gate. The flowerbeds were full of vegetables and part of the lawn was gone, replaced by small potato plants. The fence backed up to the Pleisse River's dry bed. It actually ran under Zentrum, but here it was open. So much rubble had clogged the river to the south that it was temporarily diverted. On the other side of the riverbed the park, Grosse Wiese, sprawled bigger than the whole city center.

Otto's apartment was larger than ours. Two bedrooms, a study, a bathroom with a huge bathtub, a kitchen with a door, a dining area separated from the living room by sliding glass doors, and more glass doors in the living room that opened to a flagstone deck with two wooden lounge chairs. And hot running water. Even our old apartment had lacked hot-water taps.

Otto set the table while I gawked around. A housekeeper had been and gone and had left his supper warming in the oven. "Does it pass inspection?" he asked.

"Georg was right about you being rich."

Otto motioned for me to sit and slipped into the kitchen. He returned with two beers, set them beside tall glasses, and shook out a napkin after he sat. "The apartment is only mine while I work in Leipzig. But I am acutely aware of how much better I live than most city residents, than most people in the Soviet Zone. It is because I have a skill the government needs and they don't want me to leave. Remember that, Wilm. Having a skill that is in demand can allow you to set your own wages."

He poured half his beer into his glass so I copied him. He lifted his glass. "To friends. Old and new and crazy."

I clinked my glass to his. "Especially crazy." The beer slid smoothly down my throat. No fire. No coughing.

We talked through supper, mostly about bridges. After, Otto sent me to the bath with clean trousers, belt, and shirt. I rinsed out my clothes in the same water and hung them on a rack in the corner. Otto's clothes—he had given them to me—were a little big but fit better than Father's cast-offs. I padded into Otto's study in bare feet.

Otto reclined in his chair, one leg caught on the corner of his desk, his unlit pipe hanging from his mouth. His attention didn't waiver from the papers in his hand, so I studied a map of Leipzig tacked on the wall to his left. Bridges were lettered and numbered in red ink. Looking at the map was like having my eagle's-eye view of the whole city instead of a single block or plaza. I studied the central district, especially the streets around Schupo headquarters.

"I can hear those wheels turning from here," Otto said, startling me. "What are you planning, Wilm?" I didn't respond. He joined me. "What are you thinking?"

He knew my story, maybe not details like searching for a weapons cache, but almost everything else. I had no reason to lie. "You were right that they don't think it's a game, so I don't anymore, either. Not since Ernst terrorized Anneliese. I am at war."

"That sounds serious. Is your enemy aware hostilities have been declared?"

"No."

"So this is a covert mission. You are operating ... behind enemy lines?"

The unknowing reference to Karl's game made me nod vigorously. "Exactly."

"People get hurt in war, Wilm. Even killed." Otto tilted his head and whispered, "Spies caught behind enemy lines are executed."

"I won't get caught. No one will get killed. Though if Anneliese could point out the soldiers who attacked her ..." I turned from the map. "This will be a war of embarrassment."

"A strange choice of weapons but better than Mausers, I suppose."

"My one frustration is that I can't target the person I'd most like to hurt. He'd know it was me."

"That Ernst Weber fellow."

"Yes. But every Schupo I embarrass will have his face in my mind."

Otto sat on the wooden chair beside me, rested his forearms on his knees, and gazed at the floor. "There have been a number of young people who objected to the government, who lashed out ... and who disappeared into Soviet custody. I would talk you out of this if I could."

"You can't."

"I thought as much. I would like to give you something." He took a small notepad from his pocket and scribbled on it, ripped out the page and handed it to me.

"A name and address in Munich?"

"Memorize it, then destroy the paper. It could lead back to me."

"I don't understand."

"If something goes wrong you might need a safe haven."

"I'm not leaving Leipzig. This is my home. They can leave." My voice started to rise. "The Soviets can leave!"

Otto rose and clamped his hands on my shoulders. "I understand. Now listen. That fellow was my best friend in university. We keep in touch. We even developed a simple code for sending messages. I'll let him know you might show up some day. You probably won't ever have to seek him out, but he teaches at the university in Munich and could get you enrolled. Think about it. You could learn to build your own bridges." His grip tightened. "Building is much more satisfying than destroying."

I searched his face but saw only concern. The idea was tempting. "I could learn to build bridges then work with you."

"I'd like that."

"Sure, I'll keep it."

"No. Memorize it. Destroy it. Remember: you're behind enemy lines." I nodded and he said, "One more thing?"

"What?"

"I am guessing by your red toes that your boots are too small?"

My attention dropped to the floor. "I'm used to it. I think the blisters have all turned to calluses."

"No soldier can operate without decent boots. Let me get you a pair that fits."

CHAPTER SIXTEEN

I jerked awake, stumbled out of bed, tried to recall where I was. Then I remembered: Otto's apartment. I pulled back a curtain and squinted into the darkness. The pounding rain had stopped. The silence must have woken me up.

My body was alert. No chance for more sleep. I felt rested enough that dawn must be close.

I dressed in the dark but couldn't find my shirt. I tiptoed to the door, made sure it was closed, then switched on the light. A new pair of boots sat beside my satchel. New to me, at least. They looked worn but serviceable. A pair of socks was stuffed inside. How was I supposed to pay back Otto's generosity? I knew what he'd say. Go to university and get trained.

Steinhauer & Tauber. Or maybe, Tauber & Steinhauer. T & S Engineering. That had a nice ring to it. I rolled up my old shirt and stuck it in my bag beside my book. Otto must have dreamed it would be Steinhauer & Son.

I tucked in my new shirt, cinched the belt tight, put on my new socks and boots. One final sweep of the room. A person could get used to having his own room. Better than a sofa. Or a rooftop. It might be easy to leave my family, move in here. But Otto hadn't offered that.

And Anneliese wasn't here. She had been the best big sister. If I left now, it would be admitting I was to blame for everything that happened on Wednesday. Otto was right about that too. Ernst was more to blame. I had set out with good intentions. He had not.

I shouldered my satchel and crept to the door, rolled out each step to avoid creaks. My hand was on the doorknob when a throat clearing scared the moisture from my mouth.

"Wilm?" Otto's voice was soft. I released my breath. "Don't cross a line you aren't prepared to cross. Some lines are dangerous. You might end up paying too high a price, one your friends and family shouldn't have to pay."

My fingers wrapped around the knob again. "What did you do in the war that you know so much about being interrogated?"

"I passed bridge information to the British a few times. I was questioned by the Gestapo once, but they had no real evidence so they had to release me. I was watched too closely after that to try again."

"Why didn't you go to Britain after the war ended? They must need bridges built."

"Berlin was my home. I didn't want to leave. Then the SED sent me here. To your home."

"I'm glad you came." I slipped into the darkness before he could reply.

The back gate opened to a street beside the riverbed. The rain had washed away the heat and left everything smelling fresh. I crossed a footbridge into the park and wove among the edging of trees. Across the field, the zoo inhabitants were still sleeping. Not everyone would be. The thought kept me alert and listening for the fall of boots on pavement.

I zigzagged down narrow streets, then stopped at Trondlinring, the north arm of the ring road around Zentrum. The *Bahnhof* was a few blocks east, and with the black market usually found there, this area was heavily patrolled. I listened for a few minutes, then heard footsteps. Voices.

Pressed into the darkest shadow the alley had to offer, I waited for the patrol to pass. No building excitement tonight. All I felt was a chilly calm. When the footsteps faded, I crouched low and dashed across the street.

One more patrol crossed my path before I reached police headquarters. It was quiet too. Sleeping like the rest of the city. I took the rocks I had collected earlier and targeted the one streetlamp on the north side of the building. The third rock hit its mark and broke the bulb. No one came to investigate so I watched until dawn arrived.

Four o'clock, I decided, would be the best time to strike.

And now I knew the message I wanted the Schupos to get.

CHAPTER SEVENTEEN

That evening, I waited on the rooftop for Karl. He had said he'd be here at seven and it was quarter past. I sketched ideas on the brick chimney with another piece of shale I'd brought back from the canal, and smudged each drawing when I was done.

Karl finally arrived, Georg in tow. Karl pointed at my bedding. "What's that?"

"I finally have a room of my own." I swept my arm to indicate the roof. "Bigger than I ever expected."

"Might get drafty in winter," he said.

I shrugged. "Maybe I'll be on speaking terms with my father by then." Ruth had told Georg about Anneliese's breakdown—he'd confessed at lunch—so they knew what I meant.

Karl crouched and studied my newest sketch. "A stickman? So you have a target?"

I used my thumb to smear the drawing. "Yes. But things have changed since Ernst threatened me. When I could still think of it as a game, having you along was fun. It's not a game now. I don't want you or Georg involved."

Karl's fingers raked through his hair, leaving it smooth and somehow unruffled. "Too bad. Like you said, someone needs to watch your back. Georg and I have talked. Unless it's a big target that needs both of us, I'll be your lookout. He'll help with preparations."

The lowering sun warmed my face, lit up what I knew had to be a surprised expression.

Karl sneered. "You aren't the only one who can plan. Where were you last night? Your mother was frantic. She came to my apartment after dark."

I didn't mention Otto. I'd never explained how working for him had turned into friendship. "I spent the night in the park under a bridge."

"And you found new clothes there that almost fit?"

I rubbed the knee of my new trousers. "I stole these."

Georg looked alarmed, Karl skeptical. Neither challenged me so I changed the subject. "I need a brush and some paint."

"Tired of bridge inspection? Going to paint houses?" Karl said.

"Just one."

He pointed out that paint was hard to get, which I knew. I turned the shale over and over with my thumb and forefinger. They were getting darker with each turn. "This shale, or even chalk if we could find some, works fine for small things like doors. I want this to be big."

Silence encircled us for several minutes. Karl snapped his fingers. "Does it have to be paint? Maybe whitewash would work."

I pocketed the shale. "Tell me you have some."

"That outside wall in my bedroom wouldn't be a roadmap of cracks if I had whitewash."

Georg said, "Wouldn't some factories have it?"

"We'd have to break into one," I replied, "or sneak in and out during working hours. Factories aren't my target."

Silence again. I sifted through possibilities. Otto might know where I could get whitewash, but I didn't want to involve him either. There had to be ...

I slapped my leg. "Uncle Bruno." Two questioning expressions waited for an explanation. I glanced around the roof, then felt foolish; of course we were alone. "Even when paint was available Uncle Bruno whitewashed his outbuildings. It's cheaper. I painted a shed with it last fall. But I can't remember if any was left over."

"Are you going to the farm tomorrow?" Karl asked.

"And abandon the luxury of my new bedroom for a folding cot by a stove?"

Uncle Bruno believed my story that I wanted to surprise Karl for his birthday and whitewash the cracked wall in his bedroom. He slapped gloves in my hand and sent me to clean the tool shed because that's where he would have stored any leftover lime. I found a bit, not enough to paint the shed, but enough for what I had in mind.

Uncle Bruno explained how to mix the one part salt, three parts slaked lime, and eight parts water so it didn't end up the consistency of a brick. He found some leftover chunks of salt blocks in the barn and had me grind them up with a mortar and pestle. My neck and arms were still aching when I packed up and prepared to walk back to Leipzig on Sunday.

I was halfway down the lane when Uncle Bruno called me back. He held out a worn paintbrush. "You might need this."

CHAPTER EIGHTEEN

As soon as I returned from the farm I met the guys at Karl's and explained the plan. "It has to be tonight." They stared at me as if I'd admitted I was a Soviet spy.

"It's Sunday," Georg protested. "We have school tomorrow."

"There's only a little cloud tonight. No chance of rain. And the moon won't be full for four or five nights. We'll be able to see but can hide if we need to. Tonight is the best night."

Karl gave his approval and I said, "We'll meet at three o'clock at the church in Johannapark." There was a pond nearby. We needed water to mix the whitewash and I didn't want to carry it any farther than I had to.

Georg shot a worried glance toward Karl's window. "You mean we have to go there separately? We can't go together?"

Karl rested his hand on Georg's shoulder blade. "You and I'll go together. Wilm will have the bucket and other supplies. He's protecting us. If we get caught, we can say we weren't doing anything. If he gets caught he can claim he was acting alone."

He had the reasoning right but I hated the way he had put it. I pointed at his face. "No one is getting caught."

The advantage of sleeping on the roof was that it was easy to sneak out. Even lugging a paint bucket it wasn't a problem getting to the park. I kept to the residential areas south of Zentrum, arrived early, and dozed against the church's cellar door until a noise woke me. A moment later Karl and Georg joined me.

Georg's face was dark in the moonlight. Red, I thought. He was scared. I patted his arm. "We'll be fine. We aren't hurting anything, just leaving a message."

His whisper shook. "On *Schutzpolizei* headquarters."

"It's a building, Georg. It doesn't have eyes. Remember the camp-out games in the Hitler Youth? Even in daylight, movement is what attracts attention. If someone approaches, send the signal, hunker down, and don't move."

"They'll have flashlights."

"They won't shine them in your direction unless you move." He didn't reply so I led the way to the pond, put on my gloves, and mixed the whitewash. The slaked lime wouldn't hurt my skin after the wash was mixed, and I didn't want to be explaining chapped hands to anyone. Excitement simmered underneath my actions. I tamped it down, focused on my task.

Once in position—Georg and Karl at either end of the block and me painting my stickman with strings as large as possible—my body hummed down to my toenails. I had to balance on a short wrought-iron fence edging a basement window well. Being so exposed heightened every sense. The figure finished, I sidestepped right, careful not to trip on the fence spikes, leaned against the wall with my left hand and the pail, and started the first letter.

A shorter word would've been preferable, but this was so perfect. The night was cool but sweat gathered behind my ears and dribbled down my neck. Dip, stroke, dip, stroke. I worked at a steady pace, refusing to ruin it by rushing.

My fingertips tingled. I'm sure the hair on my arms was standing at attention.

Eight letters done, three to go when a rat-like chitter came from Karl's direction. I eased off the fence and crouched in the window well, protected by the darkness but trapped by my position. A good thing it took so long to replace broken streetlamps. The cloud that had been hiding the moon drifted away and moonlight made the letters on my sign glow.

Movement. Karl darted from his hiding place. He bolted east away from the station, yelling the words from "Deutschland Über Alles." A patrol approaching from the south gave chase.

The sweat on my neck instantly dried; my mouth too. What was he doing? Of course, he was leading them away so I could finish. I climbed back onto the fence and kept painting. My ears tracked the fading sounds of pursuit while my hands worked. Dip, stroke, dip, stroke. All the while praying Karl would escape

The last line on the last letter. My heart drummed. Excitement and fear. Mostly fear. For Karl. Not for me. I was done. Retreat was the easy part, even with Georg along. I dropped the brush in the pail, got off the fence, and crossed the street to eye my handiwork.

The lettering boldly swept over stone blocks and regularly spaced windows. In the moonlight my two-meter-high stickman with strings dangled beside a single word: *Marionetten*. Puppets.

CHAPTER NINETEEN

I couldn't sleep for the rest of the night. I ambushed Karl at the edge of the schoolyard the next morning and gave him a shove. "What did you think you were doing?"

He shoved back. "Saving your scrawny hind end."

I pushed harder. He pushed back. We lunged into a clinch, grappled like wrestlers, each trying to sweep the other off his feet.

"Boys!" Ruth's hands clutched our upper arms at the same time as her yell registered. We both stepped back. She smiled at each of us. "Do you need some help?"

"No," we replied simultaneously.

Her gaze flicked beyond us and back. She patted our arms in a consoling way. Her words carried past us to whomever she saw coming. "There's no use fighting over me. I've made my choice. And I prefer a gentleman to either of you hooligans."

She turned away. That's when I noticed Georg. Ruth took his hand and he gave us a helpless but happy shrug as she led him away.

Herr Bader joined us. "Smart girl. You are lucky, Herr Tauber, Herr Heinig."

"Why? We both lost to Georg," I replied, stifling a smile.

Our mathematics instructor pointed at the ground. "Another fifty centimeters and you would have been fighting on school property. Then I would have had to punish you." He jerked his head toward the building. "Get to class."

Wondering what Georg might have told Ruth about our plans kept me alert all morning, but I slept through lunch. And mathematics. Worry can only keep you awake for so long.

After school, my route to Otto's bridge took me past Schupo headquarters. From half a block away I saw workers scrubbing and smudging my letters. But if they were still cleaning at this time of day the sign had been seen. Word would spread. *Marionetten*.

Otto confirmed I was right. He had lunched with his SED friend and people there were unhappy. First, SED headquarters had been defaced with a small insult, now the police had been hit with a larger version. Bolder. They'd already decided the two instances were linked and the culprits had to be Wolverines. But the Schupos? According to the SED man, they were furious.

"They are going to quietly increase the number of patrols, not enough to be noticed, but enough to let them cover more ground," Otto whispered, though no one was near the linden tree. I acknowledged the information with a small nod.

I stood and stretched. "I need to get home for *Abendbrot*." Mother would leave my bread and cheese outside the apartment door as she had on Friday night and last night.

Otto held out my knife. "This must have slipped from your pocket."

My stomach twinged. "Thanks." I put it back where it belonged and kept my hand in my pocket. "See you tomorrow."

"Don't come to this bridge. Tomorrow I start assessing the next one south."

I strolled halfway to the other bridge and studied it. According to the book Otto gave me, its arched design wasn't as strong as other styles, which made it more likely to need repair. I preferred the newer bridge Otto had just inspected.

I cut through the park, paused by a huge gnarled tree that rustled as the breeze sifted through its leaves. I looked up and smiled. I knew exactly what my next mission would be.

The evening breeze was cool and the chimney I preferred only partly sheltered me from it. I was tired but too wound up to sleep, and noises from the street kept pulling my attention from my bridge book. Someone shouted for her son to come inside. Farther off, the metalworks shop still rang with high-pitched hammering. Children laughed and shouted, their footsteps pattering down the pavement like hailstones.

A truck backfired. I flinched as thoughts of Karl's risky action last night shot into my mind. I rolled onto my back. I was filthy. I needed to go downstairs and bathe. Wash my clothes. But it would all be with cold water. Frau Nikel might heat water on her stove if I asked, but her summer coal ration would be small.

The beginning of June. In one month I'd be finished this grade, providing I passed, and would only have *Prima* left. Then what? I had an answer now: university. I wanted to be an engineer like Otto and build bridges. Did Leipzig University have engineering classes? Maybe Herr Bader knew. He might even be pleased.

There was one thing he would say though. I had to start doing my schoolwork. I hated it when teachers were right.

"Wilhelm!" Father called from the window I used to access the roof.

My mouth went dry. Was he going to kick me off the roof now? He called again, saying he knew I was there and I'd better get down now. I almost told him to come out if he wanted to talk to me. He might even make it with one leg, but he would be angrier than a stirred up nest of wasps. No point making things worse.

Clouds were collecting west of the city so I shoved my book into my bag and took it with me. I crawled through the open window and focused on brushing off. Otto's voice whispered from a corner of my mind: always look them in the eye. I did.

Father didn't seem angrier than normal, and I caught only a tiny whiff of *Schnaps*. He motioned for me to follow and hobbled to the stairs. He clunked down two steps, sat by the railing. I followed and pressed against the wall to get as much distance between us as possible. The feet of his crutches rested on the step below his boot. He stared at his hands holding the crutches upright. Was the tiredness I saw my fault?

His forehead folded into creases. "Move back where you belong."

Shock kept me silent. He probably still blamed me for what had happened to Anneliese. But he was reaching out. "Why?" I hadn't meant to say it out loud.

His forehead creased deeper. "The whole building doesn't need to know our business. They know it when you're sleeping on the bloody roof."

He had answered without yelling, so I pressed. "You've never cared what they thought before." I held my breath, waiting for an answer. An explosion. Neither came. I got the feeling there was more to this change of heart. "Tell me why I should move back in."

His breathing started to come in huffs. I'd pushed too far and he was getting angry. Instead of feeling panicked, calm settled over me. This was territory I was familiar with. "I'm not moving back if I don't know why."

Father thumped the crutches on the step. "You're a smart-mouthed moron." I waited. Color seeped over his cheeks. He hammered the crutches on the stairs again. "*Verdammt*, I can't stand the silence!" He shifted so the stump of his left leg was brushing my thigh and glared. "No one in that apartment says anything. One is a ghost who haunts me at the table, never looks at me, never says a word. Eats and disappears into her bedroom."

Anneliese. I hated that she was like that again, that it was partly my fault. I held Father's gaze, the same color as Anneliese's but shadowed with anger. I had never seen Anneliese angry. Not at anyone.

"The other," Father said, "is a knife-eyed witch who shoots her daggers at me every time I speak. Does whatever I say and keeps shooting daggers from her eyes."

A smile tugged at the corner of my mouth before I could stop it.

"You think that's funny?" Father leaned closer. "You think it's funny to be shunned by your whole family?"

"No," I replied. "I know what that feels like."

He refocused on his hands, forehead wrinkled again. It seemed like he was trying to apologize. I leaned against the wall and watched his struggle. My calm had turned to something almost joyful. He was sorry, even if he couldn't say it. Tone light, I said, "I don't know why you'd want me back. You know we'll end up yelling at each other again."

"Yelling is better than silence."

Maybe it was, maybe it wasn't. But I liked that he was telling me the truth, so I agreed. Father left me to gather my things.

Three nights later, a little after two o'clock, I stood beside Anneliese's bed. Her sleeping form was barely visible in the inky room. I could imagine both hands tucked under her cheek. I could imagine her at peace.

She could never know what I was doing. Ignorance was the only kind of protection I could give. She wouldn't approve; she'd think it was too dangerous. Well, I couldn't be like Mother and pretend that ignoring the attack made its pain go away. And I couldn't end up like Father, moaning over my fate, drowning my worries. I was sure that's why he drank so much. It wasn't the leg; it was not being able to protect his daughter. He hated being helpless.

Would he approve? No, he didn't approve of anything I did. He'd probably say I was a moron. I wasn't going to let that stop me.

I reached toward Anneliese's hair, then thought better of it and turned away. Anneliese's whisper stopped me. "Wilm? What are you doing? It's the middle of the night."

I returned and crouched by the bed. "I didn't mean to scare you."

"You didn't. I smelled you as soon as I woke up." Her fingers brushed my shoulder. "I'm glad you're home again. I feel safer when you're around."

A huff of air escaped. "Why? I only hurt—" My throat started to close off. I cleared it, pinched the bridge of my nose to ward off the emotions trying to leak out.

Anneliese's fingers returned, settled on my upper arm. For a minute the dark and silence embraced us the way a mother hugs her child. I could've sat like that all night.

"It wasn't your fault, Wilm. You couldn't have known we'd run into ... him."

My stomach clenched at her words. "I should have fought him off."

"He didn't actually hurt me." I started to interrupt but she continued, "It was such a shock, seeing him for the first time since ... the attack. It brought everything back, made it feel like, like it had just happened. I know I scared you, but I'm better now. Now that I've had time to think, it was good that we saw each other again."

"How could it be good?"

My voice had risen. Anneliese shushed me. "The way he disappeared from my life, I thought he despised me for what happened. But there on the street, he told me how much he'd hated himself for not being able to help. He said it had 'gutted him.'"

I recalled how green he'd looked when he'd been whispering to Anneliese. Could Ernst hate himself over that attack like I hated myself for not being able to protect Anneliese from him? I didn't want to believe it. He could be so cold, so hard. A stone man with a stone heart.

He'd probably said those things to hurt Anneliese more, to make her feel awful again. I almost said as much, then decided that if believing his lies helped her get better in some upside-down way, I'd let her keep believing. But I knew better.

I whispered that I was glad for her, told her to go back to sleep, and left.

In the living room my hand encircled the doorknob, but it took several minutes before I could bring myself to turn it. Minutes of replaying our conversation. Of wondering. In the end, it changed nothing. Karl was waiting, and Ernst was still a guy who would smile at you one instant and sucker punch you the next. And he'd still hurt Anneliese more than I could bear.

The door squeaked when I went into the hall. It was as dark as Anneliese's room. I hoped the power was out. I hoped it was out in the whole city.

CHAPTER TWENTY

Karl carried the backless chair we'd found in the rubble of a street not yet cleaned up by *Trümmerfrauen*, and I hauled a broken plank. A potato sack was tucked under my belt. I sensed the same energy in his movements that I felt in mine. It helped to know that my partner on this mission was as eager as I was. And as bold.

We could both think on the run if we needed to, which almost guaranteed we wouldn't need to. Georg ... well, if a Schupo yelled at him to halt, he would probably halt. He was too obedient for his own good. When I'd told him tonight might be dangerous, he'd been relieved to stay home.

Evading patrols was easy, and there were definitely more to avoid as we got closer to the city center. Unfortunately the power outage had only been in our neighborhood.

We skirted south of police headquarters and left the chair and plank a block west, beside an alley door so they looked like discarded items. In the park we circled, looking for the tree I had found a few days ago. Clouds retreated and the full moon turned everything silvery gray. We crouched in the shadow of a linden tree while I squinted at the silhouettes.

"There it is," I whispered. We dashed to the gnarled tree that had inspired me. I pointed up. "It's the biggest wasp nest I've seen in years. The branch it's on is starting to break."

While we climbed up, gingerly held and sawed through the branch, the nest murmured. The wasps weren't all asleep, but with luck they were too lazy to investigate. The potato sack came next, and my nerves hummed like the nest as we worked it over top so only the ends of the branches stuck out. Karl was doubtful it would save us if the wasps attacked.

His voice was tight. "Having fun yet?"

I considered that. "Yes."

Karl dropped to the ground and I inched down, sack in hand, straining to keep the branch horizontal and to make sure the nest didn't bump anything. I was sweating when I got to the grass. Karl took one end of the branch. I leaned against the knotted trunk to rest while Karl told a story about a guy who had dropped dead after being stung by wasps.

I muffled a laugh. "Beer hall nonsense."

"It's true. Some people there knew him."

"Are you afraid it'll happen to you?" No answer. I straightened. "Adds excitement to the night. We could die from bullets. We could die from wasp stings."

"But you don't think we're going to die." It was a statement, not a question.

"My father's the one with the death wish. Not me. It's a good plan."

Earlier the cloud cover had obscured the full moon. Now the stark light drove us from shadow to shadow, slowed us down. We hid from two patrols before reaching the alley where we'd left the chair and plank. The last block was doubly awkward, carrying the nest between us while balancing the other equipment.

Across from the rear corner of the police headquarters we ducked into a stairwell. An open police wagon and two troop transports with tarp-covered backs were parked in the courtyard, gateless thanks to a British bomb. A lamp by the back entrance touched only one of the trucks.

Karl spotted a patrol approaching along the north side of the building. They were talking. I caught the phrase "round and round" and something about boring. When they had crossed the mouth of the courtyard and turned to patrol the west side of the block, I understood. "They're circling the headquarters. No wonder they're bored. We'll have to watch out when we leave."

In the courtyard we hugged the darkest wall. At the transport truck farthest from the back door's light, Karl hoisted the chair over the tailgate, between the two sheets of canvas that hung like stage curtains concealing the interior. He took the plank from me and slid it silently inside, climbed in, then helped me lift the potato sack of wasps into the back of the truck. Metal ribs arched above us and canvas tarp stretched over the supports, making the interior cave-dark.

By feel, I balanced the plank on the tailgate and chair, making sure the carving I had made of a stickman with strings beside the letter *M* was face up. The chair was higher than the tailgate and gave the plank a nice downward tilt. "Okay," I whispered, "Now comes the tricky part."

"About time. This thing is heavy."

I took one end of the branch. We maneuvered to either side of the plank and carefully removed the potato sack. The humming, muffled by the sack, was now noticeable. If anyone heard it in the morning our surprise would be ruined.

We laid the nest on the plank. As we started to release the branch, it wobbled and I shot my hand out to steady it. The paper nest vibrated under my touch.

Then we heard voices. The patrol had returned. I didn't dare move. Something crawled onto my thumb, across the back of my hand. It paused between my third and fourth fingers. Then it stung me.

I inhaled sharply. Didn't move my hand though I wanted to snatch it away. The voices were still out there. The tarp moved slightly. Karl. He breathed words so quietly I almost didn't hear. "Stopped for cigarette."

The wasp crawled back across my hand. Tickled my wrist then started up my arm. It stopped at my sleeve. Stung me again. I squeezed my eyes closed. Swore in my mind. Tried not to think of Karl's story about the man who had died.

Another tickle started to roam over my fingers. I thought the wasp by my wrist might have stopped to nibble my flesh because the burning throb wasn't going away.

Karl breathed again. "Moving."

About time. Minutes dragged. The second wasp seemed happy exploring my hand so I concentrated on its tiny footsteps. Finally Karl whispered, "Clear."

I lifted my hand off the nest. It stayed in place. I batted off the two wasps. "Those beggars sting hard. Let's go."

Karl crawled out first while I held the plank steady. He did the same for me.

We raced through the night as fast as the moonlight and scattered patrols would let us. Halfway home I spotted a puddle of water and called a halt. I knelt and rested my hand, palm up, in the cool liquid. Karl squatted beside me. "Got stung?"

"Twice."

"If they yank open that tailgate without looking under the canvass and that nest falls out it could be ugly."

I imagined the swarm of angry wasps. "That's the idea."

CHAPTER TWENTY-ONE

"**Wilm, wake up!** What are you still doing at home?"

"Go away," I croaked, and rolled over. Onto my wasp-stung hand. I flopped onto my back, heard breathing. Someone was leaning over me, so I cracked open one eye.

Mother said, "It's almost noon, Wilm. You've missed your morning classes."

My eye closed again. I licked dry lips. "Georg can fill me in on history class in three minutes." I shifted so my back was to her. "Same with literature. I know more from—"

The blanket was ripped off me. "Hey!"

Mother scowled at me. "You are going to school. Why are you so tired? You crawled under your covers last night at nine o'clock."

I opened both eyes then. "Fine. I'll go. What can I take for lunch?" There had been only enough leftovers for one lunch. Father's.

A worried expression claimed Mother's face. "I'll see."

"Why are you home?" My stomach growled as I pulled on my trousers.

"I cut myself on broken glass and the foreman sent me home to clean up. I stopped at the store on the way but the shelves aren't well stocked today. It has been like that all week." Mother stood at the table and took a few items out of her sack.

I slipped on my shirt. The cuff rubbed over my wasp stings and I winced. I buttoned it up. "Have you heard why?"

"Only rumors."

"Of what?" I was awake now. Awake and hungry. My stomach rumbled louder.

Her reply was quiet. "Reparation payments."

A polite phrase for the Soviets taking our food and factory goods to pay for the war, for the pain and suffering we had caused them. "That stinks like rotten borscht."

Mother handed me a single leaf of cabbage and a single piece of bread. I almost groaned. She said, "Complaining only makes things worse."

I thought for a moment. "I'm going to help Otto at the next bridge he's inspecting, if I don't faint from hunger." I sniffed the cabbage. It didn't smell very fresh. "Do you want me to take some ration cards and try to get something from a store in Zentrum or Zentrum-West?"

"You could try." She gave me a ration card and a handful of coins. "Look for potatoes or cabbage. Turnips maybe."

The cheap vegetables. The ones I was sick of eating. I agreed anyway.

"Stop at the seamstress's on your way back from the bridge and walk your sister home."

That cheered me up. "She went to work?"

"Yes. Your father walked her there."

Maybe our nighttime talk had encouraged her. I put on my boots and left, the heat in the apartment telling me I wouldn't need my coat. Anneliese had been walking to work alone before that run-in with Ernst. Was it too much to hope that he had gotten stung?

I gobbled down my cabbage and bread on the way to school and made it to mathematics class two minutes before it began. Karl crouched beside my desk. "You scared me. When you didn't show up this morning I kept thinking about that man who died—"

My jutting finger silenced him before he could mention wasps. "I'm going to the city center after class. Can you come?"

He shook his head. "Chores."

"Everyone take your seats," Herr Bader said. "Clear off your desks so we can get started with this test."

Had he said there was a test today? I took out my stubby pencil, thankful we were still learning things that came easily. My stomach grumbled as Herr Bader handed out paper that had been erased several times. My piece was worn through in one spot. I wrote my name lightly in the top corner. Who knew how many more tests it would have to survive?

When I handed in my work, Herr Bader held up his hand to indicate I should wait. He glanced over my paper, nodding, then looked up. "You will pass this class because of these last two units, Herr Tauber. The question is, will you put your apparent talent to use in any way?"

"I want to build bridges."

"Really? That is a pleasant surprise. Homework is a wonderful bridge. It tells us that you understand the knowledge we are imparting, and it is one your history and literature instructors would like to see you building. I told them I would speak to you."

My voice dropped to a whisper. "You're a good teacher, Herr Bader." He inclined his head. I almost added that those teachers hadn't even attended *Gymnasium* themselves, then realized he'd consider that disrespectful. Instead, I asked to be released to run an errand for my mother. He agreed.

A pointless errand. By this time of day all the best produce, probably all the produce, would be long gone from any store I tried. I'd be lucky if there was anything left. Then it struck me that building bridges with my teachers meant I'd have to go to school Saturday morning instead of going to the farm. That thought put me in a foul mood.

The first store was empty, the next picked over. I managed to buy a pair of bruised turnips and stowed them in my book bag. I backtracked to the market square and strolled past the few Schupos I spotted. The third one had a red welt on his neck. I stared at it, hoping ...

"What are you looking at, boy?" the Schupo demanded.

I slid my wasp-bitten hand into my pocket. "That spot on your neck. Is it a scar from a battle?"

He laughed, an unpleasant sound. "Old scars are white, *Dummkopf*. Don't you know a wasp sting when you see one?"

"I haven't seen one in awhile. Does it hurt?" My mood rallied.

"It's on my neck. Of course it hurts. Try getting stung by a wasp and you'll understand."

I tried my best to look curious. "Where was the nest? Under your eaves? Was it big? Did they get in your house?"

"It was at head—" He stepped closer, eyes narrowed. He had to look up to pin me with his gaze. "Why the questions? Do you know something about that *Marionette* Wolverine?"

"That what?" I rounded my eyes. "I've never heard of it. Or is it a him? What's he done?"

"Get lost." He turned to scan the square.

Jubilant, I left the market square. Whether the nest had broken or not, they'd gotten the message. They knew who did it and how easily I had entered their lair. And I had a name. Like a bandit, or a worthy adversary.

I was the *Marionette* Wolverine.

CHAPTER TWENTY-TWO

Saturday morning classes were a boredom-endurance test, but I stayed awake. Barely. I had almost escaped the building when Herr Bader called me into his classroom. He thanked me for showing up. I took in his scanty lunch of white cheese and black bread, and the empty food shelf beside his cot, and a vague sense of embarrassment crawled across my skin. Idiots like me made his life miserable, yet he was thanking me. I retreated with haste.

At home, Mother was intently planning how to stretch a small chunk of sausage into something that could feed four. I grabbed cold turnip and bread and headed to Karl's, my stomach rumbling its discontent.

Karl and Georg hunkered on the steps of Karl's apartment building looking glum. Ruth was there, looking like a scarecrow in a baggy dress. Her hair poked out from her braid like straw, her nose was pinched like a narrow strip of cloth, her eyes were sunken buttons stitched in place, round and staring. At me.

They were all staring at me like I had answers to a question I hadn't even heard.

"What did Bader want?" Karl asked, his tone flat.

"He thanked me, like I'd done him a favor by showing up. What's wrong?"

Georg straightened, causing Ruth to shift away from leaning on him. "What makes you think something's wrong?"

I squinted. Georg's hair was suspiciously neat today. Ruth's influence? I resisted the urge to swear, shifted toward Karl, and repeated my question. He gestured toward the corner where his mother's beer hall was situated, in the cellar of a barbershop. "Rumors."

"Rumors that make you look like a bombing raid is about to happen? Tell me."

He picked at a loose thread on the knee of his trousers. "You know the Soviets are seizing things for reparations again."

"That isn't news. Store shelves are almost empty. So's our table." Ruth and Georg shared a look. They understood empty tables better than I did. Silence blanketed the steps. I shoved both hands in my pockets as anger stirred. I knew this rumor was going to stoke it. "What now?"

Karl snapped the thread. "They took another shipment of butter. Smaller this time, but ..."

Last year there had almost been riots when a Soviet officer had seized 1,800 kilograms of butter. It had sat on a railway siding while he'd searched for a train to ship it east. That butter could have helped feed thousands of families. Instead it stayed in plain sight, behind barbed wire, and spoiled.

"Let's go see," I said.

Smirking, Karl held out his hand to Georg, who muttered. Karl's fingers wiggled in a "give me" motion and Georg slapped a *pfennig* in his palm.

"You bet on my reaction?" I laughed. "If you're that rich, Georg, you can pay our way into the movie tonight."

Ruth snapped, "He's not rich at all, *Dummkopf*."

"Then it's a good thing Otto gave me money yesterday and told me to treat my friends." I looked down my nose at her and realized I didn't like hers because it was too much like mine—long and nearly pointed. "But I only have enough to pay for two extra people."

"Then I won't go either." Georg took Ruth's hand.

"No, Georg." Ruth cupped her free hand over their linked ones. "You go with your friends. I don't enjoy Soviet movies. But he can't stop me from going with you to the railyards."

We moved off, Georg and Ruth trailing behind, still holding hands. Karl whispered, "You could be nice to Ruth. Georg really likes her."

"I don't like not knowing what he has told her. She could be spying for the Schupos."

"If so, we'd already be arrested."

"Do you think he's telling her stuff?"

Karl shrugged. "I try not to think about it. He hasn't been so happy in a long time, Wilm."

I couldn't argue that. But I still didn't trust her.

There was a crowd at the gates to the railyards. We couldn't get near the entrance so we drifted away, along the yard's brick-wall perimeter. Every person in that seething mass had heard the same rumor we had, but the railyard guards weren't talking.

"Let's see for ourselves," I said.

Georg replied, "How? The wall is too high. The gate is the only place to see through."

I turned to Ruth. "I'm the tallest and you're the lightest."

It only took her two seconds. "You want me to get on your shoulders? In a dress?"

"I'm not interested in looking up your skirt. I want to know what's on the other side of this wall. Do you want Georg to blindfold me?"

"I'd rather he gag you." Her lips pursed. Then she agreed, and stopped Georg's protest with a kiss. He came up for air tomato red but looking pleased. It was mildly sickening.

Ruth climbed onto Karl's bent back, then crawled onto my shoulders. Her skirt folded over my face. She smelled of some herb

I couldn't place. I braced against the wall. She lifted her knee and positioned her right foot on my right shoulder, then her left foot on my left shoulder.

She sat on my head. "Do you mind?" I spoke through gritted teeth.

"Just finding my balance." She sounded smug.

I swallowed my reply and focused on staying still. Her heels dug into my shoulders as she rose. Georg kept whispering, "Careful, careful." Finally Ruth's weight stopped shifting. "Well?"

"I can see over. There's broken glass up here."

Glass to go with the two rows of barbed wire that threaded through evenly spaced shepherd-hook rods. They really didn't want anyone getting into these yards.

After a few minutes my knees started to shake. I scowled at Karl. He slapped the bricks. "Ruth? What do you see?"

Her voice wobbled. "Let me down."

I gladly complied, sinking to the ground as soon as her weight was gone. All three sat with me. Ruth's eyes leaked, though her voice was steady. "It's there. Beside the wall, three cars down from us. Just sitting on a flat deck." She stood. "I'm sorry, Georg. I have to go home."

Georg would've followed when she fled but Karl held him. "Let her go."

"But she's upset." His arm muscles clenched but he didn't try to pull away. Ever obedient.

Karl replied, "Everyone is upset, Georg. What can we do about it?"

"How do I know?" Georg replied. "I'm just so hungry, Karl. I haven't been this hungry since the winter when Mom was fired and our food ran out the first time, and we had to eat poppy seeds. Why would they take the butter? It'll be spoiled before they get it back to Russia. Maybe it would last if it was winter, but not in June."

I leaned my head against the wall and closed my eyes so I didn't have to see the hunger etched in Georg's pinched face. The anger was trying to flare up but I couldn't let it. An angry person couldn't think straight. Finally I said, "I know what we're going to do."

"What?" Georg and Karl replied in unison.

"We're going to seize some reparations back from the Soviets."

Karl whistled. "Butter?"

"Tonight."

We hammered out a plan, and then Georg and I slept over at Karl's. I woke up when his mother returned from the beer hall, listened to her rattle around for thirty minutes, go to the bathroom in the hall, come back, and enter her room with a loud click of the latch. I gave it another thirty minutes then woke the others.

We didn't have to go near Zentrum, with its high concentration of patrols, so we snuck to the railyards without incident. The warehouses that crowded the road adjacent the railyard wall, half of them skeletons, gave us shelter while we scouted the site. Three cars farther down, Ruth had said. We crouched in the alley nearest to her estimated spot.

"Sacks?" I whispered. Georg handed them over and I tucked them under my belt. "Cutters."

Karl had borrowed them from a metalworks shop. He laid them in my hand. "I still think you should let me go over the wall. You're the tallest. You could boost me easier."

"No. My plan. I take the biggest risk." The tension was starting to build in my muscles; they quivered with anticipation. Maybe Karl felt the same thing, but I knew I'd explode if I had to sit in an alley and wait. Karl was better at waiting.

"You like this kind of thing too much, Wilm," Karl huffed. "That makes me better for the job. I'll keep my head."

"So will I." The quiet was filled with doubt. I tried to explain. "When I'm on a mission, my nerves are ice. The excitement is there, but under the surface, fueling me. Every thought and action is clear. I see it from above, know every move to make. I'm doing it."

Karl released a long breath in surrender. Georg said, "You know what I think? You both like it too much. And you both scare the crap out of me."

"So let your girlfriend comfort you." What a stupid thing to say. So why had I said it? Suddenly I knew: I was jealous. Of Georg. Ruth might infuriate me, but she was a girl. And she liked Georg. Not me. I shunted the thought aside and held out my hand. "Gloves."

Karl hesitated. "You have the gloves."

"I don't have the gloves. You were supposed to bring them."

"I didn't bring them. Georg, tell us you brought them."

"Me? No." Georg poked my arm. "Let's go back. You can't do this without gloves, Tauber."

"I'm not going back. At least Karl remembered the rope."

"I have the rope," Karl growled. "Georg is right. You can't do this without gloves."

"My hands, my problem. Let's go." Neither of them moved. "If you don't help, I'll find a barrel or something and get over on my own. Are you coming?"

"*Scheisse*," Karl said. "You're a moron, Tauber."

"Like I haven't heard that before." I grabbed Karl's upper arm and hauled him to his feet. "Georg, watch for patrols while Karl gets me over the fence."

"Yes, sir," he snapped.

Karl made a stirrup for my foot and lifted me high enough so I could grip the top edge of the wall. Some glass bit my fingertips while he braced my feet on his shoulders. He grunted as he lifted me higher. Seconds later he whispered in a strained voice, "I'm up. Do it."

I rested my arm on the edge of the wall, trying to avoid the worst of the glass, and clipped each strand of wire. I tucked the cutters back under my belt with the sacks and twisted the wire out of the way. The railyard was quiet, no sign of guards.

Now came the painful part. Before I could second-guess myself I planted my hands on top of the wall and sprang up, off Karl's shoulders. My hands took my whole weight for a second. Shards of pain thrust into my palms. My boots paused on the glass, then I vaulted down.

My vision blurred as I jolted to the ground and hit my knees. I jumped up, shook my hands, and hissed air between my clenched teeth. My hands were bleeding, but they'd have to wait.

I found the butter by the smell. It hadn't spoiled yet. I flipped out my knife and cut through the brown paper, then scooped some butter onto my finger and sucked it clean. So good. I wanted to eat it by the handful. I cut big slabs of butter and slid them one by one into the first bag. No one would complain about some cloth fibers in their butter, or a bit of blood. The butter soothed the cuts a bit. I stopped at what I estimated to be five kilograms, then filled the next two bags with similar amounts.

I carried the bags to the wall and quietly called Karl. He answered right away. I lobbed each bag over the wall. Then waited.

What was the delay? Karl only had to run the bags to Georg, then return, toss the rope over, and anchor it while I scaled back over the wall. Had they been caught? I hadn't heard anything. They must have spotted someone. I stood with my back to the wall, my head twitching from side to side as I watched for guards. "Faster, Karl," I breathed. "Faster."

My heart was drumming so loud I almost didn't hear the rope slap the wall beside me. I turned my head in its direction ... and spotted a guard coming around the last car. He'd turned in my direction. "Run, Karl. There's a guard."

"Climb! Hurry," came the reply.

"Too late. Run."

I dove toward the flatdeck still piled with butter and rolled under.

CHAPTER TWENTY-THREE

Boots crunched on gravel, closer and closer. I lay under the railcar and considered my options. There weren't many. From my hiding spot I could see the rope dangling in the moonlight. The guard would spot it and raise the alarm. The only good thing was that I'd heard footsteps running away. With luck the guard had heard them too and would assume I'd fled.

My hands were greasy and hurting. I needed to get out of sight. I wedged my upper body between the railcar's front axle and the flatdeck. I held onto the coupling bar, choked on the smell of grease, and hoped the guard wouldn't look too closely.

The beam from the guard's swaying flashlight touched the rope, passed it, returned. As the light started to swing my way I raised my legs and pressed my heels against the bottom of the deck, body vibrating with the effort of keeping horizontal. The guard swore when his light found the ransacked pallet of butter. He swept the beam of light under the flatdeck then back to the rope. He swore again and ran.

I fell out of my hiding spot and rolled from under the car. The guard was probably on his way to make a telephone call. Schupos would be swarming all over in minutes. I needed to be quick.

I drew my stickman with strings half a meter from the ravaged butter, so the guard could say he hadn't seen it. I took a two-fingered scoop of butter and ate it while I scrambled to the other side of the car and paced toward the railyard's office. If I could find somewhere to hole up this could be fun. I'd never been able to stick around after a mission—to see or hear the Schupos arrive, find out how they first react. This would be way better than a Soviet movie.

My eagle's eye studied the layout of the yards. The wire cutters were too lightweight for anything like a padlock chain. The Schupos would be thorough and would search the yards. Every car, inside, under, and on top. Where could I hide if I couldn't get out?

I was at the second car from the end when a door slammed. I crouched behind a wheel and listened to two guards. They passed the gap between my hiding spot and the next row of railcars and headed down the other side. As soon as they passed I bent low and ran to the office.

A peek through the glass in the door showed an empty room. Staying low, I crept into the building and crouched behind the customer-service counter. A few chairs lined the walls, and a closed door huddled in the right corner of the room. Beside that was a doorway marked Staff Only. The exit was in the far left corner beside a bank of windows. I prepared to race toward it then froze.

A third guard blocked the exit, his back to the room. I almost groaned, and cut toward the unmarked door, hoping it was another exit, praying the guard didn't turn. I rolled out my steps as quietly as I could. And sighed with relief when it opened. Slipped through.

The room was blacker than coal and smelled like vinegar. I felt along the wall, kicked something metal, and flinched at the noise. My fingers touched a pole, ran up its length to discover a stringy mop's head. A broom closet. So much for my great escape.

I felt around to discover what else was in this closet. The back wall had some hooks with a few rags hanging to dry. And a pair of coveralls. With aching slowness I slid into them. They were too big and too short but I kept them on. If a Schupo found me I'd tell him I was a janitor and had panicked when they'd arrived. They might believe me if no guards were around.

I couldn't make out any of the voices on the other side of the door. Boredom set in, and with it, tiredness. Too many broken sleeps and nighttime missions. I needed to stay low for awhile. Let them think the *Marionette* Wolverine was gone—before I surprised them again.

I edged back over the pail, crouched beside the door, and pressed my ear to its surface. Now I could make out what was being said. Some Schupos interviewing the guards. They accused the guards of setting things up so it looked like hooligans had gotten over the wall when they had stolen the butter themselves. The guards protested loudly. The loudest one was silenced with a slap.

This kept up for several minutes before another Schupo's voice chimed in. "Sir, we have examined the top of the wall and the other side. There is blood on the wall. Someone went over it, probably with bare hands."

I closed my hands into fists. They throbbed. I could feel bits of glass embedded in the skin, but without light I could pluck out only the biggest slivers.

The first Schupo said, "Show us your hands. Hm. Clean."

Then I heard a voice that made me shiver. "We're searching the yard, sir, and have posted men around the perimeter. If he's still here we'll catch him." Ernst Weber.

"Make sure you do, lieutenant."

My mouth was dry. I briefly considered sucking on one of the wet rags, but the smell of vinegar decided me against it.

More orders flew around. I should have listened but didn't. Waiting was as hard as I'd thought it would be. It took enormous effort to not open the door and break for the street. But a bullet in the back would feel worse than glass in my hands. So I waited.

Hours. The janitor wouldn't come on a Sunday, so no one was likely to open the door if they hadn't yet. Still, I worried about it for awhile, then gave up. If the door opened, I'd try to run.

Surprise was on my side. Boredom was on theirs. I dozed off once and startled awake. My heart hammered my ribs. I had to stay alert.

The guards had long since been taken to Schupo headquarters for further questioning. It had to be close to six o'clock. I ached all over but couldn't stretch out so I stood. Rubbed my neck, rolled my shoulders. Tried to ignore the burning in my hands.

Someone reported in. The yard had been searched, nothing found. The commanding Schupo swore a rainbow-colored streak that had me grinning. Just what I'd wanted: a front-row seat to their failure.

Something crashed. Silence.

"Should I clean it up, sir?"

More silence. My muscles clenched as I prepared to race for the outer door the second this one opened. The commander swore again. "Their damned coffee. Their damned cup. Let them clean it up. Is the new railyard shift here? Brief them. I'm going back to headquarters. Leave one of our men here for the day. Damned waste of time. That Wolverine is long gone."

I sagged against the wall. Suddenly I had to urinate. But there was nowhere to go that wouldn't announce my presence like a voice over a loudspeaker.

I shifted from foot to foot. Waited. Another hour it seemed.

When the office outside the closet had been quiet for some time, I dared a peek. Empty. One railyard guard was standing outside looking over the yard. I couldn't wait. It was piss or explode. I closed the closet door, found the pail, and emptied my bladder.

No one ripped open the door so I peered out again. The guard outside hadn't moved. Likely one was patrolling the grounds.

Where was the third? I had to chance it. But not before I left another sign. I carved my stickman on the inside of the door. Now I could go.

Keeping low, I left my refuge and headed toward the exit. A guard stood facing the street, like when I'd first hidden in the closet. He had no weapons I could see. I pulled the wire cutters from my belt and tiptoed toward him. A board creaked. He started to spin; I swung the cutters. They bounced off his forehead. He sank to his knees cradling his head, dazed.

I leaped over him and fled. A warning echoed behind me. I shot into an alley and raced away. Heart pumping, body humming, boots beating the cobblestones. Left down another alley. Right through a courtyard and over a fence. Right again down a sleepy street. Another alley.

I halted, breathing hard, stripped off the coveralls and tossed them in a stairwell. There were no sounds of pursuit so I walked briskly instead of running, stuffed my injured hands in my pockets and kept to side streets all the way to Karl's.

He opened the door on one knock and yanked me inside. "That was too close. What took you so long?" Georg was nowhere in sight. Gone home with his butter, probably.

"I had to hide in a broom closet while Schupos searched the whole yard."

Karl's eyebrows rose. Then he laughed. "You have a lucky horseshoe stuck up your hind end, Wilm. I swear it."

I pulled out my knife. "I have my lucky knife. Better than a horseshoe. More comfortable."

We both laughed. Karl motioned to the sofa. "Sit. Tell me everything."

"No. I need to get my butter home before the neighborhood wakes up. I'll fill you in later."

"Fine. And clean up your hands. They look like ground meat." He gave me my sack.

When I entered our apartment, Father was eating his breakfast. He frowned at me then gave a bigger frown to his slices of dry bread. This couldn't be hidden so I didn't try. I dropped the sack beside his plate.

He gave me a sharp glance. "What's this?"

"Look."

He did. His frown deepened. "Where did you get all this butter?"

Mother appeared at his side, fear in her face. I kept my attention on Father, picked up one of his pieces of bread, slathered it with butter, and took a big bite. When I swallowed I said, "Exactly where you think it came from."

He didn't explode, didn't say anything. He just looked at me like he had never seen me before. As he continued to stare, my uneasiness grew. I headed toward the linen closet.

"Where are you going?"

"Taking my bedding to the roof and going to sleep."

"I don't recall kicking you out."

No, he hadn't. I didn't look at him. "That's okay. It's quiet up there on a Sunday morning. And you can talk about your troublesome son without him overhearing."

I went to the bathroom, cleaned my hands as best I could and cut a strip off the edge of my blanket. I wrapped each hand, using my teeth to tighten the knots. On the roof, I curled up near my favorite chimney and fell headlong into sleep.

I didn't wake up until early afternoon.

Karl came over and demanded every detail. I told them with relish, reliving the rush of excitement, remembering how danger sharpened that excitement. Realizing how much I already wanted to do it again.

For Anneliese, I told myself. But it didn't quite ring true.

CHAPTER TWENTY-FOUR

I showed up at school thirty minutes before classes started, long before any other students. Herr Bader jumped when I walked into his class. A quick glance showed there was nothing on his food shelf except half a loaf of dark rye bread.

After double-checking that we were alone, I pulled a waxed-paper packet out of my bag and laid it on his desk. He regarded it curiously. "A bribe, Herr Tauber?"

"No. Just a gift."

He opened it. His eyes grew wide and he quickly wrapped it up. He rushed to the door, closed it, and returned to sit with a grunt. He cradled his head in hands for a minute then looked up. "Let me see your hands."

I showed him my roughly bandaged hands. He grabbed one wrist and turned. His Adam's apple bobbed like a float on a fishing line. "Herr Tauber, you should know all schools were notified and all teachers ordered to watch for a student with injured hands. Something to do with theft of Soviet property on the weekend. No details given, but with rumors being what they are, none are needed." He frowned at me. "Do you have a knife?"

I got it out. He cut the bandages off both of my hands. "I will accept your gift. This is mine in return." He returned my knife, wadded up the bandages, and thrust them at me. "Get rid of these. And don't ever involve me with your foolish escapades again. I do not

want to have to choose between keeping my position and inform-
ing on a promising student."

I blinked in confusion. I'd only wanted to help him, give him
a bit of food.

He barked, "Do it now, before anyone else shows up!"

I strode home, dropped the bandages into the recently emptied ash pit in our courtyard, and paused over the acrid-smelling
manhole before I let the cover fall closed. Herr Bader was afraid.
Georg was afraid. My whole family lived in fear of one kind or
another. Everyone I knew was afraid.

Even I had been living in fear for years, during the war and
now during the Soviet occupation. Why was the fear I felt during
a mission so different? Why did it sharpen my senses instead of
dulling them the way that other fear did?

At least Karl felt the same as me. At least one other person
knew the surge of power that came with controlling that fear,
moving through it, and defeating it.

Now, thanks to the elusive *Marionette* Wolverine, the *Schutzpolizei* had learned to fear. That was the good part, the part that
made it worthwhile. They were the powerless ones here—not
knowing when I would strike again, not being able to defend
against me or catch me.

Hands in pockets, I strolled back to the school and was late for
my history class. Who cared about history? I was living history.
Making history.

After school, Karl and Georg took off while I handed in some
overdue assignments. When I got home, my apartment overflowed
with strained silence; anywhere else was a good place to be, so I
went looking for them. They weren't in their usual haunts. As I was

leaving Georg's I realized Ruth was only two flights up. Maybe she knew something.

She answered my knock quickly. I stepped inside. "Is Georg around?" The living room was empty. I peered toward the bedroom doors and craned my neck to see into the kitchen.

Fists on hips, Ruth tapped one toe. "He isn't here."

"Can I ...?" Before she could answer I crossed to the window and surveyed the street, feeling edgy like I always did around Ruth.

She heaved a sigh. "If you're going to stay, you might as well sit."

I sat and she perched on the other end of the sofa. "Georg said something about helping Karl search, but he didn't say what for." Furrows rippled over her forehead. "Did you think he and I—" Her lips pursed. I hadn't actually considered that they were fooling around, but the thought coaxed a smile. She blurted, "I hate the things you make him do."

"I don't make him do anything."

"He idolizes you and Karl. He won't refuse you anything." She frowned at her folded hands.

I leaned forward and caught a whiff of her herbal scent. "Why are you even going out with him? He doesn't seem your type."

"He's nice. Genuinely nice. Is it so terrible to want something nice in my life?" She looked up. Her eyes held a suspicious shimmer. It made them look huge. Made them glow.

Finally I managed to speak. "You're right. He's nice. He believes everyone is as honest as he is." I squinted at her interlocked fingers. "So Georg told you what we did."

She scooted across the sofa and turned my hand over, skimmed the cut-up surface of my palm. "Yes. But I would have figured it out anyway."

Her touch was electric. Did she feel it too? I gritted my teeth. "And you can't turn me in because Georg will also get in trouble.

Too bad for you." She looked puzzled. Her scent completely enveloped me now.

"I, I didn't think about that. I'm glad he has some butter..." Her tongue traced her lips as if she were imagining eating it. I swallowed, my own lips suddenly dry.

"He hasn't given you any?"

"He offered. I refused. He and his mother barely have enough to live."

I brushed a strand of hair from her brow. "So ask me. I have more to eat than he does."

She arched her brows in a mocking way. "I can't just ask you. I have nothing to trade." Her head tilted and her voice pitched low. "What do you want for some of your butter, Wilm?"

Her eyes widened as I leaned close. "What are you offering?" My whisper was hoarse. My mind couldn't keep up with the conversation. The air hummed between us.

She licked her lips again, and a guttural sound escaped my throat. I will never know how our lips met. We ended up in a tangle of limbs on the sofa. A thunderstorm of sensations shorted out my thoughts as our bodies pressed together. I wanted—

She pressed her hands against my chest, stopping me with her touch and insistent gaze. Our breathing was the only sound in the room. My weight pressed down on her as I searched her face and tried to read her expression. How had it gone from teasing to this in minutes?

My whisper was harsher than I intended. "So butter is your price? You won't ask Georg because he's too nice and too hungry, but I'm not nice so you'd really offer me a trade?"

Color drained from her face but she didn't deny it. I lowered my mouth and covered hers, kissed her hard. I suddenly wanted to punish her, for betraying Georg, for thinking I was that selfish.

More, I wanted her to be sorry when I left, sorry that she hadn't chosen me for more than a block of butter.

All at once, Anneliese came to mind. I pushed off Ruth so hard I landed on the floor flat on my back. It took several seconds before I could breathe. I covered my eyes with my arm, worked at finding some calm. Remembering Anneliese's pain drove out every feeling, every need except the need to be sick. My stomach threatened. I swallowed bile.

"Oh, God," Ruth sobbed. "What have we done? Don't hate me, Wilm. I didn't ..."

I staggered to my feet, and braced hands against knees. Sucked in air. Gathered my thoughts. Hate her? No. I hated myself, how close I'd come to losing control. To maybe doing to a girl what had been done to my sister. I hated myself with a loathing so hot that it burned through everything else.

"Stay with Georg. You make him happy, Ruth. Don't tell him about this."

From the misery on her face I knew I didn't need to say it. She looked exactly like I felt. I made it to the stairwell before I folded over with dry heaves.

I went to the park but didn't go to the bridge, didn't do anything except sit under the gnarled tree where I'd found the wasp nest and try to stop hating myself.

The sun dropped below the trees, reminded me I needed to get home soon or Mother would worry. I got there at dusk, wrapped up some butter and left. No one asked where I was going.

Ruth answered her door on the second knock. I held out the butter. She took it warily. "Do you ... want to come in?" Reluctance shaded her words, made them low and urgent. She was afraid of what I might want. A lump of self-loathing settled in my throat. I shook my head.

"I can't just take this. Not after today." Her face contorted and I knew I wasn't the only one hating the person in the mirror.

"There's one thing you could do."

"What?" The word shot out like a hand grabbing a life preserver.

"Do you remember Johanna Fahr?"

"A little. She moved away during the war."

"She's living not far south of the new town hall. She could use a friend."

The wariness returned. "Why can't you be her friend?"

"Her boyfriend is a jealous Schupo. Ernst Weber. That day you helped get Anneliese back to our apartment he threatened me because I'd walked Johanna home."

"Oh."

"I'm not the oaf you think I am, Ruth. Not all the time. Johanna is my friend, but I can't see her without angering Ernst. You could be her friend, and let her know I'm okay. If she asks."

"Why are you telling me this, asking me to do this?"

I gripped the doorjamb and squeezed my eyes shut. "Because I almost did a terrible thing today. And ... I need to know I'm not terrible."

"We both almost did a terrible thing, betraying Georg."

That's what she thought I was upset about? She didn't realize how close I'd come to hurting her? My knees threatened to give way. The vision of Anneliese's sad face came to me again. I whispered, "Will you do it? Be Johanna's friend if she lets you?"

"Yes. And thank you for the butter."

I rolled away from the door, braced myself against the wall. The thunk of a deadbolt driven home pierced my chest. I pressed my fist to my breastbone.

When I could breathe more or less normally, I walked home, head down. Part of me wanted to be caught by a patrol, to be questioned when they saw my hands. To be punished. I sat on the steps of the apartment building for a long time but no patrol came, so I retreated to the dark and silent apartment with my darker but very loud thoughts.

CHAPTER TWENTY-FIVE

Anneliese joined me in the kitchen, stood close without actually touching. I remembered the soothing effect of Otto's hand on my shoulder when I had broken down and wished our family could be more like that.

Mother and Father were listening to the radio in the living room. Some symphony of Russian music that had lots of clangs and bangs. Anneliese kept her head down and watched me butter a piece of bread I had toasted on the stove. Mother hated crumbs on her stove so I had carefully cleaned them all off. I broke the toast in half and gave a piece to Anneliese.

She took it and whispered, "Where did you get that butter? Mother and Father won't say."

I ate my toast, brushed crumbs off my shirt. "Think of me as a modern Klaus Störtebecker, liberating goods from rich ship owners, giving them to the poor."

She clamped her hand over her mouth.

"Before he was beheaded, Liese." Her wide eyes skewered me with more guilt. I started to reach out. Stopped with my hand halfway between us. Her eyes grew wider at the sight of my cut palm. I closed it into a fist. "I won't do it again. I promise." She fled to her bedroom.

I retreated to the table, flipped through the *Leipziger Volkszeitung*, saw that there was no butter allowed for any type of ration cards, then opened my history of bridges book. The evening was quiet until Father turned off the radio and stumped over to the table, leaning heavily on his crutches the way he did when he was tired. I was on his chair but he didn't order me off.

"Three days and no *Schutzpolizisten* banging on the door," Father said. "You think you're pretty smart."

"Smarter than them."

"Surely there might be one or two who are smarter than you, Wil-helm."

I hadn't realized he had been drinking while listening to the radio until he said my name that way. I closed the book. "I prefer Wilm."

"You prefer. Do you hear that, Gertrud? He prefers to be called Wilm." He knocked over a chair. Mother flinched. I stood as the calm that had eluded me since I'd left Ruth's apartment returned. I had expected this reaction on Sunday.

"Yes," I replied softly. "I prefer Wilm. If you don't mind."

"I do mind!" He roared. "I named you Wilhelm and I'll damned well call you Wilhelm if I want. It's your damned name!"

His face was red. I recalled our talk on the stairs when he had told me to move off the roof. Yelling was better than silence, he'd said. He seemed to be expecting a response so I said, "Do you feel better now?"

He heaved the table onto its side, making me jump back. He almost lost his footing, then recovered and bowled toward me, backing me into a corner. His anger plunged into a quiet, more dangerous depth. "I don't feel better. Not one bit. I want you to not bring trouble down on our heads. Is that too much to ask?"

I didn't say anything. He leaned close and breathed *Schnaps* fumes onto my face. "Is that too much to ask, Wil-helm? Could you at least try to keep trouble from our doorstep?"

I didn't know how I would react if he hit me. Was I as capable as those Schupos who had beaten him of knocking him down and taking out my frustrations when he was helpless?

"Will you answer or not?" Father tilted left and used his right crutch to raise my chin.

"I think I should sleep on the roof."

"No. Hiding is the easy way out. You'll face me. You'll answer me."

"Heinz." Mother's voice was soft, pleading.

"Go to bed, Gertrud."

She cast a worried look and left. Anneliese wouldn't come out after she heard Father yell. We were alone. He pushed the crutch higher, pressed it against my windpipe. Not hard. Yet.

"You think I don't know what you're feeling," Father said. I swallowed and the crutch seemed to press harder against my throat. He continued, "You hate the trap you're in. You hate that cruel men have power over you. And you count me as one of them."

He seemed to want an answer. I jerked my head once.

His breathing huffed out in short bursts for a minute, then finally eased. He returned the crutch to the floor and tucked it under his arm. "I was in the Wehrmacht, Wilhelm. Look at me. I was trained to fight. I did. But they were stronger. And they didn't even have the dignity to let me die. Those American pigs had to complete my humiliation by saving my life."

I braced to hear him say he'd rather be dead. At least he'd come home. Not like Karl's and Georg's fathers. I thought, Don't say it.

He didn't. Instead he said, "This is the kind of enemy you are fighting when you attack the Soviets. Know it. They want you caught because you stole a little butter. They want you whipped for it, publicly. Then they want you shipped east to a prison camp where they can starve you and work you to death out of sight of everyone you love, people who won't even know when you die. They don't want to kill you with honor. They want to degrade you. Crush you until you're more beaten than a one-legged man."

My eyes burned. I pressed my lips together until the desire to cry subsided. I shook my head. "It won't be like that. They'll never catch me. I'm going to win."

His smile held no warmth; his eyes were snow-shadow blue. "You think we didn't say the same thing? The mighty German Wehrmacht? You think you can do better? Feel free to try. But don't bring your trouble home. Don't you dare, or I will disown you. If trouble arrives on this doorstep my son is dead to me."

CHAPTER TWENTY-SIX

For three days I kept quiet. I sat with Karl and Georg but wasn't with them. In my mind I was arguing with my father, proving him wrong in every way. After school I didn't help Otto. I went to the park, but I sat under the gnarled tree and watched from a distance. Fought battle after battle in my mind.

Friday at lunch Karl pressed me. "What's next?"

I stared at him for a long time. "We're laying low for awhile."

His lip curled. "Lost your guts, Wilm?"

"You hide in an office swarming with Schupos for hours, Karl, and see how you do. You'd be pissing your guts all over the floor."

"We know you're daring," Ruth said. Her soothing tone suggested I needed to be calmed down, which cut like broken glass.

"You know nothing," I snarled.

Georg said, "Was that called for, Tauber? Ruth says something nice and you bite her head off? Apologize."

"Don't pick now to get brave, Georg. I'm not in the mood."

"Apologize," he repeated.

My fist clipped his jaw. I stalked off. And kept walking. All the way to Zentrum.

All of this thinking was driving me crazy. It was making me even more angry with myself, and now I was taking it out on my friends. Georg hadn't deserved that punch. I was the one who deserved that. I needed to do something.

Prove my father wrong.

I was passing by the ruins behind the old town hall when Johanna called my name. My feet betrayed me by stopping. I saw her coming from the direction of the Auerbachs Keller, a restaurant only the rich could enjoy. She walked with a swing in her hips and a broad smile. God, she was beautiful. Apparently, Ernst hadn't warned her away from me, just the other way around.

She was only across the street from me now, pausing as a man in a wheelchair crept past her. "What are you doing?" she called. "Skipping classes?"

Mathematics. I'd forgotten. Another sign I was going crazy. Johanna stepped into the street, clearly intending to visit with me. I bolted toward the market square, careened around the low *Suchdienst* building, wove among pedestrians, and ducked down behind a car. I saw her looking for me, turning and turning in the middle of Markt. She gave up and walked south toward the new town hall. She looked sad. I wanted to call her back, wanted to talk to her like we had the day I'd walked her home. But I couldn't. I retreated to the side steps of Thomaskirche.

I was jittery. Too jittery to think straight. Maybe Otto could give me some work to clear my mind. I headed west then took the first side street south. Slowed as I saw the police wagon parked beside my path. A glance over my shoulder confirmed I was the only pedestrian on the street. Impulsively, I crouched by the back wheel. Pierced it with my pocketknife. Carved a circle on the fender and drew a cross above it. The start of my stickman puppet. I smiled as I scratched downward, making the body.

"Halt!" someone yelled. "What are you doing?"

I glimpsed a figure in a Schupo uniform descending the stairs of an apartment building and took off. I folded my knife as I ran, shoved it in my pocket as I turned a corner. Glanced at the Schupo giving chase. He looked heavy. It might be fun to run him into the ground.

Ahead, a woman leaned her bicycle against the stairs of her apartment and carried groceries inside. I snagged the handlebars, pushed the bicycle three steps then jumped on. Behind me the woman screamed for someone to stop the thief and the Schupo yelled for her to call more police.

I zipped through the streets, turning one way then the other, closer to Otto with each corner. I shot through Johannapark and into another residential area. A few blocks from the bridge I dumped the bicycle in an alley and ran through Clara-Zetkin-Park, ducked under branches, and wove around tree trunks. I hadn't felt so alive since ... since Sunday in the railyard.

It felt good. Fantastic.

I spotted Otto, and began unbuttoning my shirt as I ran. I sloughed it off as I slid down the bank to the bridge's footings. "Give me a job. Quick."

He didn't hesitate. "In the water."

I plunged in until I was waist deep. Otto took a flashlight from his briefcase and tossed it to me. "Get under the bridge. Start describing what you see on the back side of the arches."

As I waded under the bridge I heard distant shouts. Other Schupos had responded quickly with the station being so close. They must have found the bicycle. I started telling Otto what I saw, every cobweb, every chipped bit of mortar. I could imagine him scribbling and sketching furiously. "Yes, yes," he said. "Keep going. You're doing fine ... Wilhelm."

Rapid footsteps. "Hello, there." A voice out of breath.

I kept talking but Otto shushed me. "What can I do for you, officer?"

"A hooligan." The Schupo panted. "Did you see one run by, or over the bridge?"

"Hooligan? I can't say I saw anyone run by." Otto ducked his head in my direction. "What about you, Wilhelm? Did you hear anyone run over the bridge?" He straightened and spoke to the Schupo. "My assistant. He has very good ears."

"No, sir," I replied. "No running. Some vehicles drove over—"

Otto silenced me. The flashlight beam quivered. The water was freezing under here with no sunlight to warm it up. Otto said, "I'm sorry we can't help you, officer."

Another pair of footsteps approached. The first Schupo said, "Check this man's work permit. I'll cross the river and ask if anyone saw him. He probably headed south or cut east toward the racetrack. Go that way when you're done."

The second Schupo took his time checking Otto's papers. Otto was very helpful, even wished the man luck as he walked away. Then he bent down and barked, "Get back to work, Wilhelm. I don't pay you to stand under there and do nothing."

He made me continue reporting for ten more minutes, then called me out. I was surprised icicles weren't hanging from my trousers. He noticed my shaking and his salt-and-pepper eyebrows merged into one long fuzzy caterpillar. "Boots and socks off. Stretch out in the sun. Let it warm you and dry you off."

Otto sat beside me but continued to scribble in his notebook. I noticed him glance at my chest several times then realized he was looking at his ring on its leather thong. Had he thought I would sell it? Slowly the increasing warmth on my chest became noticeable, but it was awhile longer before my legs felt like their ice blocks were melting.

"So," Otto said, "what have you learned today, young friend?"

I thought about it, not liking that I hadn't been able to finish scratching the puppet stickman. "To not give in to impulses. Follow the plan."

"Plans can go wrong too. Always have a backup plan." He set his notepad on the grass. "Have you warmed up?" He took my wrist and turned it over. One brow rose slightly as he stared at my palm. The cuts were mostly healed but still visible. "You took the butter. I feared it was you when I head the tale from my SED friend. *Marionette* Wolverine. What nonsense."

I jerked my hand free.

"You like that name? Do you fancy yourself a folk hero? I hope not. Those railyard guards spent half the day in unpleasant interrogations because of you. Collusion. Do you know that word? It means they thought the guards were working with you. They raided their houses looking for stashes of butter. Unfortunately for one of them, they found something else. A closet of boots, if I recall. He had been selling them on the black market."

"That's not my fault."

"Indeed. But sometimes we don't see the ripples that flow out from our actions." Otto took out his pipe and went through his loading ritual, then slid it back in his pocket.

"Why don't you ever smoke it?"

"My pipe? I used to smoke it, but after my son died the tobacco tasted like ashes so I stopped. Now it seems a waste of money given conditions in the city. I still buy tobacco, but now I tap it out of my pipe where keen, hungry eyes are watching. It's a simple way to let a few pennies end up in needy pockets without reducing the person to begging. Selling dribs of tobacco on the black market is somewhat more dignified, don't you agree?"

"Begging is awful. I did it once, right after the war ended. Anneliese and I went into the country, from farmhouse to farmhouse, but barely got a handful of poppy seeds." I sniffed. "That was the only time we ate them. But Georg brings cooked poppy seeds to school sometimes. I can always tell when he has them because he tries to hide what he's eating."

"You speak a lot about Georg. Sometimes I think he might be a younger brother."

"He needs someone to look out for him. He's nice. Too nice for a mean city like this." Too nice for a friend like me.

"Was it always mean?"

"No. But now it's broken and beaten up. Parts are missing ..." I stretched out again and covered my eyes as my own words sank in. "People with missing parts can be mean."

"People? Cities, you mean. Or maybe the people living in those cities?"

"Take your pick."

A few minutes silence, then Otto said, "You told me your father was missing part of his leg. Has it made him mean?"

"Yes. No. I don't know. It's made him ... bitter. Frustrated. Maybe scared."

Otto sighed. "But you won't be like him, will you, Wilm? You won't be scared by anything."

I rolled onto my stomach, propped up on my elbows, and let the sunlight heat my back. "I guess I won't."

"My son was fearless too. Nothing scares a father so much as a fearless son."

"You're saying I scare my father?"

"You terrify him, Wilm. You must. You're terrifying me."

I furrowed my brow, squinted at my fists. "Why?"

"Think for a minute, and give me your best guess. Why do you terrify me?"

I thought of the thrill of the chase. It felt good to escape those Schupos. But ... I knew I would get the same thrill from hunting as evading. Like when I had snuck up on that railyard guard and dazed him with the wire cutters. And then there was Ruth and how close I'd come to hurting her.

I squeezed my eyes shut and said, "I'm becoming like them."

"Tell me that scares you, Wilm. Tell me you don't want to cross that line." There was an urgency in his voice that made me sit up and scan his face.

He had always been honest with me. I had to be honest with him. "I'm not sure I can tell you that, Otto. I'm not sure I want to."

CHAPTER TWENTY-SEVEN

On Monday, Georg still wasn't talking to me and his chin sported a fading bruise. He even refused my food. By Wednesday, I was desperate to bleed off frustration, so Karl and I snuck out in the night and left drawings of my stickman puppet and a capital M on the doors of government buildings, including the *Schutzpolizei* headquarters. Four easy strikes that felt hollow.

Finally I tried to apologize, but Georg wouldn't accept it until I apologized to Ruth. So I did, but it came out something like, "Stay away and we'll get along." What if we slipped and Georg found out what had happened between us? Better to keep our distance.

On Saturday night Georg agreed to come with us to the cinema since Karl offered to pay his and Ruth's way in. We didn't tell them it was with money Otto had given me. Georg sat as far from me as possible. Ruth sat between him and Karl and made a point of not talking to me. Maybe I made her as nervous as she made me.

The cinema was full of younger people. Loud, bouncing off walls. Karl joined in the hooting when the film started but soon fell quiet. I dreamed of watching something fun. An adventure movie. Even a musical would be better than a documentary.

But no, it was the typical Soviet documentary. Karl and I had made certain it wasn't anything about the Great Patriotic War. Neither of us wanted a repeat of his reaction to seeing German prisoners of war. But this? About farming and productivity and happy Soviet farm workers? Why did they need to take all our food if they were so happy and productive?

The audience's restlessness matched mine. I was about to tell Karl I was leaving when a bit came on about the Soviets sending loads of grain to their German comrades. A tomato hit the screen. The splattered fruit plopped to the floor leaving the screen looking bloodstained. Another tomato, thrown from somewhere behind us, joined the first. Splat! I started laughing.

Then someone in the back howled like a wolf. My laugh cut off. Wolverines? Real Hitler Youth with a grudge? I grabbed Karl's arm. "Stay low. Tell the others we're leaving."

I ducked down, pushed past hollering boys. They thought it was funny. They wouldn't think so in a few minutes. Three of us stumbled out the back exit and into the alley just as police wagons screamed to a halt at the alley's mouth. "Where's Georg?" I said.

"He was right behind me," Ruth replied. She peered back inside. "He's fighting his way past boys tipping over benches."

Some Schupos started toward us. Karl and I looked at each other and both said, "Run." I took two steps. "Ruth. Run!"

She glanced at the door, nodded. We raced away, Schupos ordering us to halt. People poured outside and barred pursuit. Two blocks later we stopped in a courtyard entrance, beside its locked gate. Still only three of us. I slapped the stone wall. "You said he was right behind us."

"He was!" Ruth shouted back. "He must have gotten caught in the crowd."

I spun, pressed my forehead and hands against the cool stone. Behind me Karl paced and Ruth tapped. Karl said, "I'll go check. He probably ran a different direction."

His footsteps retreated. I turned so my back rested against the wall, propped one foot against the stone, and jutted my knee out. Folded my arms and prepared to do what I did worst. Wait.

Ruth planted herself in front of me. Light from a streetlamp almost reached us, enough so I could see irritation written on her face. "You're just letting him go?"

"He knows the risks."

"And Georg? Does he know the risks?"

"Not so much. That's why Karl went back."

"Why didn't you go?"

I closed my eyes, inhaled slowly. I wasn't going to get angry. "This is a scouting mission. One person can go unnoticed easier than two."

"You think it's all a game."

I cracked one eye open. "I know it's not a game."

"I wish those kids in the theater knew that. Throwing tomatoes. Stupid."

"What do you expect when they have to watch those kind of garbage movies? Happy Soviet farmers producing piles of grain. They show that, claim to feed us, then steal our food? I might've thrown a tomato too, if I'd had one."

Ruth fell silent for a moment. "Maybe the movies are putting on a good show so the world won't know the truth."

Her thought hung between us. What truth? That they were liars and thieves? When I didn't answer, Ruth added, "Maybe they're all starving. Like us. Maybe they are so desperate for food that they're forced to take ours. Maybe they're worse off than us."

I wished she hadn't said that. It made a twisted kind of sense. I didn't want to think of them like that. I preferred them as monsters. Not people like us, struggling to survive.

"No," I whispered, thinking of Annaliese. "I don't care how much they might be suffering. That doesn't give them the right to do the things—" I clamped my jaw shut.

Footsteps. Too soon to be Karl. Too heavy to be Georg. And there were two pairs. Schupos might be arresting anyone anywhere near the cinema, and we had nowhere to run. I shoved my emotion aside. Why would two people be here at this time of night? My gaze fell on Ruth.

Before I could think better of it, I pulled her to me, wrapped my arms around her waist. She started to struggle until I whispered, "Someone's coming. You're my girlfriend."

"If it's Georg I'll never forgive you."

"Neither will he." I kissed her. Her arms curved around my neck and she kissed me back.

A flashlight played over us. "Break it up, you two, and get off the street."

I looked up, felt muddled. Didn't have to fake it, not with how Ruth had thrown herself into that kiss. She hid her face against my chest as if embarrassed. The flashlight's beam made me squint. A pair of Schupos. They nudged each other, laughed, and walked off.

I rested my cheek on the top of Ruth's head and willed my breathing to slow. "We can't do this again."

"No. I don't like you much, but I like your kissing too much," she whispered.

Her herbal smell wafted around me. I swallowed. She hadn't been acting. Neither of us moved. I said, "In your apartment? I ... never meant to get so carried away."

A long pause. Ruth's arms lowered and she rested them against my chest. "Apology accepted. Will you accept mine?"

"I thought I had." I leaned my head against the wall, sought to change the subject. "Did you meet up with Johanna?"

Ruth stepped out of my arms; cool air replaced her warmth. "Yes. She's nice. I called on her the very next day and we arranged to meet. When we did, Wednesday evening, her Schupo boyfriend showed up."

I tensed. "What did he say?"

"When he found out I was from Johanna's old neighborhood he asked if I knew you."

"And?"

"I told him yes. And said you were an idiot. He liked that answer and invited me to their apartment for tea tomorrow."

"Fool him with the truth. Good one."

"It worked. And it wasn't ... completely true."

I straightened at the sound of hurried steps. Karl stumbled into the archway, panting. He coughed, leaned against the wall, and slid to the cobblestones. Ruth and I crouched on either side. He said, "Saw them loading guys into two wagons."

"Georg?" I asked.

Karl nodded. "He looked back as they pushed him in, like he was looking right at me."

"Did he see you?"

"Don't think so. He looked scared." Karl covered his face with his hands. "He won't last under questioning, Wilm. They'll see he's hiding something as soon as they sit him down."

"Then we have to get him out," Ruth replied.

We both stared at her. Karl said, "They will take him to Schupo headquarters, not some makeshift holding cell. How exactly do you propose we get Georg out of there?"

"You're the planners."

"Small bits of vandalism isn't the same thing as breaking someone out of a busy jail."

"Maybe we could bribe someone," she said.

Karl's lip curled. "We might have a whole Deutschmark be-tween us. Some Schupo will gladly take that in return for letting a prisoner go."

"Quiet." I pressed my thumb and forefinger against my eyes. "This isn't helping. I need to think." Silence. I opened my eyes. Their faces were pale in the dim light. Pale and blank. I sighed. "I'll go in."

"Go in?" Karl repeated. "You mean walk into Schupo head-quarters? Well, that will make it easy to arrest you. What will you do there?"

"Talk them into letting Georg go." This was stupid. I knew it. They knew it. "Any chance you saw a Schupo we might know?"

"Like maybe the one who chased you to the canal when you skipped school?" Karl was starting to sound angry. "Sorry, I wasn't there, didn't see him. Should we ask around? How about the one who interrogated us about your father's beating? I'm sure he'd help."

"Wait." Ruth popped to her feet. "Johanna told me her boy-friend is working evening shifts this weekend. That's why I have to visit her in the early afternoon tomorrow instead of the regular time for *Kaffee und Kuchen*."

"Ernst Weber?" I closed my eyes. *Scheisse*. "Okay. I'll throw myself at Ernst's mercy." If he has any. "Georg better appreciate this."

Karl pushed fingers through his hair. For once, it stayed messy. "What if you can't convince him?"

"There is no can't here. I can't can't." I gripped Karl's shoulder. "Take Ruth home. Patrols will be swarming Zentrum all night."

"But how will I know ..." Ruth began.

"I'll tell Georg to stop by your apartment after he's released."

"But if you fa—"

"Don't say it."

The police building was a stirred-up anthill. From outside I could hear the chaos. My nerves tingled with painful intensity. I had to walk into the enemy's lair—and stay calm.

Too much thinking and I'd bail out. I walked up the steps, held the door for a Schupo in a hurry, and entered the lobby. High counter, people on telephones, others waiting. A clamor came from the back, beyond a propped-open door. Shouts. Slammed doors. Clangs. I caught sight of Schupos manhandling men and boys into rooms. Orders flew back and forth.

One handcuffed boy tried to run, was tripped by a Schupo and sent sprawling. The Schupo laughed and turned toward the front. Ernst. His gaze touched me, moved on, snapped back. After a moment, his expression changed to amusement. He motioned me to join him.

I barged through the half gate and was grabbed by a burly Schupo with a matching frown. "Where are you're going?"

I pointed. "Ernst Weber. He's expecting me."

The man looked over his shoulder. Ernst nodded. Sausage fingers fell away from my arm and swatted the back of my head. "Don't be long. We're busy."

I scrambled sideways between clusters of people, wove down the hall to where Ernst lounged against the wall. Someone pounded on the door beside him, begged to be let out. He banged back with his fist. "Quiet in there, boy. We'll deal with you when we deal with you."

He turned his attention to me. "What brings you to *Schutz-polizei* headquarters, Wilm? Evening stroll?"

"No. I was at the cinema."

"Oh? Then why aren't you in an interrogation room, or in a cell downstairs?"

"As soon as those tomatoes hit the screen I took off."

"You were a good shot. They were almost dead center."

"Wasn't me. Someone behind me threw them."

"And, of course, you couldn't see who did it."

"Lights being off makes things hard to see." I shrugged. "I heard someone howl though."

"Again, not you."

"No."

He straightened. "Not a Wolverine then?"

"No."

"Never in the Hitler Youth?"

"You know I was, Ernst. Everyone was. But I was fourteen when the war ended."

Another Schupo pushed past us with a guy maybe three years older than me. He shoved him into the next interrogation room. I glanced at the door Ernst was guarding. The boy behind it was no longer pounding. He was sobbing.

I suddenly asked, "Why are you even talking to me? Last time I saw you ..."

"I wasn't happy with you. I remember." His smile was thin. "But a week ago Johanna told me how she saw you and you ran off. She was upset. I enjoyed comforting her. And I like that you learned your lesson."

My gaze flicked to the door again. Ernst stepped forward so we were almost nose to nose. "You know him?"

"No. He ... sounds young."

"You don't think they can cause trouble when they're young?"

"I suppose." I understood then that Ernst wanted the boy scared half to death before he started peppering him with questions. Was someone doing that to Georg right now?

"You look serious, little brother," Ernst whispered, still in my face. "Why are you here? You got away. Why come back?" I couldn't help it—I glanced at the door again. Ernst's voice went quieter. "You don't know him, but you know someone we brought in. Right, little brother?"

I gave a jerky nod. "Please, Ernst," I breathed back. "Help me get him released."

He narrowed his gaze and I used every bit of willpower to keep looking into his granite-blue eyes. He stepped back. "Talk to someone at the desk. We have procedures. Follow them."

"Please." I grabbed his jacket sleeve. He eyed my grip with a look that said, "let go." I didn't. Instead, I closed in so we were nose to nose again. The urgency I felt leaked into my words. "He doesn't belong here, Ernst. He'd never do ... anything."

"Then he has nothing to worry about. Let go."

I did, but stayed where I was. "I can't let him end up like that." I waved at the door with the crying boy behind it. "He's one of my best friends."

"Can't? I don't think that's a word you are in any position to use here."

I squeezed my eyes shut for a second. "I know that. I am ... powerless. But you're a lieutenant, Ernst. You tell other people what to do. You have power."

"Why should I do anything for you? What was it you said that day our unit took you boys on in soccer? Something about selling out to the Soviets?"

"I was angry. I said something stupid. Boys do that sometimes."

"And now you're desperate. Why? Maybe your friend threw the tomatoes and you're trying to save his hide."

I laughed. A single explosion of sound that made several heads turn. "Georg is starving more often than not. He'd never throw food away, not even rotten food."

Ernst smiled. "I always liked you, little brother. You've turned into a cold one. Calm as a sheltered pond. If you want my help, be honest. Tell me why you'd be angry enough to say something really stupid?"

He'd deserted then harassed my sister, but that wasn't what he wanted to hear. I worked my jaw while I thought furiously. I'd been trying to ignore his calling me "little brother," but maybe I could use that. "Because you left."

"Your sister?" He sneered.

"No." I had to force the words out. "You left me. You were like a big brother to me and you just left." I wanted to plow my fist into his face. Partly because he was toying with me, but partly because it was true. I continued pushing words through clenched teeth. "I loved you like a brother and you ... *Scheisse*. Forget it." I turned, didn't want him seeing my struggle to stay calm.

He jerked me back. There was something in his eyes, something uncertain. The mask was gone, I realized. "So this Georg," he whispered. "Do you love him like a brother?"

I stared at the doorjamb above his head. "Not in the same way. You idolize a big brother. He's more like a little brother, I guess. I look out for him." I locked my gaze with his. And started to tremble at the sadness I saw there. As if he were sorry he hadn't looked out for me. "He's nice, Ernst. Too nice. He needs a big brother." Had I said too much?

Ernst's voice stayed low, soft. "What would you do to save this friend who needs you to look out for him? Would you take his place, Wilm?"

"Yes!" Then quieter. "Yes."

"Nothing to hide?"

"I didn't have anything to do with tonight. Interrogate me all you want."

"I have a better idea." I held my breath. "You could be by my side again, little brother."

"What do you mean?" Someone bumped my shoulder, pushed me, but all my attention was on Ernst.

"Apply to the *Schutzpolizei*. I'll put in a recommendation and make sure you get in. You have guts, you can stay calm. We'd be a great team." Enthusiasm radiated out from his eyes, as if he'd suggested we join a soccer team together.

I couldn't find my voice.

"Well?" Ernst gripped my arm now. "Do we have a deal, little brother?"

"I can't." I spat out the first excuse that came to mind. "Mother wants me to finish *Gymnasium*. She'd never forgive me if I didn't."

"How close are you to finishing?"

"One year." I fought the urge to swallow. I couldn't betray my growing nervousness. There had to be another way to get Georg out.

Ernst nodded. "It's good you want to respect your mother's wishes. Here's what we'll do. I'll get your friend out. Consider it an apology for deserting you, little brother. Then, starting in the fall, while doing your final year of school, you'll train with the auxiliary police on weekends. That way, when school is finished, you'll be on your way to becoming my assistant."

"I usually work on my uncle's farm on the weekends." His expression began to close, like a door in a tinker's face. The mask would be back in seconds and my chance lost. "But I could work something else out," I said in a rush.

Ernst offered me a smile—a real smile—and his hand. "Together again, little brother?"

I didn't dare hesitate. I gripped his hand hard. "Together again. Big brother."

CHAPTER TWENTY-EIGHT

I knocked on Otto's door. It was Sunday and I hoped he was home. I straightened my jacket collar and knocked louder. Someone inside called, "Coming. Be patient."

Otto opened the door and surprise stamped his face. "Wilm. I wasn't expecting to see you on such a fine day. I thought you would be off with your friends."

At the mention of friends my forehead rippled into a frown. "Are you alone?"

"I am. I was about to go outside and enjoy the morning sun on the patio. Wait out there. I'll get us both a drink."

One chair had Otto's pipe on its arm. I sat in the other. Otto returned and handed me a cup of coffee. "Best thing to drink on a warm morning, don't you think?"

"Don't know. I usually just have water." I took a swallow. The mellow flavor lingered. Real coffee, not *Ersatz*. I relaxed and sipped the warm brew.

Five minutes of silence later, Otto asked, "Did you come only to drink my coffee, or is something on your mind? You seem to go quiet when you are troubled."

"I did something last night ..."

"Serious?" When I nodded he said, "Was anyone hurt?"

I shifted to look at him. "It wasn't like that." Another swallow of coffee and I started again. "We went to the cinema. There was trouble. Not us. We snuck out the back but Georg wasn't fast enough. He was arrested."

"You want me to see what I can do?" Otto's tone was dubious.

"No. I got him out. I talked to someone I knew."

"Just like that?" I frowned at my coffee and took another drink. Otto said, "I see. You paid a price to free your friend. Judging by your expression, I'd say it was a high price. I did not realize you were on good terms with any police officers. The only one you have mentioned by name—" Otto gripped my wrist. "Is that who you spoke with? Wilm, have you become like Faustus?"

That name sounded familiar. Something Mother and her reading circle had studied when I was young. "I don't know. What did he do?"

"He made a bargain with the devil." The warmth bled from my face. Otto sighed. "And so, I see, did you. What kind of bargain, Wilm?"

"I ... agreed to join the *Schutzpolizei*." Dead silence. I focused on my finger circling the lip of the cup. "I can finish school, but in the fall I'll start training on weekends."

More silence. I finally looked up to see that Otto's eyebrows had merged into one, and it shadowed his eyes. "Do your friends know?"

"I couldn't tell them. I told them I'd begged. That Ernst got so much enjoyment from my begging he released Georg."

"You can't lie to them, Wilm."

I jumped up. The almost empty cup fell onto the flagstone deck and broke. I scowled at the pieces. "But maybe it's a good idea. Best way to learn their methods."

"You don't seem like double-agent material. I don't think you have the stomach for it." Otto stood and held my shoulders in his muscled grip. "Do you have the stomach for this?"

I frowned past his shoulder. "I think I'd be good at it." Then looked him in the eye. "I already admitted I'm becoming a lot like them. This would be another step. I could train with them ... then turn the knowledge against them."

"Do not lie to yourself about this, Wilm. Why would you be good at it?" When I didn't answer he gave me a little shake. "Why?"

I wrenched free. "Because I like it! I like the hunt. Is that what you want me to admit? Well, I do. I like evading the hunters. But I like hunting too. I'd be good at hunting down criminals."

"Except some of them wouldn't be criminals. Some of them would be young men like you, young men whose sisters were raped and who need to find some kind of justice, young men who want some freedom. I thought that's what this was about. Not about the hunt." He sighed. "If you join them, Wilm, our friendship will have to end. You are telling yourself you could spy from the inside, but I cannot watch you become what you hate."

"I had to get Georg out of there. He would've talked. All of us would've been arrested."

"You have made your decision, Wilm. I have made mine. Good-bye."

I stood outside Otto's gate in a stupor. He had turned his back on me. I couldn't believe it, even though it was as clear as Frau Putt-kam's store windows. He wanted nothing to do with me.

What did I care about a crazy duck-loving engineer? I didn't need his good opinion any more than I needed my father's. I was old enough, man enough, to make my own decisions. I bent down to pick up a rock. When I straightened, Otto's ring, still on its leather thong around my neck, tapped me. He had no right to judge. I'd done what I'd done to save a friend.

It was too warm for a jacket but I didn't want to carry it. I stuck two more rocks in the jacket pocket and whipped the first one at a sign. It ricocheted into the street. Like a bullet. I tried to imagine being the one holding the gun, the one walking his rounds. Couldn't.

The rest of the way home I targeted anything metal with rocks and bits of broken brick. I liked the hollow plink each hit made.

Karl was waiting in my apartment foyer on the stairs. "Where were you?"

"Otto's."

He slapped my shoulder. "Come on. There's something I have to show you."

"I'm not in the mood, Karl."

"You will want to see this, Wilm. Trust me."

"Fine. Let's go."

Karl almost bounced as he walked, kept punching me lightly on the arm and shadowboxing with lampposts. "I still can't believe you talked Ernst into releasing Georg."

"Me neither. Maybe they caught a Wolverine in the sweep and it put him in a good mood."

"Do you think there are real Wolverine groups? Sure there are some former Hitler Youth who are pretty angry at losing, but resistance groups? I don't believe it."

"Maybe I should work for the Schupos undercover and find out."

That sent Karl into waves of laughter. For the next block, every time he looked at me he started laughing again. We stopped outside the entrance to the Stag's Horn, his mother's beer hall. "What are we doing here?"

"I told you I had to clean up. Mom left me a note. There was a brawl last night. Big mess." He trotted down the few steps to the entrance. Before I could object, Karl said, "You want to see this, Wilm."

I waved my hand in defeat and followed. Karl unlocked the door and we entered the dimly lit room. "Leave the shutters closed." He went behind the bar, returned with a flashlight, and motioned toward a booth. "Sit."

I slid into the high-backed padded booth. Comfortable leather. Heavy wooden table. The whole room smelled of stale beer and smoke, but the booth seemed even more thickly saturated. "Nice booth. Why are we sitting here?"

"I told you about this booth, remember? This is the one Schupos like to sit in."

Heat licked up my neck and over my cheeks. Had he sat me here because he knew about my agreement? I peered into the gloom. This would be my view some day. You could see the whole room. I understood why the Schupos chose it.

"Wilm? Don't you want to know why I sat you here?"

I'd play his game. Pretend he didn't know for a little longer. "I figure you'll tell me. Do I have to ask? Beg like I did last night with Ernst?"

Karl whistled lowly. "You weren't lying that you aren't in the mood." He leaned forward. "You'll be in the mood for this." He set the dark flashlight on the table and interlocked his fingers. His voice dropped to a whisper. "I found the weapons cache."

"You what?" I gaped at him.

"You heard me. It's not enough to start a war, but it's real. I've seen it."

"Are you pulling one over on me?"

He grinned. "No."

"Okay, where is it?"

"You're sitting on it."

I raised my eyebrows. Karl nodded. "I was cleaning. A bottle had broken on the back corner of your bench so I had to crawl under the table to get all the pieces. One was wedged between the end of the bench and the wall. Cut myself getting it out." He held up his left hand to show off the bandage I hadn't noticed. He admired the white cloth. "When I was pulling out the glass, I triggered a hidden latch."

My whole body tensed. A familiar thrill prickled my hairs. "Show me."

He grinned again. "I knew you'd say that. Take the flashlight and crawl under the table. I'll slide onto the bench and find the trigger."

I grabbed the flashlight and eased under the table, stretched out so my head was near the wall and my legs were sticking out into the room. "Ready."

Karl crawled onto the bench I'd been on and lay prone, then reached down the crack. "Watch your head." A click and the front of the apparently solid bench fell open. I jerked back to avoid getting hit. Karl laughed. I switched on the flashlight.

The space under the bench was packed three-quarters full. Neatly stacked Mausers, a handful of various pistols, some ammunition boxes, some long-handled grenades. It was my turn to whistle quietly. I ran a finger along the barrel of a Mauser. It needed cleaning.

"Isn't it perfect?" Karl asked.

I knew what he meant. "Right under the Schupos' noses."

"Their hind ends, actually."

We both chuckled. I picked up a grenade, felt the weight of it.

"We have a problem." Karl's tone had turned serious. "The plan was to lead the Schupos to the cache so they'd think they could trust us. We can't do that. Mom might know about this. Even if she doesn't, as one of the owners she'd be arrested."

The light switched on. Karl jumped. I froze.

"And as the other owner," a male voice said, "I would be arrested too. And I wouldn't like that at all. Tell me, Karl, why do you need the Schupos to think you're their friends?" Before Karl could reply he added, "Tell your friend to switch off that light and get up."

I handed the flashlight to Karl. Turned onto my hands and knees to back out, used the movement to hide the grenade under my belt so my jacket covered it. When I stood, Herr Schink, who was also the bartender, pushed me aside and closed the compartment's door.

He repeated his earlier question. This time, Karl answered. "Because Wilm is the *Marionette* Wolverine."

"That vandal who's embarrassing the Schupos so regularly?" Herr Schink ran his hand over his bald head and smiled. "Then we each know a secret about the other."

"We won't tell," Karl laid his hand on his chest. "I swear."

"I know I can trust you, Karl. What about your friend?" He squinted at me. "Isn't your dad the one-legged—"

"Yes. And you can trust me too. I'm not going to any prison camp." The grenade's canister dug into my side. I kept my arm loosely against it to hold the jacket in place. Why had I taken it? I didn't know. But I knew the danger of having a live grenade under my coat was honing my senses to an edge sharper than Krupps steel.

It occurred to me that, as a good Schupo in training, I should tell Ernst about this. I guess I wasn't a good one yet. I hadn't crossed the line that made it okay to betray my best friend.

Herr Schink grabbed both of us by our collars. "You don't tell anyone. No friends, girlfriends, lovers, sisters, or parents. Talk to each other and I'll throttle the pair of you."

I stuck out my chin, wanting him to know I wasn't afraid. "What are you planning?"

"You won't ask that again if you know what's good for you."

"Karl and I are both good at getting around by night. If you ever need help ..."

"I don't need the help of two overgrown turds. Get out of here." He pushed us away and we dashed out the door.

We ran half a block, then collapsed against brick wall, laughing.

"What are you planning?" Karl mimicked in a high voice. I hit him.

"I can see why you didn't ask Georg along. He couldn't keep a secret like that." I rolled my shoulders. "I need to get home. I promised Mother I'd do literature homework for a change."

"Homework? You? Did they brainwash you in that Schupo building?"

He had no idea. "There's a first time for everything."

"Right. You're acting strange today." Karl shrugged to indicate he wasn't angry. "So you go discover what homework is like and I'll track down Georg. Wish I could tell him, but you're right." He punched me in the arm one final time and jogged down the street.

The grenade dug into my side uncomfortably. Why hadn't I told Karl? Probably because it had been a stupid impulse. I glanced at the beer hall's door. It wasn't like I could walk in, hand it back, and say I was sorry for stealing their potato masher.

And Herr Schink couldn't report the grenade stolen. Which made it mine.

CHAPTER TWENTY-NINE

The sun beat down on the rooftop. I lay shirtless on my jacket with my rolled bedding as a pillow. Heat enveloped me. Otto's ring branded my skin, yet I couldn't bring myself to take it off. Being a Schupo was a life sentence. It's not like I'd ever get to be an engineer now—the ring was a searing reminder of how alone I was at this moment.

My father was on the verge of disowning me. I couldn't tell my friends what was happening. And the one friend I had told had ordered me to leave him alone. My life had blown up, even without ever using that grenade.

It was hidden. I had found some loose roof tiles with rotten boards underneath. After making a hole I'd wedged the long handle between two attic boards.

I couldn't leave it there, couldn't risk someone finding it. If nothing else I would take it into the country, maybe blow up a tree. It might be fun to throw a live grenade, just once.

The scratching and clinking of someone climbing out of the window and up the short ladder to the flat roof pulled my mind away from visions of exploding trees.

Anneliese appeared at my elbow. She sat and hugged her knees to her chest. "How can you stand being up here in this heat?"

"I like it."

Her gaze dropped to my chest. "You have a pool of sweat."

She started to reach out then pulled her hand back. "What is that ring? More Störtebecker booty?"

My lips pressed together for a few seconds. "A friend gave it to me." A former friend. The backs of my eyes started to sting. I blinked rapidly. I wasn't going to cry over that loss. It was nothing. As soon as Karl and Georg found out what I'd done I wouldn't have any friends. They'd call me a traitor.

They'd be right.

How had things gotten to this point? My gaze slid to Anneliese. She was staring into the distance and didn't seem to want to talk. At least she had sought me out.

Curse those Soviets for attacking her. For ripping up her spirit so badly she didn't seem to want to live. Father was right. She was a ghost, haunting him, haunting me. Reminding us how little we had done, could do, to protect her.

I had been targeting the Schupos because Ernst hadn't done anything to protect her either. But maybe I had been targeting the wrong people. The Schupos were puppets. They might even be good policemen, if not for their puppet-masters. I had to believe some of them were decent if I was going to be one. I had to believe I could wear that uniform and still be honorable. I couldn't bear to be a puppet with Soviets pulling my strings.

I had stolen the butter from the Soviets, but I'd have done that no matter who owned it. Georg had needed the food. Maybe it was time to scout out the puppet-masters, to see if they had any weaknesses.

I sat up so fast I startled Anneliese. I raised both my hands. "Sorry. I need to go for a walk. I might be late. Tell Mother I'll try to be back before dark."

"Where are you going?"

"Nowhere important."

"I wanted to ask you something." I searched her face for a clue. She said, "I'd like to go to the park with you and see those ducks."

Why now? Otto wasn't even talking to me anymore. But I couldn't refuse her, not when she showed even this small sign of life. I nodded. "Next weekend." I grabbed my shirt and headed for the window. She called after me that she would take my coat and bedding downstairs. I waved in acknowledgment.

Taking a long route, I went northeast and crossed a wide stretch of train tracks over a kilometer away from the *Bahnhof* and well beyond the yards. There were several stretches where the only barriers keeping people off the tracks were wire fences, and they had holes. On a Sunday the tracks weren't busy so I loped across the gauntlet. Only one train was leaving the station and it hadn't gotten up any speed.

I cut back northwest, crossed more tracks. I had never been here but knew roughly where I was headed, the west part of the Gohlis-Mitte district. It took over half an hour to walk the distance but the Soviet barracks were easy to find, in an old military compound. It was protected. Of course it would be. Wire fences without holes. Barbed wire along the top. A guarded gate. Signs in Russian and German to keep out.

I crouched by a hedge and watched for awhile. Troops in diarrhea-brown uniforms walked the compound, went to outbuildings that were probably storage, worked on troop transports, talked, and smoked. Never looked beyond the fence.

"What do you think you're doing?"

I popped to my feet and spun around. The man in front of me was maybe three years older, half a head shorter. He smelled of confidence as he tipped up his cap so I could see his face, see the scar that ran a millimeter away from his left eye. His lip curled. "You can't get in, if that's what you're thinking. We've watched. We know."

"We?" I smiled. "You're a Wolverine. A real one."

"You a Schupo spy?"

I shrugged. "Not yet."

"Joining them?"

"Not yet."

"I was watching. You move like you've snuck up on enemies. Maybe you'd rather join us."

"You planning an attack?"

The sneer returned. "Not yet."

"So you must be coordinating with other groups, planning something big." I licked my lips, slid my hand in my pocket, and twirled my knife. "I'd join for something big."

"That's a good way to get caught. The more that know of a plan, the more chances they will learn about it." He jerked his head toward the Soviet compound.

"You don't work with other Wolverine groups?"

He shook his head slowly. "Better this way. Want to meet the others?"

"Have you ever done ... anything?" I stilled my hand, clutched my folded knife.

The sneer turned to a snarl. "We will."

I laughed. "I always thought that Wolverines were vicious resistance fighters. The war's been over for two years and you haven't done anything? You're just shadows flickering on the wall. Not real. A myth." My thumb jabbed my chest. "I've done more to boost your reputation than you have. So no, I don't think I will join you."

He swept back his baggy military jacket and braced his hands on his hips. He had a Hitler Youth knife strapped to his belt. "And who the hell are you?"

"The Schupos call me *Marionette* Wolverine. That's funny. They think I'm one of you."

The suspicion in his face eased. "What are you looking for?"

"Just looking."

"Yeah? Well, if you decide to do more than look, we aren't going to help you."

"I didn't expect it." Especially now that I'd met him. "But will you tell?"

The sneer returned. "We never cooperate with the enemy." He pulled his cap low over his eyes. "Good luck, boy. You'll need it. And find a different name."

"I didn't name myself." But I was talking to his back as he jogged down the alley.

CHAPTER THIRTY

The week oozed along slower than a snail. Dull nights were all Karl and I had on our three outings. No close calls. Not one heart-pounding, electrifying moment of excitement. I yawned and Herr Bader shot me a look.

"Class," he said, "I know it's Friday and you're excited to start part one of your examination, but I have an announcement to make before we begin."

Groans swirled around the room. I joined in.

"All schools have been notified that a special visitor is arriving in Leipzig tonight. A high-ranking Soviet general whose name I cannot pronounce." That drew chuckles from the back rows. Herr Bader held up his hand. "According to our information he will be landing at nine o'clock, and no doubt his arrival will be greeted with much pomp and ceremony."

"Why do we care?" Karl called out.

"Because, Herr Heinig, the authorities want the cavalcade route, from the airport to the hotel where he is staying, to be lined with his adoring and grateful German comrades."

His sarcastic tone cut off any potential snide comments. I narrowed my eyes. Pomp and ceremony would mean soldiers, all in a row, buttons polished and rifles gleaming.

"Why the long faces?" Herr Bader continued. "They especially want young people. Surely you can see this as an excuse to get out with your friends and have a party? I'm told that there will be refreshment stations for those who attend. It could be diverting."

I had never heard Herr Bader use such a wheedling voice, like he was pleading. He was making it sound like an honor, but I was starting to think he was under a lot of pressure to make sure students showed up. "Any good refreshments?" I asked. "Like beer?"

The guys laughed. Some girls giggled.

Herr Bader's smile relaxed. "You'll have to show up and find out, Herr Tauber."

I returned the smile. "I guess I will."

He cleared his throat. "So much for announcements. Now for part one. And make sure you study over the weekend. Part two is Monday afternoon and I know you are all looking forward to your very last test in this class." That brought several cheers.

It was good I had studied. I handed in the test papers fairly sure I'd passed. Herr Bader followed me into the hall, wanting a moment, and asked if I recalled telling him I wanted to build bridges. I didn't have the heart to tell him that my plans had changed. I touched the ring under my shirt, realized what I was doing, dropped my hand. "What about it?"

"I have given it some thought, especially in light of ... the gift you gave me." Herr Bader swallowed. "I think you should study structural engineering."

"Do you have a place in mind?"

"I do. I think you should go study in America or perhaps Canada."

I laughed. "Canada? Why would I want to go there? My home is here."

He cupped his hand over my shoulder. "I think it would be safer. North America has a lot of rivers. You would have more bridges to build than you could manage in two lifetimes."

"I see what you're trying to do, Herr Bader, but I know where my life is going." I just needed to come to terms with it. "I'm glad you also teach mathematics in *Prima*. You'll make my last year bearable."

His hand dropped. "I won't be here this fall. I asked for a transfer to Weimar."

I could feel the frown but couldn't seem to make it go away. "Because of my gift?"

"No. No, of course not." He rushed his words, too quickly to be sincere. "My aunt lives in Weimar, and with my cousin now in prison camp ..." He sighed and turned back to the classroom.

When Karl and Georg finished the test, Ruth was already on the steps beside me. A good distance away, not touching, not looking at me. As soon as the guys sat, I stood. "I have an idea."

Karl beamed. "I knew you'd come up with something. Is it big?"

"Maybe. I think we'll need your help, Georg." He looked worried, but agreed.

"I'm coming too," Ruth said. She took Georg's hand and relief washed over his expression.

I considered arguing but, truth was, she'd keep Georg calm if anything happened. I shrugged. "I have something to do, then I'll meet you at Karl's. If what I'm thinking works, we need to move fast. It has to happen tonight."

CHAPTER THIRTY-ONE

Hands in pockets, fingers worrying my knife, I stood by the bank of the canal until Otto noticed and hiked up to join me. We watched a flock of ducks paddling along the edge of the far bank, beaks darting into the reeds as they fed.

"I hope you've come to say you have had a change of plans," Otto said.

"I don't know how to get out of it. Ernst made me shake hands. It feels like I've signed a contract." I pulled the ring from under my shirt collar. "I wanted to give this back to you."

Otto studied me for an uncomfortable moment, then shook his head. "Please keep it. Send it back to me when you've found a way to start building instead of destroying. Then I will know my young friend has found his way home." He rested his hand on my shoulder. "I know I must seem harsh to you, possibly at a time when you need help. But I cannot support the decision you've made. Working for this government is hard enough, but I am building things, fixing them. Your choice will turn you into an oppressor."

"Never!"

"It will happen. I saw it with the Nazi government too. You will end up doing things you never dreamed possible. You should have trusted your friend more, and trusted that he would not betray you when they questioned him. People can find great depths of strength when they need it."

I walked away. There was nothing else to say.

The map I'd drawn of the Soviet compound was on Karl's bed. We each sat at one corner, studying the brown butcher's paper. I rubbed my neck under my collar. It was too hot for a jacket, and Ruth had given me a strange look when I'd kept it on, but I didn't want all my secrets revealed yet.

"This is impossible. How are we even going to get through the fence?" Karl said.

I pulled the wire cutters from inside my coat. "I never got around to returning these."

Karl eyed the cutters doubtfully. "So we get through. The place is swarming with Soviets. We'll only get caught."

"Not if we do it tonight." They all looked at me in expectation. "Pomp and ceremony. You heard Herr Bader. Every Soviet in the city will be at the airport greeting that general. Except maybe for a sick ward, the place will be empty. Wouldn't surprise me if they replace the guards at the gates with some Schupos."

We turned our attention back to the map. I explained the layout, how we could approach the north barracks between some outbuildings, do our deed, then melt away to join the civilians on the parade route, cheering the Soviet general as he came to town.

"And you'll leave the message?" Karl said.

"I'm not asking any of you to take that risk. You only have to be lookouts. Georg and Ruth, you can position yourselves here"—I jabbed the paper—"so you can see if the guards at the gate decide to do a round. And Karl, you can watch my back while I go in."

"Simple," Karl said.

"That's how I like it."

"But these aren't the puppets, Wilm. It doesn't make sense to leave your usual *Marionetten* symbol." Karl flicked the map. "What kind of message are you planning to leave?"

"They need to know that not everyone wants them around."

"You could write, 'Go away,'" Ruth said. "And if you say please maybe they'll consider it."

"You could be quiet," I replied, then caught Georg's frown and raised my hand. "Sorry. I'm a little edgy. I didn't mean to be rude."

Georg relaxed and Ruth inclined her head in acceptance of the apology.

"Do you have a message in mind?" Karl asked.

"Yes." I pulled the long-handled grenade from under my coat and dropped it onto the map.

CHAPTER THIRTY-TWO

"You guessed right. The guards at the gate are Schupos tonight. Ruth and Georg are in place," Karl whispered. "Now call it off."

"Why are you here if you don't want to do it?"

"I'm watching your back. I knew you'd do this on your own if I didn't come."

"And the second I tossed the potato masher onto the map I knew you wanted out." They had all jumped away from the grenade, like they expected it to blow up right there.

He grabbed my collar. "Why did you take it? You must have a death wish, like your father."

I smacked the hand away. "I'm nothing like him. I'm doing something, not getting drunk every night. Ever notice how people don't have enough money for food, but they all have enough for beer or *Schnaps*? You must have noticed. Your mother makes her living from it."

"Leave my mother out of this."

"Leave my father out of this."

Karl sighed. "A grenade. *Scheisse*. Explosives were never part of the game."

"It hasn't been a game for a long time, Karl. Not for me." I took the cutters and bit through the first wire. "You're starting to worry almost as much as Georg. All I'm going to do is toss the grenade into an empty building and run. We get to hear a big bang, know that we caused it, and wish like crazy we could tell someone we did it."

I cut more wires, pulled at the gap, cut more of the crisscrossed mesh until the opening was a meter high. "That'll get me through. Make it bigger while I'm gone so it's easier to retreat."

Karl took the cutters. "Last protest. Please don't."

"Protest noted. See you in a few minutes." I squeezed sideways through the gap.

My eagle's eye had shown me the best spot for getting into the compound. The storage sheds I slipped between hid me from any guards looking this way. I figured they'd only be watching for approaching vehicles. The light on the corner of the barracks created a swath of shadow that let me sneak to the building in safety.

An old German *Kuebelwagen* was parked by the barracks. I crouched and sliced the back wheel out of habit, then skirted around it and plastered myself against the side of the brown bricks. I took out the last of my chalk, only a marble now, and sketched my puppet stickman on the foundation, under the bricks. It was like a signature. Otto had shown me how bridge builders left their signatures on what they had built, often by attaching a cast-iron plate or by carving into the stone. For me, chalk would have to do.

The windows were open to the night breeze. Could they have made it any easier? I pulled the grenade from under my belt and gripped the long wooden handle. Let the excitement frizzle over my skin and coax sweat out of hiding. It dripped under my collar.

It was hard to keep my breathing even. I stood, peeked into the room, ducked down. A stove and rows of cots. I hadn't seen much but the silence told me all I needed to know.

Tension wrapped my muscles tight. Karl would come looking soon if I didn't act. I took a deep breath, exhaled slowly. Then I unscrewed the metal cap on the end of the grenade's handle.

I felt the string that ran up the hollow handle. This was going to be so good.

I pulled the string, threw the grenade in the window, sped around the *Kuebelwagen*, and ducked by its wheel. The concussion boomed in the quiet night. Glass shattered outward. I sprinted toward the sheds.

The screaming yanked me to a standstill. I turned, not understanding. The room had been empty. I thought. My hand slid into my pocket, seeking the comfort of my knife. The screams grew louder, more pained as I watched the flames dance.

My pocket was empty. I patted it, patted my jacket. Panic wrenched my gut. My knife must have fallen onto the ground. I had to get it.

I took one step and was jerked around by Karl. He dragged me to the sheds, pushed me into the wedge of shadows. "Do you want to get caught?" I started back but he blocked my way. "We have to run."

"I dropped my knife." I sidestepped but he blocked me again.

"Run! No one cares about your bloody knife."

"I do!"

Karl punched me. I staggered back. He spun me around and pushed. "Move! Hear the sirens? They'll be here in minutes."

He was right. I knew he was right. But my knife.

"Now!" He hit me again.

I started running. Heard my jacket rip on the wire as I scrambled through. We ran for blocks. I followed Karl, not able to think about anything except the trouble lying on the ground beside that burning building.

We dove behind a half wall as a fire truck wailed past, then cut across and wove our way through side streets. Finally Karl pulled me into the remains of a bombed-out house. We both dropped to our knees, gasping for breath. I fell onto my side, then rolled onto my back and pressed my fists into my gut to stop it from churning.

"You said the place would be empty. Didn't you check?"

"I looked. I thought it was clear." Those screams had sounded like more than one man. "If I killed them ... No one was supposed to get hurt." My stomach seethed into a whirlpool.

"We can't worry about that now. But what the hell was that about your knife?"

"It fell out of my pocket." I pressed harder, willed myself not to vomit.

"So what? It's just a pocketknife. Lots of people carry them."

"With the initials W-T scratched on one side?"

A moment of silence. "Lots of people in Leipzig have those initials."

"You don't remember what it looks like, do you?"

"How could I? You hardly ever let anyone touch it."

I could picture the day I had gotten it, the ceremony of scratching the initials on its handle. "Ernst Weber gave it to me, for my twelfth birthday. It had been his, and his initials are carved on the other side. E-W. Do you think lots of people in Leipzig have a knife like that, Karl?"

He had no answer.

"As soon as Ernst sees it, he'll know who did it. And he'll come after me."

CHAPTER THIRTY-THREE

We met Ruth and Georg at our agreed-upon rendezvous, beside the rectangle of tumbled down wire where we had crossed the second set of train tracks. The slope was dark and we huddled halfway up it in a tight circle. Sounds drifted from the yards along the track.

Karl clapped Georg on the back. "I knew you'd get out of there when things went boom."

"Did it go okay?" Ruth asked.

I didn't answer. After a long pause Karl told them what had happened.

Ruth exhaled loudly. "We're in a lot of trouble, aren't we?"

"I am," I replied. "Not you. None of you will admit you were there."

"Shut up, Wilm," Karl said. "We're involved. The Schupos will ask around and someone will tell them we're always together. Ruth could maybe stay out of it, but not Georg and me."

"W-what are we going to do?" Georg whispered.

My breathing huffed into the silence. Karl said, "You're planning something, I can hear it. Going to get noble and turn yourself in?"

"No. Ernst would crucify me."

"Ernst? Not the Schupos? Just Ernst?" Karl said. "What aren't you telling us here, Tauber? There's something you haven't been telling us all week."

It didn't matter now. Nothing did. I rubbed my cheek. "I made a deal with Ernst."

"A deal with him? What kind of deal?"

"One that got Georg released. That's all that matters."

"What kind of deal?" Karl insisted.

I sniffed. "I agreed to join the Schupos, after school is finished, and eventually I'll become Ernst's partner." The relief at finally saying the words didn't last long. The silence was so deep, so filled with shock and disbelief that I wanted to escape. Tension coiled around my limbs.

Then Karl said, "I think your application might be denied."

Laughter exploded out. I couldn't stop. I fell over, rolled down the slope, and sprawled at the bottom, helpless with laughter. My friends gathered round, but they weren't laughing.

Ruth said, "I think he's gone crazy. Send-him-to-a-mental-institution crazy."

A distant siren cut me off in mid-laugh. I chuckled one last time. "One good thing came of this disaster, then. I don't have to become a Schupo."

"You would've made a terrible Schupo," Ruth said. "You're a vandal."

"That would've made me a good Schupo. Hunted and hunter. I know how they think."

"And now you're hunted. So get thinking," Karl said. "What are we going to do?"

"We need to get out of Leipzig."

"How far out?"

"Far."

Georg said, "We'll be back on Monday, right? We have our last examinations on Monday."

I blew out my breath. "I don't think we'll make it back for them, Georg."

He moaned his dismay and Karl said, "You have somewhere in mind?"

"Maybe. But I can't tell you yet."

"Why?"

"Because we aren't even out of the city, Karl. If we get caught, or only one or two get caught, then we can't tell what we don't know."

"So where should we meet? My place is out. Mom's having some kind of party tonight. Birthday for a friend or something."

I knew Georg wouldn't want us to meet at his home. "Get your stuff. Come to my apartment."

"Won't your father cause trouble?"

"We won't be there long enough for him to bother. Besides, as of a little over an hour ago, I'm no longer his son."

CHAPTER THIRTY-FOUR

I walked into the apartment and kept my coat on. Father was in his chair with a *Schnaps* in hand, the radio turned low. Anneliese and Mother were at the table mending clothes.

"How did the parade go?" Mother asked.

"I never got there." I hefted my satchel. The bridge book was still in it. I wanted that. But what else should I take? I rifled through my bedding, rolled one blanket as small as I could, and stuffed it in the bag.

"Going somewhere?" Father asked.

My mouth was dry. I swallowed before I looked up. "It's not your concern."

"So long as you live under my roof, you will answer my questions."

I stood and tried to think what else I could take that might help. "Give me ten minutes, then I won't live under your roof."

Mother gasped, started to stand, but Anneliese pulled her down. Father got his crutches and heaved himself up. In four swings he was in front of me. "Then you'll answer my questions for the next ten minutes. Where are you going?"

I blinked rapidly. I couldn't think with Father glaring at me. What had he asked? Where I was going? "Away."

"What have you done?" His voice was deadly quiet. I couldn't stand how calm he was.

I yelled, "I don't answer to you! I'm not your son anymore!" I heaved air and watched understanding dawn on his face.

At the table, Mother started crying. I could hear Anneliese trying to comfort her.

I nodded. "Trouble is coming. I'm sorry. But saying sorry means nothing."

"What have you done?" he whispered.

I rubbed my eyes and whispered back, "I think I killed some Soviets."

Our voices were pitched so Mother and Anneliese couldn't hear. Father replied, "Maybe they won't know it was you."

"They'll know. I dropped my knife."

He knew what knife I meant. I'd been so proud of it. Had showed him the second he came home on leave from his Wehrmacht unit. Had explained the significance of the two sets of initials. His face went flinty and he brushed past me. "Come with me."

He led me into his bedroom and sat on his bed, then pointed to the closet with one crutch. "Get down that box under your mother's two hat boxes."

I set it on the bed, and when he motioned to do so, opened it. A green canvas bag was inside.

"Take it out." I followed his instructions as he spoke. "It's a British bag called a rucksack. They carried ammunition inside. Open it. The only things I saved from my uniform when I was released were my belt and knife. Take them. The bag too. It's sturdier than your school bag."

I removed my belt and replaced it with his, adjusting the knife sheath to rest comfortably at my hip. I examined the long pointed blade, touched the spot where the Nazi emblem had been pried off, then slid it into the sheath. "Why are you doing this? Why are you being like this?"

Father snorted. "I feel useful for the first time in two years and you have to question it."

"What do we tell Mother?"

"Don't tell her about the Soviets. And don't show her the knife. Keep it covered. I have to live with her after you leave, and I have the feeling that's going to be a hard task."

"That's my fault, not yours." I buttoned my jacket to make sure the knife was hidden.

"Doesn't matter." He jerked his head at the door. "Go face her. Say your good-byes."

I left him on the bed rubbing his forehead, his lips pursed tight. Where had this man come from? He looked a lot like the father I used to know.

I gave Mother a brief hug then transferred my book and blanket to the rucksack. "I did something stupid tonight, *Mutti*. Police will come. You didn't know what I was doing so you'll be fine. Tell them what you know." Which was nothing, thankfully.

Anneliese ran into her bedroom and slammed the door. I squeezed my eyes shut, pressed against them to try to stop the headache that was growing. I slung the rucksack so its strap cut diagonally across my chest and the bag rested against the back of my hip.

Someone knocked. I opened the door to Georg, Ruth, and Georg's mother. Frau Rohrbach crossed to Mother and they embraced. I gave Georg a dirty look and mouthed, "Your mother?" He lifted his shoulders helplessly.

Ruth whispered, "She wanted a few more minutes with her son."

Karl walked in without knocking. "Mom fired me. Said if I wasn't sticking around she was going to get someone more responsible to clean the Stag's Horn."

I grinned and tapped his shoulder with my fist. He took the wire cutters from his bag.

"We might need them."

Karl shrugged and shoved them back in his bag. His eyes widened. I turned to see what he was looking at. Anneliese stood in the hall, dressed in her boy clothes.

"What are you doing, Liese?" I marched over to her.

"I'm going with you."

"No." I shook my head hard. "There will be men with guns tracking us. No."

"Yes. Those men are coming here too, Wilm. I ... I'd rather be out with you in the darkness than here, having them leer at me."

"Don't do this, Liese. I can't be responsible for you. They'll arrest us if they catch us. You'll be safer here. You'll find the courage to face them. I know you will."

"I won't," Anneliese replied quietly. "I think I need to leave Leipzig. There are too many bad memories here. I don't care what you've done, I feel safe with you."

How could she still trust me? I searched for the words to refuse her. Couldn't find them.

Ruth sidled over and took Liese's hand. "I'll look after her. We can't leave her, Wilm, not with you-know-who on the rampage."

Ernst. How could I forget? He would interrogate Anneliese mercilessly, would make that incident by the tobacco shop seem mild. I nodded at Anneliese; she nodded back. Mother started crying again. Anneliese rushed over and hugged her. Frau Rohrbach patted both their backs and tutted. It was too much. I'd done this. Torn up four families. Devastated my mother. My control was cracking like thin ice under a heavy load.

Father swung his crutches and landed in front of me. I startled, not realizing he had left the bedroom. He said, "You're looking battle-fatigued, soldier. Can't give in to that in the middle of the fight. You and your unit have to move out. You don't know how much time you have."

I stared, uncomprehending. He slapped me. My hand covered the stinging cheek and I blinked the fog from my vision. From my thoughts. "We have to go," I whispered.

"Right. I'll delay them as long as possible when they get here. They'll never meet such a pig-headed, one-legged *Arschloch* as me."

"I don't understand. You said you'd disown me. I'm not—"

His one crutch clattered to the floor as he grasped my chin. "You will always be my son. Nothing will change that, no matter what I said before. Bringing trouble wasn't the problem. It's already here, all around us. My fear was the problem. You shouldn't have done what you did, but I can't hide from it. I can't deny it. And I don't want you paying the price they'll want to make you pay. I named you. I raised you. And I want you to live. Hear me? Escape and live."

"What about you?"

He took his crutch from Anneliese. She kissed him on the cheek and rejoined Ruth. He touched the spot, almost smiled. "Doesn't matter. They want a fight, I'll give it to them."

"Couldn't you follow? Later?"

"No. Half a leg is my trap, Wilhelm. There is no escaping that."

"Don't do this."

"Do what?"

"Turn back into the man I remember. Now. How am I supposed to leave when I finally have you back?" I hugged him.

He pushed me back roughly. His voice cracked. "Get going. All of you."

I felt everyone watching. I didn't care. I only cared that my father had returned, just in time to help me leave. "I hate that you're doing this. You could at least make it easy for me."

"How?"

I thought for a few seconds then stomped over to his *Schnaps* bottle and poured a bit of golden liquid into his glass. He said, "What do you want, Wilhelm? Should I toast your health?"

"I prefer Wilm." I downed the liquor in one swallow. It burned going down but I didn't cough. I slammed the glass down. "Hear me? I ... prefer ... Wilm."

Mother whispered, "Wilm, don't make trouble."

"I've already made the trouble, Mother." My voice rose as I gave my frustration rein. "I am trouble! I've been nothing but trouble from the moment I walked!"

Father said, "At least you didn't have such a smart mouth back then. You think you're a man just because you can drink like one? Drinking doesn't make you a man. Doing what's right. That's what makes you a man, Wil-helm."

I knocked over his chair, thundered across the room, bellowed in his face, "I prefer Wilm!"

Smile lines creased out from Father's eyes. He yelled back, "Get the hell out of my house, you moron! Get out! Now!"

I flung the door open. My friends and Anneliese scurried out, looking shocked, almost terrified. I paused in the door. "Thank you."

Father inclined his head. "You're welcome. Write when you're safe, Wilm."

CHAPTER THIRTY-FIVE

"Roadblock," Karl whispered.

"I see." Two Soviets and two Schupos. They were working together. Not good.

We settled back below the ridge of broken wall. The others were waiting at the west end of the block in a courtyard. I said, "They must be covering every road out of the city. Even if they know it's us, they can't know which way we'd go. But they shouldn't know it's us already. What are the chances that Ernst is one of the Schupos investigating?"

"They'll call every man in for something like this."

"Okay. Worst scene: Ernst already knows. Father said he'd delay them as long as possible."

"You going to tell me what that yelling was all about?"

I shook my head then realized he probably couldn't see. "Easier than saying good-bye." Leaving would have been easier altogether if Father had stayed in his chair and stayed miserable. At least he hadn't talked about dying with honor on a battlefield, but Ernst could turn Leipzig into a new battlefield for my parents. Maybe Father wanted that.

"I'm thinking too much," I whispered. "Let's go."

"Where?"

"We'll head northeast, to the factories that were bombed. There's enough rubble and mess there, and not many roads. We should be able to sneak through."

"Why are we going east?"

"For one, they'll probably expect us to head straight west and get out of the Soviet Zone. We're going to Uncle Bruno's farm."

"Won't take them long to track us there. What then?"

"We'll be gone."

"Where? I know we can't come back, but it'd be nice to know where we're going."

"I have a few ideas. I need to talk to Uncle Bruno."

"I don't like being left out like this, Wilm."

"You'll be in on the planning at Uncle Bruno's. We all will be."

An old truck rattled down the street. Middle of the night it had to be a delivery truck picking up a load. We poked our heads up as it stopped at the roadblock. Two men were ordered out, made to stand with hands on heads in the light of the truck's headlamps. The police began searching the vehicle. I tapped Karl's shoulder. We crawled back from the wall, then ran in a crouch down the street, keeping close to walls and dodging pools of light.

The others were eager to move. Anneliese was still holding Ruth's hand, and had been since we had left the apartment.

We moved out single file with me leading, the girls behind me, then Georg and Karl at the back. The narrower and darker the street, the better I liked it. The first major street we had to cross had a military truck cruising by slowly. We hid in a stairwell, ducking when a floodlight on the truck swiveled in our direction. The sweep of light didn't slow.

There was probably a truck like this on every main road. I waited until it was three blocks away, then signaled for Ruth to run across with Anneliese. They disappeared into the shadows on the other side. The truck continued its slow crawl east.

Karl sidled up to me. "Having fun, Tauber?" There was an edge to the question.

"No, but I'm staying calm." Icy, like the cold fish Ernst had accused me of being. The fizz of excitement had been replaced by unrelenting tension. My muscles might never relax again.

I waved Karl and Georg across. Waited for an alarm. The night stayed silent. I joined them.

Some of the factories were running despite unrepaired bomb damage. Others were slowly being stripped of windows, bricks, and anything else that could be used by others. We stuck to the shadows of deserted buildings, hid to avoid guards at operational factories.

The third time we hid, Karl pointed out noises behind us in a derelict factory with no windows or doors. Scraping. Whispers. Maybe refugees from the eastern land Germany had lost to Poland after the war, people who couldn't find decent homes and didn't want to live in the refugee camp west of the Elsterflutbett. They wouldn't report our passage to anyone.

Beyond the factories, open fields. Wooded patches and farm sites dotting the countryside. We kept to trees as much as possible, skirted farmyards. At the first village we came to I scouted the signposts to figure out where we were, then led everyone south. Other than a few farm dogs barking at us, our journey went unmarked. I hoped.

We arrived at Uncle Bruno's farm at half past three. Had it really only been six hours since I'd tossed that potato masher into the barracks? Everyone was exhausted.

Uncle Bruno wasn't happy to be pulled from his bed. He wouldn't turn on lights until he had drawn all the blackout curtains he had never gotten around to removing. He fed us drying bread and hard cheese, boiled up some stinging-nettle tea. When we had eaten and were drinking the bitter tea, he said, "Why are you here?" His shuttered look said he knew it was bad news.

"My fault," I said.

He thumped the table. "Then why aren't you alone? Why would you include your friends and your sister in your stupidity?"

I closed my eyes. The world was turning inside out again. This was the reaction I'd expected from my father, not my uncle. I was too tired to deal with this. Large hands hauled me from my chair and slammed me against the door. Anneliese cried out. Uncle Bruno half lifted me and shoved me against the door again. Hard. My air huffed out.

My toes were barely touching the floor. Uncle Bruno said, "Your sister wouldn't be with you unless you brought trouble, real trouble, to this family. What have you done?" He banged me against the door to underscore the question.

"I killed some Soviets."

Anneliese gasped. Uncle Bruno's hold relaxed. "Soviets? And you left my sister to deal with your mess?" I saw his fist coming and jerked aside. It clipped my ear and thudded against the door. The pain that had to have shot up his arm seemed to give him pause. He glanced back at my friends, glowered at me. "I want you gone."

"We need your help."

He took a minute to consider that, eyed Anneliese for several more. "I'll help, but because of her, not you. Girl," he said to Ruth, "take Anneliese to my room. Try to sleep. Both of you." Ruth led Anneliese from the room.

Georg yawned, then Karl. I clenched my jaw and the pain of not yawning rang in my ears. Uncle Bruno pushed me to the table and sat across from me. "Do they know it was you?"

"If they don't, they will. I dropped my knife."

"Then you can't stay in the Soviet Zone. Your life isn't worth a *pfennig*."

"What?" Georg said. "I thought we would just hide in the countryside for a few days."

The way his mother had been hugging mine, she had known Georg wasn't coming back. "Sorry, Georg," I said. "We have to get to the American Zone."

Karl snapped his fingers. "I knew it. That's where Mom hoped we'd go." Georg's hair stood on end. "Your mom can follow after we get word back to her, Georg. It'll be okay. Wilm has never steered us wrong."

"Don't say that, Karl. Not after tonight," I whispered. "Uncle Bruno's right. I should never have involved you in such a dangerous plan."

"Then why did you?" Uncle Bruno asked.

"I wanted to hit the Soviets and ..." I released a breath. "I thought it would be fun."

"Thought what would be fun?"

"Throwing a potato masher into empty barracks." I squinted one eye, expecting an eruption.

His voice was as tight as his expression. "Where'd you get a grenade? No. Don't tell me. So the barracks weren't empty?"

"I thought they were. But ... there were screams."

Uncle Bruno slapped the table. "Not another word." He pointed at a bookshelf in the hall. "Bottom shelf, right side. There should be an old map. Get it."

I draped the rucksack over my chair, then my coat.

Karl whistled. "Where did you get the knife?"

"My father. He had it hidden in his bedroom."

"Better than the one you lost," Karl commented.

"I'd rather still have the other one. Then we wouldn't be in this mess." I got the map.

"Give me the knife," Uncle Bruno said. I handed it to him and he used it to point out Leipzig. "Here's where your life ended." He touched the knife tip farther west. "And here's where your new life will begin, if you get there. We're here." He tapped just east of Leipzig. "How to get there?" He put a hole in the map at the border of Saxony and Bavaria, the border between the Soviet and American Zones.

"I think we should swing south around the city," I said.

"How far?" Karl asked. "Markkleeberg?"

I glanced at Uncle Bruno, who was frowning as he studied the map. "Farther south, I think."

"Let's figure out a route," Uncle Bruno said. "Then we'll worry about supplies."

My muscles relaxed, just a little, for the first time all night.

CHAPTER THIRTY-SIX

Uncle Bruno set a handful of bullets on the map. He nodded, indicating I should take his Luger from the barn. "You have food, water, compass, map, rope, blankets. Hide in the trees all day unless unwanted company arrives. If no one comes, I'll feed you before you leave. Don't come to the house until it's dark."

He turned to Anneliese. "*Liebchen*, you weren't involved in this. You could stay here. Cook. Help with the animals. I'd like you to stay."

She reached out, lightly brushing our uncle's sleeve. First that kiss on Father's cheek, now this. "Thank you, Uncle. But I'll go with Wilm. He would do anything to keep me safe."

Uncle Bruno jabbed his finger in my face. "Make sure she stays that way."

He herded us outside. Dawn had broken but it was still too early for most people to be out. I stopped in the barn for the Luger, also took the cleaning kit but left the oily cloth. We stayed low along the fence line until we were in the trees and then settled at the base of a squat oak.

"Anyone else so far beyond tired they're cross-eyed?" Karl asked. He lifted the coils of rope off his shoulder and scratched his neck.

We all agreed except for Ruth. "I slept a bit. I'll keep watch." She shinnied up the tree and settled in a branch.

I hadn't even noticed that she was wearing trousers. Both she and Anneliese looked boyish. That was good if the Schupos were looking for a group with two girls.

I rolled into my blanket and crashed into sleep with the unloaded Luger in my hand. I woke early afternoon. Ruth slept while the rest of us waited, the uneventful day making us restless. We tried to sleep some more, but with no success. Darkness was a relief.

Uncle Bruno ushered us inside and we shared a silent *Abendbrot*. Bread, cheese, a bit of meat. Milk. It was a feast after weeks of turnips and cabbages. Georg's burp of satisfaction signaled an end to the meal.

Uncle Bruno rose. "Time to go. This is your last chance to stay, Anneliese."

She shook her head and joined Ruth at the door. They linked hands. I set my rucksack on the table. "Can you do something for me?"

"Something else?"

"I'll try to repay you, after we get across the line." He motioned for me to continue. I pulled the book of bridges from my rucksack, removed the leather thong and ring, and laid them on the book. "These belong to a man named Otto Steinhauer. A friend. He's working in Leipzig, inspecting the bridges on the Elsterflutbett, working on the Rennbahnsteg right now." I pictured Otto filling a pipe he would never smoke. "Could you return these? Tell him I remember the address. Tell him I'm ready to build." His eyes narrowed. "Should I write it down?"

"Nothing in writing. I'll remember."

"You'll do it?"

"Yes. Go."

The lines of trees on both sides of the road cast it into shadow. The moonlight shone down in spurts because of scattered clouds, but barely touched us. The night was uneventful. Near dawn we found cover in a half-collapsed cowshed in the far corner of a farmyard. We had eaten some bread and cheese while walking so Georg and Ruth took one blanket, Anneliese took one, and I rolled into one. Karl took first watch.

Anneliese lay almost touching my back. "I like being out of Leipzig," she said. "I can breathe better."

"I'm glad," I whispered before sleep ambushed me.

A snuffling noise woke me somewhere around midday. At first I thought it was a pig but a low growl told me it was a dog. Then I thought the Schupos had found us. Another growl. No, a low-pitched whine. I didn't know much about dogs but this one sounded curious.

Everyone was sleeping. I thought about nudging Karl and hassling him for not waking me up when he got sleepy, but what was the point?

I crept to the door and peered through a partly broken board. A furry head jerked up. Brown eyes stared at me, kept staring for several minutes until the dog's ears perked and it turned its head at a sound only it heard. It trotted away.

I found a hole that gave me a view of the farm, kept watch, studied the map, and wondered how far we'd walked. The American Zone was more than one hundred kilometers away. Was that three nights of walking? Four?

Before we began our second night of travel we ate the meat Uncle Bruno had given us. We took small country roads west, south, west some more. We had already left the flat plain around Leipzig behind, but weren't moving as fast as I wanted.

In the northern sky the clouds' bellies were lit by a glow—the lights of Leipzig. We rested, no one speaking as we faced the pale yellow clouds. It felt like the truth now: we wouldn't be back. Johanna came to mind. The first girl I'd ever talked to without feeling foolish. I wish I'd kissed her. I wish we'd snuck off somewhere, maybe to the Battle of the Nations monument. I would've held her hand and talked, and walked with her through the neighboring cemetery until we found a secluded spot. Then I would've kissed her. It would've been worth the risk.

My pigheadedness had wrecked that and everything else. I'd been too sure nothing could touch me. But this had exploded in my face and the shrapnel had hurt everyone I cared about. Why did they still trust me? I had killed men. I'd barely had time to think about that, but now, watching Leipzig's glow, the reality started to sink in. Two men, maybe more, dead because of me. Did they have wives? Children? For sure they'd had mothers who would be crying for their lost sons like mine was probably crying for hers.

I lurched to my feet, unable to stand my thoughts, and roused everyone. Clouds turned the landscape murky and indistinct. The air was moist and once I thought I heard the plop of something landing in water. We trudged along in silence, for hours it seemed. I couldn't fight the odd sensation of drifting in and out of sleep even as my feet kept moving.

The truck was almost to us before the sound cut through my daze. Karl and I simultaneously cried, "Take cover!"

I swerved right. Two steps off the road the ground sloped down. I started to fall. Instead of fighting it, I dove and rolled down the slope.

Landed in water. The mucky bottom made it hard to get my footing, but it wasn't deep, only to my armpits. When the grumbling grew louder and the headlamps visible, I took a breath and submerged. Vibrations from the truck shuddered through the water. When I couldn't stand another second without air, I surfaced gasping. The truck was gone.

"Wilm?" Karl said. "Are you okay?"

"Only wet. The others?"

"Fine. We lounged on the bank instead of going for a swim."

I crawled out of the shallow bog and flopped onto my side. The Luger would need a good cleaning. I patted my pockets to make sure I hadn't lost anything. My hand paused over my jacket's inner pocket. I groaned and slid my hand inside.

Uncle Bruno's map had been old and tattered. Now it was mush.

CHAPTER THIRTY-SEVEN

An owl hooted. The police we were watching snapped to alertness and swept their flashlight beams over the fields. Flat on the ground, Karl and I barely dared breathe. One shaft of light traveled over our heads, tickling the tops of the rye hiding us.

We waited until the Schupos' vigilance relaxed a notch, then backed away from them and their infernal roadblock. The others waited in a depression at the far end of the field. They were huddled, Ruth in the middle, Georg and Anneliese squeezed against her sides. Unfortunately, moonlight made it easy to see. Karl sighed as we sat.

Georg asked, "More roadblocks?"

"Yes." I pulled Father's knife from its sheath and poked at the ground. We couldn't go north, back toward Leipzig, and every time we tried to go west we ran into another roadblock. They'd woven such a tight net that you couldn't burp without a patrol arriving to check out the disturbance. "We'll have to go south some more, then try again."

"How much farther south?" Karl asked.

"I don't know. Once we get to Plauen we only have to go a short distance southwest to reach Bavaria. Since Plauen is west and south of Leipzig I think we're still fine."

"We'd be more fine if we had a map," Ruth said.

"So go ask those Schupos. They might have an extra one you could borrow."

"Quiet, both of you," Karl said. "If we had a map we'd still have to go south, so let's go."

There was no break in the wall of surveillance to the west. When the sky lightened to gray we found ourselves in a triangular valley of open fields with villages at each point. No wooded areas. We cut to the nearest village and took refuge in a haymow inside a sagging barn that housed the scrawniest cow I'd ever seen.

"I'm hungry," Georg said.

"We're all hungry." Ruth snuggled against his side and he settled with a sigh.

"Wilm?" Anneliese asked. "Will we get to Bavaria tonight?"

My response was cut off by the squeak of the barn door. I pulled the Luger from under my belt and carefully reached for the rucksack so I could get the magazine. Why hadn't I reloaded the pistol after cleaning it? I released the catch and slid the magazine into the handle but not so far that it clicked in place.

Below, feet dragged over the floor. Slowly. Anneliese hid her face against Ruth's stomach. Georg looked pale as a corpse. I could smell my sweat over the dusty hay.

A loud scrape. I flinched. My hands weren't very steady. Could I finish loading the clip, flip the safety, load a round, and fire before I got shot? I doubted it.

Below, the quiet voice of an old woman rose up, filled the breathless silence. "Dear Brunhilde." A patting sound. "My old eyes might be failing but I saw shadows flit across my yard. If Wolfgang had heard he would have barked up a storm. Did the shadows come in here?"

The sound of milk squirting into a pail was rhythmic and calming. Uncle Bruno had taught me to milk his cow but I was never any good at it. I always preferred watching him, watching the metronome switch of the cow's tail, watching the steam rise from the pail.

The swish-swish stopped. "A shadow could join me," the old woman said. "Shadows have nothing to fear from me. I live my days with ghosts." She resumed milking.

Go down or not? As I was trying to decide, Ruth brushed past me. She paused on the ladder, motioned me to move closer so I could watch, then climbed down silently. I shifted onto my stomach, pistol in hand.

A head of thinning gray hair rested against the cow's side. Ruth moved to stand near the animal's tail. The gray head turned toward Ruth. "You're skin and bones, almost a real shadow." Half a dozen more squirts of milk. "Only a child. Surely they can't be hunting for children."

"Who?" Ruth whispered.

"The *Schutzpolizei* and the Soviet Army say they are holding joint training exercises. 'In case the Western capitalists invade,' is the market gossip." She cleared her throat. "I have seen enough of such things to know they are seeking someone, or setting a trap."

"Why would you tell me? I might be a Schupo spy," Ruth said.

"And so might I." The woman cackled and patted the cow's skinny flank.

"You could get in trouble for help—" Ruth cut off. She had practically admitted we were the fugitives being sought.

"Trouble? I am too old to care, child. I have lived through four governments: Kaiser Wilhelm, hopeless Hindenburg and his Weimar fools, the furious Fuehrer and his Nazi fools, now this company of SED fools. They are all the same. They all take my milk and butter and make me live by their rules."

The old lady pushed slowly up from her three-legged stool so I could see her stooped form from the waist up. "After eighty-seven years of rules I know I will not have to suffer many more. And no government will get today's milk." She laid a knotted hand on

Ruth's arm. "You share it with your other shadows, and that loaf of bread I set on the shelf." She cleared her throat again. "Hunting children. Shameful."

The old woman disappeared from view, then reappeared as she backed her cow out of the stall. As she led the cow out of the barn she said, "Farmers to the west say the exercises are worse there, with more soldiers. Wise shadows will stay off the roads."

CHAPTER THIRTY-EIGHT

Bread sopped in warm milk tasted heavenly. We saved half the loaf but shared all the milk. At dusk the old lady returned her cow to the stall, milked it again, and left four finger-sized Thuringer sausages, all without speaking. After she left I kicked myself for not asking how far it was to Plauen. We cut each sausage into five pieces and ate slowly to trick our stomachs into thinking it was more.

We had just left the barn when a red dot glowing in the darkness made us take cover behind a hedge. Steps crunched closer, stopped immediately on the other side of the hedge. The red tip winked through silhouetted leaves, rose, brightened, lowered. Repeated several times. The red circle dropped to the ground half a meter from my nose. A shadowy boot snuffed its light.

Another set of footsteps grew louder. The man by the hedge said, "Any luck?"

"They haven't seen anything. You ask at the next house."

"What are the chances the fugitives would come through this village?"

"Doesn't matter. Our orders are to ask at every house. The next one is an ancient grandmother. Do you need my help or can I watch from the street and have a cigarette?"

The first fellow swore and the second laughed. They moved toward our kind hostess's house. We crept away, breaking into a run as soon as we were sure it was safe.

The night was a blur of racing through rolling countryside, resting, running more, collapsing in exhausted heaps. Plauen had to be straight west now, but with roadblocks and roving patrols, we couldn't get to it. When we finally thought we'd found a hole in their net, a farm dog caught our scent. Its barking summoned a patrol.

We continued south, wasting half the night backtracking. The land became hillier, with fewer fields, more wooded areas. In a forested gully, we drank from a rill until our stomachs sloshed, sagged against the trees and each other.

Anneliese shared a tree with me, our shoulders touching. "Wilm, do you have any idea where we are?" In a scant whisper, she added, "I'm afraid."

I ignored her question. "Don't be afraid, Liese. You aren't part of this. If we don't get away ... You truthfully never knew what I was doing. They'll return you home with a stern warning to avoid troublemakers."

If we don't get away. It was the first time I had admitted that we might not succeed. I wondered if I could distract the Schupos by surrendering and give the others time to escape. I couldn't let everyone suffer for my actions more than they already had.

Anneliese said, "I don't want to go back."

Neither did I. For me, the trip would be made in chains.

We decided to continue south for the rest of the night. Then one of us would sneak into a village and find out where we were. The scattered bits of forest grew together; we had mostly left farmland behind. Our slow progress, hampered by backtracking, became slower still. We came to a road and followed it, ready to dive into the forest if a vehicle came along.

The moon had long since set, leaving thick darkness. I took one end of Uncle Bruno's rope, Karl the other, and everyone

grabbed it. I led. Sometimes I didn't know I was walking off the
road until branches grabbed at me and I veered away.

The realization it was getting lighter came gradually. Staying
on the road became easier. Then Ruth noted that the jagged slice
of sky above us was gray. We came to a bend and the road ended
in a small yard with a black rectangle of a house, another that was
probably a barn. There looked to be a clearing beyond the barn,
a pasture of some sort.

We puzzled over the compass, almost impossible to see. Karl
figured south cut right through the pasture. We snuck along the
edge of the forest near the house. No dog barked. We came to
a fence beside the far building. Cords and cords of wood were
stacked against it. A woodcutter's cottage, then.

Karl whispered, "We're all exhausted, Wilm, but we need to
put some distance between us and this place. Let's just cut across
the paddock."

"I agree," said Ruth.

They were the only two who ever gave their opinions. Georg
always agreed with Ruth and Anneliese with me. I was so tired it
was hard to think. "Fine. Do you want to lead?"

"No," Karl said. "You go and I'll guard the rear."

Anneliese bent, scooped something from the ground. "It's
getting awfully light."

Karl replied, "Let's move fast."

We climbed through the fence and struck out. Halfway across
the pasture loud angry howls started up behind us. We all looked
back. I stopped, startled by the sight of three stubby ghosts skim-
ming over the ground toward us with phantom garments flapping.

"Geese," Anneliese cried.

Honks, not howls. Wings, not garments. And an unearthly
racket. Lights came on in the house.

We tore across the pasture, stumbled on uneven ground. At the fence I helped Anneliese, then clambered over. Ruth and Georg both scrambled to safety. Karl yelped. Anneliese spun, flung something toward Karl. He vaulted the fence. The geese ran into the boards, honking, flapping, stretching long necks between the boards to reach us. We dashed into the forest, all thoughts of sleep banished.

Minutes later, Karl called, "Slow down. I can't go that fast. *Scheisse*."

We waited for him. I asked, "What happened?"

"Those were meat-eating geese. Look." He turned around. "They tore my trousers. I must be bleeding. If Anneliese hadn't knocked that one away with whatever she threw, I'd be in pieces in the paddock. Nice shot, by the way."

"They bit you?" I said.

"Right on the hind end." We all smothered laughter. Karl snapped, "Sure, laugh. It hurts."

"You're right," I said. "We shouldn't laugh. Let's get farther away and find somewhere to hide. At least that shouldn't be hard in this forest."

"And we still need to find out where we are," Ruth said.

We found trails through the forest, kept south, had to skirt west to avoid some roads, some houses, more houses. It started to sprinkle. Our path took us higher along the side of a huge hill that seemed to be vying for mountainhood, until we reached a clearing. From its upper edges we overlooked a town that sprawled across the valley floor and reached into the surrounding hills like the arms of an octopus.

Downhill, across the clearing, a manor house reigned over manicured lawns and what looked like swimming pools. We shrank under the trees, from the rain and unwelcome eyes.

Ruth said, "I'll go into town and find out where we are. Maybe find some food."

"Why you?" I asked. "By now, the Schupos know we've all missed our last day of school. You included. They might have posters up with our pictures."

"That's right," Anneliese said. "You're all part of this. But as Wilm reminded me, I am not. I have to be the one to go."

CHAPTER THIRTY-NINE

Morning rain left the air thick with moisture, especially in the forest. I hunkered behind a screen of trees and watched the road winding out of the hills into the town below. Anneliese only had to find out the name of the town and the direction to Plauen, but I was still jittery.

Wrecking the map had been disastrous. I was sure we had missed Plauen. I could picture the map but could only put names of bigger cities on it. None of these villages meant anything.

The sun was burning off the wisps of low cloud feathering over the hills. Karl had lit a sputtering campfire, knowing the clouds would camouflage its smoke. We needed to dry out. If the clouds evaporated we'd have to douse the fire.

A familiar figure hiked around the corner at the bottom of the hill. Finally. It looked like Anneliese was carrying something. Food, I hoped. What I wouldn't give for a slice of warm bread topped with raspberry jam. My stomach grumpily reminded me of the scant handful of wild strawberries Ruth had found for breakfast. I tried not to think about food.

Someone appeared at the bottom of the hill. The road curved so Anneliese wouldn't see him, but my lookout was above the road, and I had a clear view. He followed slowly. The way he stood was familiar ...

Ernst. The one person who had seen and could recognize Anneliese in her boyish garb. My muscles strained with wanting to jump up, shout at Anneliese to run. My breathing sped up but I only watched. That's all he was doing too.

He wanted Anneliese to lead him to us. I touched the Luger under my belt. Could I use it against someone I knew? Anneliese trekked uphill, oblivious to her shadow.

Ernst seemed to be alone. He followed at a distance, keeping half behind trees, hedges. Had the way I'd injured his pride by tricking him into releasing Georg led to him wanting to catch us single-handedly? Could we capture him?

I hared back to camp and told the others what was happening. Karl helped me fix a blanket so it looked like someone was in it. I said, "You all pretend you're sleeping. Karl, stay awake for Anneliese, and tell her I went back to sleep." I pointed at our rigged blanket. "Urge her to sleep, say you'll watch, then fake going to sleep. I'll hide and ambush Ernst." It was the best I could come up with. All three warily agreed.

I swung into the tree above my sleeping form and loaded the Luger, but left the safety on. I didn't want it accidentally going off when I jumped.

The hunted was hunting the hunter. No electricity buzzed through my body at the thought. Instead, certainty settled over me, a sense that I was risking a lot, but not for the thrill. Risking because I had no choice. Because my friends were depending on me. The thought made my jaw clench. I refused to fail them.

Anneliese arrived. Below, Ruth and Georg snuggled like spoons with his face hidden in her hair. Karl rose to meet Anneliese. He took her bag and wrapped her in a blanket before she knew what was happening. Whispered. She gave a nod and lay down.

Karl sat at the base of the tree beside Anneliese. He watched for maybe three minutes, then stretched and pretended to nod off. His head drooped forward. A smile lifted one corner of my compressed lips. We were a great team.

Ten minutes passed. I started to worry Ernst had returned to town for help. My legs stiffened from balancing. My knuckles ached from gripping the branch I planned to swing down on.

Undergrowth rustled. Ernst appeared below me, pistol pointed at my decoy. His thumb, on the safety, started to slide—

I swung down, my feet crashed into Ernst's shoulder. He fell onto his side and began to roll. I thumped down beside him, landing hard on my knees, and stuck the Luger against his neck. Flicked off the safety. He froze. Karl grabbed his pistol.

Ernst was practically snarling. And he looked terrible. Strips of tape curved over his nose. His eyes were centered in bruised circles.

I rose, keeping the Luger trained on his chest. "Rope." Ruth scrambled to Karl's pack. "Tie him up, but use as little as possible," I said. "We don't want to waste it on him."

Karl helped Ruth tie Ernst's hands behind his back, and made the knots so tight Ernst grimaced. They also tied his ankles. Karl searched him, found handcuffs and a knife. He kept the knife, tossed the handcuffs in the smoldering remains of the soggy, dying fire.

Ernst looked uncomfortable, half on his hands in the hollow of the tree I had hidden in. I put the safety back on the Luger and squatted beside him. Hate rolled off him like heat off a stove.

"Where are we, Anneliese?" I asked.

She said, "Bad Elster."

I tried to picture it on the map. "How far from Plauen? Did you find out?" She shook her head.

Ernst snorted. "You're lost."

"Then how did you find us?"

"Once I remembered the uncle you and Anneliese used to visit it was easy, even if he wouldn't talk. We cut off every western route. Your only choice was south. I've been waiting in Plauen. Ironic that's where you were headed. When a woodcutter reported his geese raising the alarm this morning I knew it was you."

I touched the barrel tip to Ernst's neck. "Where is Bad Elster?"

Unconcern replaced his anger. "Thirty kilometers or so southwest of Plauen. Mostly south."

I pictured the map. We had gone a night's journey too far south. We had to be almost at the Czechoslovakian border. We'd need to backtrack north-northwest at least twenty kilometers to get around the odd finger of Czech land that poked into Germany. Around that tip would be the Bavarian border, where the American Zone began.

"Do you know where we are, Wilm?" Karl asked.

"Yes. Now."

Ernst inclined his head. "Glad to be helpful, little brother. If only your family had been half so helpful you'd have been in custody days ago."

My mouth went dry. "What did you do to them?"

"I didn't do a thing to your wily uncle. There was no proof you'd been there. Closed-mouthed beggar. Not like your father."

That Ernst was enjoying telling me this was easy to see. But I had to know. "What about my father? What did he say?"

"He said a lot and nothing. Refused to be questioned in his apartment so we took him to headquarters. Refused to tell us where your mother was, or Anneliese. The women never told him anything, he insisted. It took us half a day to track her down to a Frau Rohrbach's home. Know her?" His gaze flicked to Georg, who went pale. Ernst sneered at me. "Your mother wept and wailed so much, kept asking what you'd done. Not helpful. Smart of you to not tell her about the barracks attack. Though she admitted you were our elusive butter thief. The confirmation was nice but I didn't need it. I knew when I saw the knife. The knife and that stickman you drew on everything, each one a signed confession. I thought you were smart. They gave me the case. Easier to catch a culprit you know. Once I thought about it, I knew you'd go to that uncle."

He was enjoying this, performing for a spellbound audience of one. I felt the presence of my friends, of Anneliese, but I knew he was only talking to me. Ernst said, "Your father ... I'm not sure he liked me when I was dating your sister." He didn't look at Anneliese. "You idolized me, but he probably thought I only wanted to get into your sister's skirt. He didn't like being interrogated by me. I admit I was surprised by his reaction when I asked about you. I've never heard a father swear so vividly when talking about his son. He wanted us to find you. Little moron is nothing but trouble, he said. Wanted us to bring you back so he could beat the snot out of you." The near snarl reappeared. "I might have believed him if he hadn't broken my nose with his crutch. Stupid fool made me shoot him."

I couldn't hear over the ringing in my ears. His lips formed the words, in the shoulder. Then his voice cut through the ringing. "He wouldn't stop coming at me. You have to believe, little brother, that I didn't want shoot him again, but he kept attacking me. I had to kill him." He said it with a sneer.

I stared blankly while my stomach was invisibly ripped open. Behind me Anneliese started to cry. I couldn't give Ernst the satisfaction of seeing my pain. Gut-ripping, heart-stopping agony. I found my voice, though it wasn't working very well. "Thank you," I croaked.

Ernst's head jerked back. His jaw slackened.

"All he wanted"—I swallowed, fighting the lump of grief swelling to close off my throat—"was to die an honorable death on the battlefield. You gave him that."

His mouth snapped shut. His lip curled. "There's no honor in dying to protect a traitor. That's what you are, little brother. A filthy traitor."

His tone startled me. It had jumped from cold to scalding. Ernst's mask was gone, his fury so visible he didn't need words. He had trusted me and I had betrayed him. Together again, big brother. I had lied to him. This wasn't about bringing me to justice. For him, it was personal.

I was hammered again by what he'd said. He'd killed my father. I shoved the Luger so deep in his neck he gagged. "You're the traitor. A puppet working for the Soviets. They rape and kill and steal from us. We get no justice. And you just watch." I kept the gun jammed in his neck and grabbed his chin. My spittle dripped on his face. My voice started to crack. "You stood and watched. You watched while four Soviets attacked my sister."

His blue eyes shimmered like twin lakes. "I didn't watch. I couldn't. Don't you think I wanted ...?" The mask slammed back into place. In a blink his eyes were dry, stony orbs. "She was stupid to go to such a dangerous place alone."

I drew back and punched him in the mouth. And again. He spat some blood and sneered. I switched off the Luger's safety. Pressed the barrel against Ernst's forehead. My finger trembled against the trigger. I wanted so badly to kill him.

A minute ticked away. I lowered the pistol, flipped on the safety. Ernst barked out a single laugh. "I knew you didn't have the guts."

"No," I whispered. "I have the guts. But pulling that trigger, killing an unarmed man, would make me ... just like you. And I refuse to become that." Refused to think I might already be like him after I'd killed those Soviets. But I hadn't meant to kill those soldiers. I had to hope that intentions made a difference.

Karl cleared his throat. "Wilm? Why would he bother to tell us all this?"

Other than the enjoyment he got from ripping my heart out? I frowned at Ernst's stony expression, at the blood oozing from the corner of his mouth. His unconcern with being captured. I jumped up. "Pack. We have to leave. He has men who'll show up soon if he doesn't return with us." If I had shot Ernst, the sound would've brought his men running.

Everyone scrambled to stuff supplies into our bags. I kicked Ernst's thigh. "How long did you tell them to wait?"

He squinted up. "Why would I tell you that?"

I gripped the barrel of the Luger and whacked him on the temple with the pistol's butt. He slumped sideways. I kicked him again and got no response.

Karl punched my arm. "Got everything. Which way?"

I pulled the compass from my pocket and tossed it to him. "West to the Czech border. We'll follow it around the corner into Bavaria. With any luck, Ernst will head back toward Plauen and miss us. You lead. I'll watch our backs." If I went last, the Schupos would catch up to me first. Get them out if I get caught, I wanted to add.

Karl tucked Ernst's pistol under his belt and nodded, as if he'd heard me.

We plunged into the forest.

CHAPTER FORTY

We followed hiking trails that crisscrossed the hills. I didn't pay attention to where Karl led us. I was too busy looking over my shoulder. Too busy trying to contain the wild animal of my grief in a back room in my mind. I wanted to howl. Couldn't.

Karl stopped us in the U of a thicket and shared out the small loaf of bread Anneliese had gotten in Bad Elster. I forced myself to focus on surveying our surroundings. To think of anything but the caged animal.

An alley of grass swept between us and another forest. A sign was posted off to the left, and another sign maybe fifteen meters away. I squinted. There was German on the sign, but also another language. The Czech border. Ruth tapped my shoulder and pointed in the other direction. Two soldiers patrolled along the grass borderland. Soviet soldiers.

I was mostly hidden from their view. If I ducked now they'd spot the movement. They walked slowly, glancing back occasionally. Ruth and I kept immobile. The soldiers passed. Finally, trees blocked them from sight. But now I could see a pair of soldiers advancing along the forest on the other side of the clearing. Czech soldiers. I dropped to my knees.

Karl kept his voice as low as possible. "How are we supposed to follow the border if it's guarded? There might be a lot of patrols between here and Bavaria, more the closer we get."

A lot more once Ernst gave the alarm. What were our options? Go back to Bad Elster and steal a car maybe. But the town would be crawling with Schupos. And none of us could drive. I closed my eyes and imagined the map.

Wind rustled branches while I considered possibilities. "I've got it." I opened my eyes, took out my father's knife—the only keepsake I'd have of him now—and swept debris from the ground. I used the knife to draw the border. The smell of damp earth floated up. "See this finger of land? We're west of Bad Elster so we're beside the finger. It's Czechoslovakia. From what I remember of the map it isn't even thirty kilometers across, maybe less. And on the other side: Bavaria. The American Zone."

Karl's frown was as deep as Bad Elster's valley. "You mean we're going to cut across Czechoslovakia? What about the Czechs?"

"We'll get across before they know we're there."

"There's no fence. What will stop the Soviet patrols from chasing us?"

"I don't know if anything will stop them. Do we have another choice?"

"Shh," Ruth hissed. "The soldiers are coming back."

It had barely been ten minutes, fifteen at the most. There had to be a lot of border patrols closely spaced if they were back so soon. Anneliese took my hand. Hers was cold. Grief was written in her face. I mouthed, "I'm sorry." She squeezed my fingers.

The ground muffled the soldiers' footfalls. They stopped near the clearing for a few minutes, probably by the trailhead we had been on. Then they moved away.

"Okay," I said. "We have to time our run across the border so no Czech or Soviet patrols see us. We'll have to run like we've never run before. Together. No looking back. Just run."

The others followed me to the trail's end. The Soviets had disappeared around a curve but some Czech soldiers were still visible. I grew edgy waiting for them to disappear. Finally, no one was in sight. I motioned. "Now."

We burst from the trail and charged across the grass, our feet pounding the rough ground. Surely they could hear us back in Bad Elster.

My toe caught in a hole. I somersaulted, scrambled up. I glanced behind and saw the Soviets coming back into view. They shouted, but we were already across the clearing.

A shot rang out as I dived under Czechoslovakian trees. A flock of startled birds burst skyward.

The forests in Czechoslovakia had fewer trails. Heading west, we crossed a road almost immediately but then slowed down, had to blaze our own path or follow faint game trails. Karl continued to lead. I took the rear, continually looked back, dreading Soviet pursuit.

At another road, we watched plodding horses pull a farm wagon toward us. The farmer seemed half asleep, hat low, reins slack. When the wagon finally passed, we sprinted across the road one by one. The farmer never looked back.

We came to a clearing that opened to a swath of farmland. Rolling hills, little cover. A spire indicated a village near the middle of the valley. The higher hills behind us were forested and continued to the southwest. We rested under a canopy of spruce trees.

"When do we get to stop?" Georg asked. "We only slept a few hours this morning."

"We have to keep going," I replied. "It's not far."

"We're turning southwest, so it'll be farther than you think, Wilm. And we're hungry." He licked cracked lips.

"Isn't this part of Czechoslovakia German-speaking? The Sudetenland?" Ruth said. "I could ask for food at a farmhouse."

Karl shook his head. "Not a good idea."

"Why?" Anneliese asked.

"Things I heard in the Stag's Horn."

"More rumors?" Georg said. "We investigated the rumors about a weapons stash and nothing turned up. Why should we believe any other rumors?"

Karl and I stared. I said, "Georg, where did I get that long-handled grenade?"

"How should I know? I—" Georg's mouth snapped shut, opened, closed again. "There really was a weapons stash? And you didn't tell me?"

"We couldn't tell anyone," Karl replied. His fingers raked his hair, now as messy as Georg's. "The cache was in the Stag's Horn. My mom would've been arrested."

"What else did you take from it?" Ruth asked.

"Nothing," I said. "Karl didn't even know I took the grenade until I dropped it on that map."

"What rumors did you hear, Karl?" Anneliese changed the subject.

"That after the war the Czech government took away German land and property in the Sudetenland. That they kicked out the German speakers. Millions."

"That can't be right," Anneliese said. "Millions?"

Silence reigned. I wondered about those people hiding in the derelict factory. Ruth said, "So we have to act like the rumor is true and stay away from everyone."

The slosh of an almost empty canteen made us look at Karl. "Everyone gets a sip. There'll be streams in this forest. We refill at every chance, watch for berries, keep moving."

Georg groaned but didn't protest. We passed the canteen around, emptied it. Karl suggested we rest for ten more minutes. I called him aside. We sat under a spruce overlooking the fields.

"Let me see Ernst's pistol." Karl handed it over. "Walther P-38. Do you know how to fire it?" He shook his head. I examined the pistol. There was a round in the chamber, five in the magazine, two missing. "Uncle Bruno once explained how it's different from his Luger."

I had Karl hold it as if he were going to shoot at the field, and pointed as I talked. "Safety here. There's a round in the chamber so keep it on S unless you're going to shoot. If a round wasn't loaded, you'd pull back and release the slide. But it is, so you just thumb the safety up, point, and pull the trigger."

"I feel like I'm back in Hitler Youth."

"Except this time you're listening. You might need to use this."

"I won't hit anything."

"Doesn't matter. Pistols have a small range. But fire in the direction of anyone and he'll dive for cover. If he's hiding, he isn't shooting at us."

"*Scheisse*. Do you think ...?"

"No. Let's get everyone up and moving."

There was no way to go fast and keep out of sight. We found a stream, a few strawberries. We were exhausted. Hungry. I glimpsed a rabbit but it fled so quickly I might have imagined it. Rabbit over an open fire, fat dripping, making the flames sputter and flare. Ruth found some wild raspberries. With each unripe berry, sourness burst in my mouth. We ate as many as we could. I went back to dreaming about rabbit.

Again our heading was west. We crossed another road and climbed another hill, caught glimpses of open land to the north and south. Straight ahead was forest.

I pushed everyone to keep moving as dusk fell. We came to another field. In the dark we couldn't tell how wide it was, but a short distance to the north lights shone from two windows. Warmth, food, shelter—that farmhouse might as well have been in Spain for all the good it did us.

"We have to stop, Wilm," Karl said.

He was right. Darkness, weariness, and obstacles had slowed us to a crawl. And we all had stomachaches from the unripe berries. We took turns retreating into the forest. Ruth was gone when I found a tree to urinate behind, and still gone when I returned to camp. We all settled down, except Georg, who wanted to look for her. I was considering it when she finally returned.

The waxing moon filtered some light onto our circle of blankets. Ruth stepped into the center and dumped an armload of carrots onto the ground. She waved something long and dark and told us to eat. I sighed. "You raided that farm's garden."

"Don't worry. I went down the rows, pulling one here, one there. They'll never notice. I only took one cucumber from their greenhouse." She handed it to me. "Their dog was friendly."

A good thing or we'd be running again. The others were already rubbing dirt off carrots and chomping down. I sliced the cucumber into five pieces. The only sound was crunching. Those carrots tasted better than chocolate. We ate our cucumber chunks for dessert.

I woke with a start hours later. Snuffling sounds. A dark form. I squinted, fearful it might be a wild boar. A Luger's bullet wouldn't save us then. But wild boars didn't have tails that flipped like a windscreen wiper. The dog. It finally left but took with it any chance of sleeping.

We had fallen asleep without setting watch duty. I put a tree between myself and the group, leaned against it, and kept an eye on the farmhouse, barely visible.

Soon the horizon beyond the farmyard began to lighten. I had slept longer than I'd realized. I hadn't noticed the chill of the night, but now it crept into my bones. I shuddered. Regrets and guilt swirled around me. Without warning the animal grief lunged out and closed off my throat. I fought to breathe, to stay calm, but especially, to not think.

Vati. I hadn't called him that since I was twelve. Why couldn't he have bluffed his way through the interrogation? What had Ernst said to make him attack? I had killed two men, and because of that my father was dead. All my fault. No. Father had wanted Ernst to pull the trigger, had wanted to die in battle. But it felt like my fault. I had started the chain of events.

The cold shivered over my skin. My breath came in gulps. I couldn't fall apart now. I had to get everyone to safety. No more deaths. But death wrapped its clammy hands around my throat and blew fetid air on my face.

Someone sat beside me. Ruth tilted her head, watched me with a puzzled curve of her brow.

I stared back, still gulping for breath. For life. I needed to know I was alive. Needed to feel something other than numbing cold. I cupped my hand along Ruth's jaw and kissed her. Inhaled the warmth of her breath. I imagined I was kissing Johanna and deepened the kiss, wanting ...

Ruth's hands on my chest nudged us apart. "Don't," she whispered. "Never again." Her expression suggested she'd slap me if it weren't for the noise it would make.

My hand still rested on her neck. I wanted to kiss her again, to recapture the sensation of being alive.

Behind Ruth, a twig cracked. I jerked my head up. Georg stared at us through a break in the branches. Ruth popped to her feet. I followed. She hit my chest. "You've ruined everything." Her voice rose. "Everything!" She spun and ran into the spearhead-shaped field. We were close to the tip where the field narrowed to a point.

Georg glared at me, fist curled. I said, "That was me, Georg, not her. She likes you. Get her."

Confusion replaced anger in his face. I gave him a shove. "Go after her. Now."

He raced after Ruth. She sprawled onto the ground, started to push to her feet.

A dog barked. It galloped across the field from the farmyard, as if it had spotted an old friend. A large figure stalked behind it. Raised something.

A rifle.

"Gun!" I yelled. "Get down!"

The man swiveled his rifle toward me. I probably blended with the trees. He swung it back. Ruth and Georg hadn't taken cover. She was rabbiting toward the trees with Georg trying to catch up. He kept glancing at the man with the rifle.

Georg lunged to push Ruth down at the same instant the rifle shot shattered the morning. Ruth fell. Georg jerked as if pulled by a puppet string and crashed to the ground.

CHAPTER FORTY-ONE

The Luger jumped into my fist. I flicked the safety, shot in the direction of the man with the rifle. He dove to the ground. Ruth crawled toward Georg, turned him over.

Karl arrived at my side. I pointed. "Use the P-38. Shoot at him if he raises his rifle. Keep him pinned. Tell Anneliese to get our bags. Follow under the trees."

I sprinted across the field, Luger in hand. Remembered to put the safety on before I hit my knees beside Georg.

Another gunshot. I ducked, then realized it wasn't loud. Karl had fired the P-38. I glanced toward the farm but didn't see the rifleman. "How is it?"

"Arm. On fire." Georg's eyes were wide. His coat arm was dark, the smell of blood strong.

"I think it went through," Ruth said.

I passed the Luger to her. "Get to the trees." I flung Georg's uninjured arm around my neck and pulled him up. He yelped. I ran, half dragging Georg, who was stumbling and swearing at me. For good reason. My fault again. Always.

A branch slapped me in the face as we ducked under the trees. A second branch swiped me; a brittle twig cut my forehead. Karl and Anneliese caught up, each carrying two bags. Anneliese had a blanket slung over her shoulder.

"We have to stop," Ruth said.

"No." I dragged Georg through the forest. "If that farmer has a telephone we only have minutes to gain some distance."

"Georg is bleeding."

"Cut that blanket and bind the wound as we go. When you're done, we run."

Georg whispered, "Let me go, Tauber. I'll keep walking."

I released him and took my Luger back. Karl cut a strip off the only blanket we had left. At least they'd saved the bags and supplies inside them. I urged Anneliese to keep up and dropped behind to watch for pursuit. Karl and Ruth tied the rough bandage over Georg's coat tight enough that he complained. "Okay," I said. "Faster."

"Will we make the border today?" Anneliese asked.

"We'd better."

Karl gave Ruth the compass, pointed and said something that I couldn't hear. He waited until I reached him then fell in beside me. "I told her to go as fast as possible."

"It won't be fast enough."

"Why were they out in that field?" I ducked around a tree. Karl pulled me to a stop. "I heard Ruth yell, then sat up to see her running." I yanked my arm free and started walking. He caught up. "What did you do, Wilm?"

I swatted a branch aside. "Acted like a moron." I called ahead, "Speed up, Georg. You're not gut-shot."

Karl muttered, "You're sure being one right now."

I hit his arm. We both stopped. "I'm trying to get us to safety. Even if the Schupos or Soviets didn't follow us across the border, the Czech police will be hunting us now. They'll follow our trail from that farm. Understand?"

"I have a brain, Wilm. But Georg was shot and you don't seem to care."

"It was my fault! Of course I care. But one bullet in the arm will be nothing if we're caught."

Karl grabbed my collar. "Why was it your fault?"

"Because Georg saw me kiss Ruth."

His hand dropped away. "*Scheisse.*"

"Always so good with words. At least she didn't kiss me back." I jogged to catch up with the others as they hiked up a hill. Karl passed me and took the lead. It felt like he had declared his allegiance. And it wasn't with me.

I walked beside Anneliese for awhile. Kept watch behind us. The thin underbrush made it easy to see if we were being followed, but that worked both ways. Fear thudded through my veins. I quietly asked Anneliese how she was doing. She said she was afraid but doing better than she'd expected. It was the trees. Their peacefulness. Her cheeks were pink under the filth of five days' travel. She looked healthier than I'd seen her in ages.

The unsaid hung between us. Father was dead. Anneliese took my hand. Her attempted smile faltered. "Will Mother be okay?" she whispered.

"Probably. Maybe Georg's mother will move in with her. We'll write as soon as we can."

She nodded and held my hand until a tree blocked our path. I stepped behind and stayed there. The trees fell away at the crest of the hill. A road ran along the ridge. We hid behind a screen of raspberry canes. The trees opened to expose a wide hilltop to the southwest. Three military vehicles were parked on the crown. We saw two Soviet uniforms, a few we didn't recognize that were probably Czech. One Schupo uniform. That person was turned away but his stance said it was Ernst. He had gotten the Czechs to help search for us.

Karl pointed north to where the road dipped off the hilltop and into trees. I nodded and waved for everyone to follow him.

The calm that came with risk was back. Uncle Bruno had given me enough bullets for a full magazine. I had used one. I would use the other seven if that's what it took to buy my friends time to escape.

Below the crest, at a bend in the road, we crossed safely to the western side. And ran. Georg clutched his elbow to hold his arm steady and never complained. Maybe a kilometer farther on we crossed another road. All these ways through the forest made it easy for Ernst to get around. He'd find our trail eventually.

Georg finally collapsed. He sagged against a half-rotted tree trunk and sucked air into his lungs. Ruth rubbed his good arm. Karl pulled the canteen from his bag, shared the water, and slipped away to find more.

I crouched in front of Ruth and Georg. She glared; he didn't look at me. "I'm sorry," I whispered. Georg studied me from the corner of his eyes. I had to try to explain. "I was thinking about my father when Ruth sat beside me. I kissed her because ... I felt death choking me and needed to touch something alive. It wasn't Ruth. I was even imaging someone else. But she was there and ... warm." That sounded stupid. "You have reason to hate me, Georg. I hope you won't, but I deserve it. She didn't kiss me back."

His voice was shaky, quiet. "You're such a moron, Tauber."

"I hear that a lot. It must be true." I tried to smile but failed.

"It is," Ruth said. "That's why I like you, Georg. You are a gentleman."

They kissed. I exhaled. "Rub it in. The nice guy wins the girl. He's not always nice, you know."

Ruth kissed him again. "He is to me."

I wanted to roll my eyes. "Give him another kiss. Maybe that farmer realized you were his garden thief or just didn't like trespassers. If Georg hadn't pushed you right then, you would've taken that bullet in your back." Her eyes rounded into saucers. This was

CHAPTER FORTY-TWO

Fear gave wings to our feet. We pushed as hard as we could. Collapsed only when we couldn't go another step. Continued after a few moments rest. I hadn't realized how slowly we'd picked along yesterday. Our timidity had cost us a lot in time and distance.

The hills rolled away to the west. Climbing slowed us; we made up for it on down slopes. In a shallow valley we rested by a stream. Karl filled the canteen, passed it around, filled it again.

Georg leaned against Ruth and immediately fell asleep. Anneliese curled up and laid her head on Ruth's lap. I crossed the stream, sat, and leaned against a beech tree so I faced the group and could watch to the east. I rested my forearms on raised knees and held the Luger loosely.

Karl joined me and sat facing the other way. Our shoulders almost touched. He pushed his fingers through hair that had darkened more each day. "Tell me we're close."

"We must be. Three kilometers at most. I'm hoping less."

"Hoping?"

I squinted at the overcast sky and scratched the itchy fuzz on my jaw as I tried to imagine the map. "I think the map showed the finger getting fat at the bottom. If Bad Elster is near the base of the finger like I recall, then we might reach the border sooner if we angle northwest."

"Might?"

"That's all I can offer, Karl. Might. What do you think?"

He chewed his lip for a moment. "We head northwest. Do you think they're following us?"

I didn't want to say what I thought. Karl nudged me. "I think they'll have someone following us, and people waiting for us." He started to spew his favorite swear word. I gripped his shoulder. "Don't keep reminding me what we're knee-deep in. Please."

He pulled the P-38 from under his belt and ran a finger along its barrel, gripped it, aimed it behind me, his frown growing deeper. He laid down the pistol. "You're scared."

I hesitated, then nodded.

"You never act scared. Back at that farm, you shouted a string of orders and ran into the field like a crazy man. You could've been shot."

"That occurred to me after."

"But not during."

I shook my head.

"Were you scared when you were pulling those pranks in Leipzig?" I shook my head again. His voice dropped lower. "But now you're scared." He snorted. "There were times in Leipzig I was almost crapping my shorts, but I hid it because you were fearless. Do you have any idea how much more terrifying it is to have you admit you're afraid?"

"That was for fun, Karl, for the thrill. This—" I grabbed his shoulder again. "When Georg got shot it was my worst nightmare. You're here because I messed up. I have to get you all to safety. Don't you see?"

"I think I do. You don't care if anything happens to you, right? So long as we're okay. That's beautiful. Noble. Except you're my best friend and I don't want anything to happen to you. Understand? You made us memorize that address in Munich so if something happens to you we can still go to your safe haven. Right?" He encircled my wrist, pulled my hand down, and leaned close. "Well that stinks more than a mountain of dung. We're in this together. We have to get out. Together."

"If we can."

He gritted his teeth and squeezed my wrist hard. "Together, Tauber." He released me.

I rubbed my wrist and echoed, "Together. Let's wake Sleeping Beauty and his fair maidens so we can get moving."

Minutes after we headed out a drizzle started. A heavy rain might hide our tracks; all this did was make us miserable. We seemed to be trudging uphill more than down, each shallow valley higher than the last. We came to another road, took cover. One vehicle with Czech police cruised by, heading north.

I waved Ruth and Georg across. Then Anneliese and Karl. I was two steps from the western edge of the road, almost under cover, when a vehicle crested the northern rise. We didn't wait to see who was driving.

My heart thumped with the speed of a panicked rabbit as we raced up the hill, dodged trees, ducked under branches. Karl started pulling Georg. Ruth pulled Anneliese. I had the Luger in hand, looking back, always looking back.

I ran into Anneliese. Grabbed her so she didn't fall. I was about to yell at them to move when the sound of water registered. And the fact that there was no ground beyond Anneliese.

Sidestepping, I peered into a gorge. It wasn't deep, maybe eight meters, just deep enough that it would hurt to fall. And it wasn't wide, maybe three meters, but too wide to jump. This is how it would end? By a puny river, barely more than a stream, on a hill in a land where the farmers would toast the deaths of a few German teenagers?

I kicked a rock. It bounced over the edge of the gorge.

"There might be a bridge," Ruth said.

"Yes," Karl replied. "But which way?"

The fear receded. My eagle's eye soared above us. The hill sloped down to the north, where we had glimpsed farmland earlier. "If there's a bridge, it'll probably be north. But there are more people that way too, and they'll expect us to look for a bridge. Let's go uphill and hope the gorge closes enough to get across. More forest. Easier to hide."

Georg stepped close, searched my face. Nodded. "You haven't led us wrong, yet."

I poked the shoulder of his wounded arm. "When did you turn into a liar?"

"Hey! That hurts. Touch it again and I'll punch you."

I tilted my chin, offering a target. After all these years he looked like he was ready to fight. I grinned. "It would almost be worth it, Georg. I wish we had time."

Karl swatted my head. "This is why you get called names. You like to bait people. I'll lead." We sped along the gorge's edge. Jogged east, west. The gorge narrowed, but not enough.

Karl held up his hand to stop and pointed. A tree had fallen across the gap. A bridge. I skirted past the muddy hole left when the roots had upturned. The far end was balanced on a small notch in the gorge shaped like a comma. Rot had set in near the now-vertical roots, which meant the whole trunk might be soft.

"What do you think?" Karl asked.

"We cross," I replied.

"It's beech so the trunk is nice and straight, but those branches are long dead," he said. "We can't grab them if we lose our balance, and we'd break our necks on the rocks down there."

I crouched and peered along the length of the trunk. We needed to repair this bridge, or reinforce it. What would Otto do?

"Running out of time, Wilm."

I held up one finger. All those nights poring over that book on the history of bridges paid off. I jumped up. "The Incas."

"Who?" Karl and Georg asked together.

"South Americans. They built rope bridges across gorges. How much rope do we have left?"

Karl flung open his bag and reeled out rope. "Your uncle gave us a lot. Must have been ten meters. We didn't use much on Ernst."

"What's your plan?" Ruth asked, hands on hips.

I tied a knot in one end and handed the other end to Karl. "You go across, Karl. Tie this end high up on a tree. I'll wrap my end around a tree on this side and anchor it. Each of you will go across hanging onto the rope above your heads. If the tree gives way you can still cross hand over hand. I'll bring the rope across with me so no one can follow."

"Georg can't do that," Ruth said.

"Yes, I can. I have to." Georg hugged his arm to his side. Otto's voice whispered inside: *People can find great depths of strength when they need it*. I gave Georg a nod.

Anneliese took my Luger. "I'll cross second. I'm the best shot. I can cover you." A shadow seemed to flicker through her eyes, and I almost reached to get the pistol back. But she stepped back, her face unclouded.

"You got lucky hitting that goose. That doesn't mean you're the best shot," Karl muttered.

"She is," I said. She seemed so much like the old Anneliese right now. "What are you waiting for, Karl? Go."

I fastened the rope to a tree so it was looped around itself but not tied. I braced one foot against the trunk, gripped the rope. Karl flipped the line so it ran between the upraised roots and cradled in a Y. He was almost across when a supporting branch on the underside broke and the tree dropped a notch. He fell to his knees, crawled the rest of the way.

He leaped to the ground on the other side and waved. In minutes he had the rope pulled tight and tied off. Anneliese tucked the Luger inside her trousers and jumped up. Her hands walked along the rope above her head in time with her feet—right foot and left hand, left foot and right hand. She stepped over protruding branches, never hesitated. She took Karl's outstretched hand and jumped off the bridge.

"Go Georg," I said. "If you get in trouble, Ruth will be right behind you."

Georg started out, then slowed, looking down rather than ahead. When he was halfway across I told Ruth to go.

She caught up to Georg, barely holding onto the rope where Georg clung to it with his good hand. She was whispering. He slid his foot forward. Then his other foot. My arms started to ache. The stink of my sweat was worse than it had been in days, and that was saying a lot.

Two steps from the other side, a loud crack reverberated. The tree shifted sideways. Georg lunged toward Karl, who pulled him to safety. Ruth dangled from the rope until she found her footing, then followed. Karl ushered them under the trees.

I unlashed the rope and stood by the fan of roots. I could see the spot that had broken, about three-quarters of the way across. Instead of a nice straight trunk, the surface dipped down then up to where Karl waved frantically for me to come.

Were there any other options? I tied the end of the rope around my waist in what I hoped was a secure knot. I'd never been great with knots. Fear wasn't rooting me in place; it was common sense. That bridge wasn't safe. Then I heard a distant yell and barking. The sound of a trail being found.

My choice was made for me. I hopped up on the base of the trunk, found my balance. Ran.

A step before the weakened spot, the trunk gave way, lurched to the side. Bucked me off. I arced away and down, rope losing slack fast. The cliff rushed toward me.

I had time for one thought: I hoped the knot held.

CHAPTER FORTY-THREE

The rope played out. Jerked. Spun me around, carried me toward the western face of the gorge. I slammed into the wall of earth and jutting roots. My breath punched out. It took a few seconds to realize I wasn't holding the rope. My knot had held.

Blood in my mouth. I licked more off my lips. One hand gripping the rope, I wiped my mouth. Now I could feel blood pouring from my nose.

A voice swam through the angry buzz in my ears. "Wilm? Wilm?" The voice was hushed but urgent. "Are you okay? The dogs are getting closer. I sent the others ahead. I can't haul you up by myself. You have to help."

I coughed, spat blood. The buzzing was making it hard to think. Why would I have to climb? Why was I concerned about the knot? I remembered being on the bridge.

The rope cutting into my chest rolled a centimeter toward my armpits. Hanging. I was hanging. I had fallen, hit the cliff.

"Wilm! We're running out of time."

Give me a minute, I said. No, the words hadn't come out. I tilted my head back to search out Karl. Blood ran down the back of my throat. I swallowed it.

"They'll see where you are by the rope," Karl said. "What should we do?"

I peered east but couldn't see the tree bridge. I had swung

to the inside curve of the comma of land the tree had rested on. They might not see me with the rope gone. I tried twice, found my voice. "Cut the rope. Under the knot on the tree so they see it. Toss my end off the cliff, then go."

"But you'll—"

"I'll hang on. There are roots." One of which might have broken my still-bleeding nose.

I kicked around and found two footholds, one on a root, one in a hole of some kind. I looked up. Karl was still there, wearing his most worried face. The barking got louder and helped chase away the wasps in my head. I grabbed hold of a root by my shoulder. "Do it."

He pulled his knife and cut the rope below the cliff's edge. He disappeared.

The cut section of rope coiled down, struck my shoulders and rucksack, and fell to dangle from my waist. It almost made me lose my balance. I grabbed another root and pressed my cheek against the cliff. Whiffs of damp loam sifted through the stench of blood.

My right hand was already aching from gripping the root by my shoulder. Higher would be easier but there was nothing in reach.

The barking rang clear. They were along the gorge. I licked away more blood. My jaw was sore. I poked around with my tongue and found a broken stub where my left eyetooth had been. The touch stabbed pain up into my jaw. I hissed.

Voices yelled over the dogs' frantic baying. Not Russian. Czech, maybe. The clamor was so loud I figured they had reached the tree bridge's roots. My foot slipped out of its earthen stirrup. Every muscle, knuckles to toes, clenched. My jaw tightened too, which almost made me yelp. I opened my mouth and pushed my boot deeper into the hole. Aching corkscrewed through my neck and arms.

More voices. German this time. "Tell him to silence those dogs." Ernst. Keep the dogs by the bridge. Don't take them farther along the gorge where they'll see me.

A centipede crawled over my fingers then under the root I clung to. The dogs had quieted but still whined, gave the odd bark. Did they smell our scents on the tree? My blood?

A German voice I didn't recognize said, "See that rope, sir? I think they got across."

"I'm not blind, you *Dummkopf*."

A Czech voice babbled, then Dummkopf said, "He wants to know what crime such wily criminals committed that his government gave permission to chase them across his country. Should I tell him about the injured Soviets, sir?"

"Don't tell him anything. Ask him where the closest bridge is."

Injured Soviets. Not dead. Relief swept over me with such force that I almost cried out. I wasn't a murderer. Hadn't destroyed any other families. Thank God.

I tried to focus on what was being said. *Dummkopf* had spoken in Czech and was translating the reply. "Almost six hundred meters downstream. This path follows the river all the way to it."

The Czech said something else. *Dummkopf* spoke again. "He says it's no use, sir. The border is less than a kilometer away. We'll never catch them."

"Maybe he can't," Ernst said. "But I will. Follow me."

Footsteps pounded away. Now that Ernst was gone, my muscles started quivering. *Dummkopf* and the Czech moved off with dogs barking again, trying to warn their master they were going the wrong way.

I turned my attention to hanging on. Sweat slicked my palms. My legs shook. I didn't dare look down, didn't want to see the rocks below.

A rope hit my back. Above me Karl said, "There's a knot in the end. I'll pull but you have to climb."

I grabbed the rope and was reaching for a new handhold before Karl even started pulling. Urgency drove me up and over the edge. I rolled away from it and rose on shaky legs. Karl cut the rope from my waist and helped me into the forest.

The hillside plunged down. We scrambled along, grabbed branches for balance. If there was a path I didn't see it. I caught glimpses of a road curving along the hill's base. Karl pointed to a screen of bushes by the road. Georg and Ruth were using it for cover.

I slipped. Karl grabbed me. "Let go," I whispered. "I'm okay."

Before he released me, he said, "Did you hear? Those Soviets were only injured." He grinned. "We aren't killers."

He meant I wasn't a killer. "Great. But Ernst is running to catch us."

Alarm crossed Karl's face. He released me and we snuck down the hill to join our friends. I slid to the ground beside Georg. "Where's Anneliese?"

"What happened? Your face is covered by blood and dirt."

I touched my nose. The bleeding had stopped and it hurt to touch, but the pain was mostly a dull throb. "Where's my sister?"

Ruth pointed down the road to where Anneliese crouched behind a boulder. "She said she was going to distract the patrol we spotted. They're standing, just watching the road."

My gaze jumped farther down the road to a pair of Soviet soldiers. I didn't think the Czechs usually had Soviets hanging around. These men were working with Ernst. West of the road, one hundred meters across a clearing, a line of posted signs marked the border. The Soviets had a view of both the road and clearing.

"I'll help Anneliese distract them. You three get across that road and run for your lives."

Before I could figure out what Anneliese had in mind, a pistol shot rang out. One of the soldiers fell. The other took cover behind a tree.

"Run!" I pushed Georg. Ruth and Karl leaped after him and raced across the road toward the clearing and Bavaria beyond.

What had Anneliese done? The Soviet behind the tree took a shot at her. She was twenty meters away over open ground. I kept to the forest and stole closer, hid behind each tree.

Anneliese shifted from the southwest side of the boulder to the southeast. She took aim and fired. Caught the Soviet in the shoulder. He fell from behind his cover and she shot again. He hit the ground. Didn't move.

I rested my head against the smooth trunk and inhaled sharp short breaths. I didn't think Anneliese could ever kill anyone. That darkness that had flickered across her face when she'd taken the pistol had been real. She had shot Soviets. Had she pictured the faces of her attackers when she'd pulled the trigger?

No time to wonder. Ernst was coming. Pull yourself together, Tauber. Still gasping, I gripped the rough bark, straightened. Anneliese began to rise. Turn. Her face was grim.

Then small flames spouted against dark foliage. *Choo-choo-choo. Choo-choo-choo.* The rapid sneezing of a machine gun. Anneliese lurched and jerked in a hideous dance.

CHAPTER FORTY-FOUR

Shock turned me to stone. I wasn't breathing. Couldn't breath. Couldn't think. Anneliese was on the ground. Blood darkened her coat. Horror gurgled in my throat.

A Soviet emerged from the forest. His machine-gun barrel bounced as he walked. The road curved behind him. He must have cut through the trees when the first shot was fired. He reached Anneliese, nudged her with his boot. Pressed his heel against her shoulder and shoved.

She fell onto her back and the Luger spit fire. The Soviet flew back, his chest exploding with red. She was alive!

I bolted to her, took the Luger from her limp grasp, and tucked it under my belt. Two, three bloodstains were growing. Shoulder, stomach. She needed help but wouldn't get it on this side of the border.

She tried to speak but coughed. I hushed her, told her what I was doing as I dragged her up to sit against the rock, then hoisted her over my shoulder. The Luger fell. I left it, latched my arm over the back of her knees, and took off across the clearing.

Karl, Ruth, and Georg stood at the line of border signs. I kept my attention on them. I couldn't look back. Someone would be there soon enough. The P-38 slipped from Karl's hand as all three stared at me with gaping mouths and round eyes.

Shouts behind us. Karl startled, pushed Ruth, who grabbed

Georg's hand and ran. Ernst bellowed across the clearing, "Halt, Wilm Tauber. You're under arrest!"

I clamped down on Anneliese's limp form and tried to run faster but my legs were getting shaky. Anneliese flopped like a ragdoll, bumped my rucksack.

"Halt!" A bullet whined to my right. Ernst was too far away to aim accurately with a pistol or I wouldn't still be moving.

I passed the signs, stumbled out of Czechoslovakia, and fell. A bullet thunked into a sign to my right. Anneliese rolled onto the ground. My chest and shoulder were stained with her blood, and she was still bleeding. Her face was snowy, lips pale. I got up, gripped her wrists, and backpedaled three meters to a boulder, pulled her to its sheltered side. Only then did I look up. Ernst had stopped halfway across the field. He raised his pistol, aimed at me. Shot. I flinched. The bullet ricocheted off a boulder to my left.

Karl joined me.

"What are you doing?" I snapped. "Run."

"We're across the border, Wilm. Why is he shooting?"

"I don't think he cares about a line of signs, Karl."

Anneliese groaned. I scrunched down by her side. She opened her eyes. "Wilm." Her voice was weak. "Did we make it?"

"Yes."

"Good." Her eyes closed again.

"Liese? What were you thinking? We could have snuck through the forest." I laid my hands along her face. Our noses almost touched. "Liese?"

Her eyelids fluttered open. "It's okay, Wilm. Better ... this way."

"No, it's not."

A smile flitted, disappeared. "Like Father. Have ... honor ... back."

"Father didn't want us to die. He wanted us to live. Escape and live!"

"Please, Wilm ..."

It sounded like she wanted to ask me something. "What?"

"Said you'd ... do anything." Her breathing was shallow.

"Yes. I will do anything, Liese. Anything for you. Anything." Just live, I wanted to add.

Her eyes closed as she took a gasping breath. She squinted her eyes open, like it was taking a lot of effort. "Live for me. For *Vati*. Live, Wilm."

"Live for yourself!"

"Love you." Anneliese's eyes drifted closed. I searched her face for any sign of life. Held my cheek against her mouth and nose, prayed for the slightest breath. I was shaking too hard to tell.

Another bullet chinked off the rock. Karl said, "*Scheisse*, Wilm. Ernst is walking toward us again." Another ricochet. "He's going to shoot us. Walk right up and shoot us."

I pressed my forehead against Anneliese's, begged her to live. Karl yanked me away. I fell onto my backside. He pointed at Ernst. "He's going to kill you, Tauber!'"

Ernst walked toward me with deliberate steps. Ejected a magazine from his pistol butt. Inserted another. Paused. Loaded the chamber and aimed. Fired.

I jerked. My hand flew to my chest. The bullet buried itself in the ground beside me, but I felt where it should have hit. That wasn't his pistol. That's why his aim was off. I clenched my jaw. Anneliese wouldn't want me to just let him execute me. Energy surged into my limbs. "I'm not leaving her." I cradled Anneliese's limp form and rose. Wobbled for a few steps then found my stride.

Ruth and Georg stood hand in hand in the middle of the field watching us. Karl raced toward them and I marched forward. Another shot from behind us. My rucksack jumped. I wove left, right, knowing he was gaining with each step.

From around a stand of trees an American jeep roared toward us. A soldier stood in the back manning a mounted machine gun. When they passed Georg the gun burst to life.

I halted. They were shooting at us? Energy snuffed out like a candle. I dropped to my knees, pressed my cheek to Anneliese's forehead, and struggled to stay calm. After all we'd been through the Americans were going to kill us? My gut wrenched.

The jeep swung halfway around us and skidded to a halt. The machine gun rat-a-tat-tatted. The sound battered me. Why was I still alive?

The driver jumped out. I heard the American word *kid*—the word they'd used for "boy" when they had been in Leipzig.

My God. Leipzig. Would Mother ever know?

"What's happening?" A German voice.

Anneliese. My God.

The wild animal rammed against the door in my mind and it started to crack. I gasped, couldn't get air. I held Anneliese tightly and stared at the two Americans. "Don't shoot!" I cried. "Please don't shoot. Don't let her sacrifice be for nothing!"

"Sacrifice?" the one soldier asked in German and knelt to touch her throat. "This girl's badly hurt."

"She's his sister. Is she—" Karl's voice opened the door.

Wild grief scattered my thoughts. It wrapped a band around my chest and mashed it tight. Noisy gasps escaped with each attempt to breathe. Agony exploded inside. I lowered Anneliese, fell beside her. Wanted to howl. All that came out were choking sobs. Tried to stop. Couldn't.

Awkward pats on my shoulder. English words I didn't understand. "We scared those Commies off. Let's get to a doc."

Anneliese. We were supposed to escape and live. Both of us.
Not one.

Both.

CHAPTER FORTY-FIVE

I leaned over Anneliese's hospital bed and kissed her forehead. "The doctor says this second infection will gone in less than a week. Then you can join us."

She gave me a weak smile. "Stop stalling. Go."

My friends were waiting outside the hospital. I checked the hand-drawn map and pointed left down the Munich street. We started out. It had been a long journey. Only ten blocks to go.

For four and a half weeks we'd lived in a tent city with other refugees from the Soviet Zone. There were a lot this summer, more than usual. Something about people avoiding recruitment to the new border police and some mining village. I didn't pay much attention.

After Anneliese was out of danger I wrote to Mother. Since Schupos watched the mail, I figured Ernst would read it, but I doubted that Mother ever would. So I wrote to Otto as well. He could get word to her we were safe. Uncle Bruno got a separate letter saying only that we'd gotten to the American Zone. He wouldn't be happy I'd let Anneliese get shot ... but maybe he'd like that I'd carried her to safety. In the end, we'd saved each other.

We would've had to stay longer in the camp but we kept pestering the authorities. We wanted to be settled and in school in September. Georg was especially anxious about that. The authorities gave us our papers and let us go after they confirmed that Otto's friend in Munich really was expecting us.

Munich was worse than Leipzig for bomb damage, but I felt the difference in the way people walked without fear and didn't cringe from the American soldiers or the police.

We reached a street only partly damaged, and lingered across from a townhouse with a green door and the address Otto had made me memorize.

I was afraid.

Being in the camp had been a kind of limbo, where I'd sat by Anneliese's bedside, let grief about Father roll over in waves and it didn't matter. I'd come so close to losing her too, the doctors said. No surprise since I'd thought I was carrying a corpse across that field. I think she'd wanted to die; it took her ages to heal and was taking her longer to rediscover reasons to live.

Why is this so hard? I only have to cross the street. But knocking on that green door was moving on. Letting go.

Somehow, Ruth knew what I was thinking. "You'll both take your father with you wherever you go."

I stuffed my hands in my pockets. No knife to occupy fidgety fingers. I wondered if Ernst had kept it. I forced calmness into my voice. "A kiss for luck?"

"My boyfriend would beat you up."

I grinned at Georg. "He would try."

He frowned. "Get your own girl." Ruth took his hand.

Karl said, "Good advice. You and Ruth are too much alike to ever get along."

I shrugged. He had a point.

"You're wasting time," Karl said, no heat in his words. "If I didn't know better, I'd say you were scared."

Our gazes held. I couldn't bring myself to admit it, not in front of Georg, who thought I was fearless. "What do I have to be

afraid of? We're together, right? Together we can face anything."
As soon as the words were out, I realized they were true.

My friends escorted me to the bottom of the stairs. I climbed
the six steps, paused on each, ran my hand along the stone balustrade, halted before the door.

Green. The color of life. And behind this green door, where I
would find Otto's friend, was the start of my new life.

One more year in *Gymnasium*. Then ... university. Bridges.

Father had rediscovered his honor in death. I would find mine
in life. A life spent building bridges. The first bridge to build, from
old life to new, was summoning the courage to walk through this
door.

I raised my hand, took hold of the brass knocker, exhaled
slowly.

With a final glance at my friends, I knocked.

HISTORICAL NOTE

Wilm and his friends live in Leipzig, in southeast Germany. The story takes place in 1947, when World War II had been over for two years. At the time, this eastern area of Germany was controlled by the Soviets (the now-defunct U.S.S.R.), and would be until 1949, when it became the country of East Germany. Other parts of post-war Germany were controlled by the Americans, the British and the French; combined, those zones became the separate country of West Germany.

Life in Europe after World War II was difficult for everyone, but even more difficult for Germans. It didn't matter if a German had believed in or supported Hitler and his Nazi government (and many did not), and it didn't matter how young or old a German was. The victorious Allied governments wanted to punish the German people, whom they believed responsible for starting the war. This was especially true for the Soviets. Their communist government was completely opposed to the fascist beliefs of the Nazis, but more than that, the Soviets had suffered a great deal when the German armies had invaded in 1941. There were a lot of hard feelings, and the Soviets were very cruel to the people living in the Soviet Zone of eastern Germany.

Many of the incidents in Wilm's story are based on actual events, some described by people I interviewed and some taken from books. *Trümmerfrauen*, reparations, New Teachers, rationing, fear of attack from Soviet soldiers—these were all realities in Wilm's world.

While Wilm's story is fiction, two specific incidents included in the book did happen. In 1946, 1,800 kilograms of butter (3,960 pounds) were indeed confiscated by a Soviet officer and left to spoil when he couldn't find transportation for it to be returned to his homeland. And a train full of German prisoners of war, released by the British, did go into the Soviet Zone in 1947. Whether the British intended those prisoners to return to their homes, I don't know, but the Soviets took control of the train and refused to let the occupants leave. The train was directed to the east border of Germany, where the POWs were off-loaded and sent to prison camps. I do not know the train's route, so gave it a fictitious stop in Leipzig.

One historical change I made should be noted. The Germans generally referred to the Soviets as Russians, and that is still the case today when Germans speak of the war and the years immediately after. But since the Russians were only one of many people groups who made up the U.S.S.R., I decided to use the more correct term, Soviets, in the story. In the one case where I used the term Russian, it referred to one officer who was indeed from Russia.

The Soviet government was very secretive, and finding information about the Soviet Zone in Germany was difficult. Two specific books helped: *The People's State* by Mary Fulbrook (Yale University Press, 2005), and especially *The Russians in Germany* by Norman M. Naimark (Harvard University Press, 1997). Two people I interviewed gave me a lot of useful information: Mr. Alfred Walther, who shared his story of living in Leipzig during that time, and Herr Christoph Kaufmann at the Leipzig City Museum, who answered pages of questions and pointed out several German books filled with photographs of Leipzig during and after the war.

Looking at those photographs, one thing becomes perfectly clear: it doesn't matter which side of a conflict a person is on, war makes victims of us all.

ACKNOWLEDGMENTS

The initial act of writing is solitary, but creating a book is definitely not. More friends than I can list encourage me on each writing journey, but I do want to name Marsha Skrypuch, for her mentorship and advice. Thanks, cuz! And, as always, thanks go to Mike, my "patron of the arts," for encouraging me to keep striving toward my goals.

To Gail Winskill and the whole team at Pajama Press: thanks for believing in *Graffiti Knight* and for pulling all those strings behind the curtain that turn a manuscript into a book. And thank you for giving me the opportunity to work with Linda Pruessen, a talented editor and tireless cat-herder. Linda, many thanks for keeping me on track and helping to whittle Wilm's story into its final form.